BATTERED EARTH

D. HILLEREN

iUniverse, Inc.
Bloomington

Battered Earth

This is a work of fiction. All of the characters, names, incidents, organizations, and dialogue in this novel are either the products of the author's imagination or are used fictitiously.

iUniverse books may be ordered through booksellers or by contacting:

iUniverse
1663 Liberty Drive
Bloomington, IN 47403
www.iuniverse.com
1-800-Authors (1-800-288-4677)

ISBN: 978-1-4620-0379-2 (sc)
ISBN: 978-1-4620-0378-5 (hc)
ISBN: 978-1-4620-0377-8 (e)

Library of Congress Control Number: 2011904274

Printed in the United States of America

iUniverse rev. date: 5/24/11

Prologue

In the new decade, the average global temperature has risen to new heights, further melting glaciers and ice caps. Violent and unpredictable storms increasingly plague the earth. Sea levels have encroached on coastal shorelines, forcing picturesque seaside towns to be abandoned. Large sections of the Louisiana coast, including half of New Orleans, are under water. Even the seemingly impregnable New York City has suffered massive flooding in the low-lying areas of Battery Park City, Tribeca, and the West Village. Across the nation, money has been poured into the construction of levees and dams to fight the losing battle with erratic hurricanes that cause flash floods and rivers to over run their banks.

Casualties have become so frequent and personal that there is an unusual outcry from the people. A climate summit, something which used to be a curiosity, has turned into a global media event, with the hopes that a breakthrough can be found.

Chapter One

Russian Orthodox Church

It was a bright and promising morning in the Voleostrovsky District in St. Petersburg. The sun was already catching the towers of the Russian Orthodox Church, where workers were slowly beginning to climb up the scaffolding to begin their workday. The onion-shaped cupolas reflected a blinding gold that stood out as a beacon, distinct from all the other drab and dirty buildings in the neighborhood surrounding the church. The restoration workers were methodically making their way down to the lower reaches of the building, where only small sections of the cupolas remained to be gilded.

During the Soviet times, this particular church had been transformed into an ice skating rink for all the young people of Leningrad to enjoy. Many citizens had the best memories of their Soviet childhoods skating with friends and holding hands with their first sweethearts in the rundown shrine. But when the ceilings began to crack and the stones began to crumble, Soviet officials shuttered the doors.

The church ultimately survived the Communist era and was now a cultural icon, welcoming wealthy tourists to the city. The travelers came on private yachts and boutique international cruise ships that would dock at the busy harbor directly across from the church. They gazed out at the pale yellow exterior with the striking gold cupolas. It was a stunning example of Russian architecture and a logical pick to undergo complete renovation by a government interested in promoting tourism.

A man opened the heavy wood door and entered the dim interior of the church with confidence. He turned to his right, ducked into a doorway, and began climbing the winding, circular staircase on the north side of the church. His drab coveralls and cap were the same as all the other workers, and he carried an old paint tarp on top of a cardboard box. He climbed the jagged stone stairs until he reached an archway where an even steeper staircase branched off to the left. He was confident that this would take him to the smaller, more isolated tower he was seeking.

The climb was not an easy one, but he was in good physical condition. His steps were rhythmic until the end of the journey, where the circular staircase narrowed even further. It became difficult to carry the cardboard box without bumping into the coarse stone walls. Finally, he reached the cramped tower room in the secondary cupola.

He put down the box and tarp and looked out the unobtrusive opening that he had noticed while scouting the exterior of the great church. He smirked and licked his cracked lips in pleasure since the view of the ships in the harbor was even better than he had imagined. In the small space, he laid out the paint-splattered tarp and opened the cardboard box to reveal a partially assembled rifle. In a few deft moves, he completed the rifle assembly and peered through the high-powered scope.

He focused in on a luxury cruise liner that had just docked in the harbor, and noted the bright blue and yellow flag waving toward him in a slight breeze coming off the water. He expertly gauged the distance and determined the adjustments he would have to make to execute the perfect shot.

From this vantage point, he could see the passengers who had gathered on the main deck to watch the ship's arrival. A middle-aged woman who appeared to dominate the conversation with her friends caught his eye. She wore a white pant suit with excessive amounts of makeup and jewelry, including an ornate diamond cocktail ring that flashed in the sun. He targeted her forehead in the cross-hairs of the scope and slowly squeezed the trigger of the unloaded rifle. In satisfaction, he thought of the exorbitant sum of money that he was going to get paid.

Exhaling forcefully, he lowered the rifle, knowing he wasn't going to experience the pleasure of the kill today. He reluctantly pulled himself away from the perch, disassembled the rifle, and put it back into the tattered cardboard box. He put the box against the stone wall and covered it with the paint tarp, knowing this section had already finished restoration.

He began the return journey down the irregular, winding stairs. When he reached the bottom, he walked out the massive front doors and nodded at a "fellow" worker coming in. He proceeded down the block of the blossoming, academically oriented neighborhood and only paused for a brief moment to look at his reflection in a cafe window.

Chapter Two

Seattle

The town car would be there in ten minutes and Nicole was still throwing clothes in the suitcase. After all these years of travel, she should be a pro at packing, but it was still a major chore. She indiscriminately pulled clothes out of the drawers and closet, leaving a jumbled trail of clothing behind her. This trip would be a couple of weeks long, including an excursion on a ship in the Baltic Sea. There would be the standard business meetings, cocktail parties, and various informal gatherings in variable weather conditions: a packing nightmare.

She looked at the chaotic piles of clothes and sighed. She impatiently pulled back a lock of her dark wavy hair that had fallen over her serious blue eyes and began packing with more determination. She was dressed in her standard travel attire: comfortable black jeans, low-heeled boots, and a fashionable, one-button jacket.

The buzzer rang, so Nicole threw in an extra black sweater and hurriedly closed the suitcase. She made a mental check of the absolute essentials: passport, credit cards, cell phone, and laptop. She had packed a large bag and a barely legal carry-on—way too much for a seasoned traveler.

She walked out of the lobby of the residential tower located in the trendy Belltown neighborhood of Seattle. She was welcomed by the fresh sea air and the cries of the seagulls hunting for fish in the nearby bay. Nicole enjoyed living in this area because she could walk to unique restaurants and coffee shops or browse through the numerous boutiques and art galleries. She really loved being home, which made it even harder to leave on another trip.

The town car driver pleasantly greeted her, opened the passenger door, and put her bags in the trunk. They drove past the Space Needle and headed to the freeway. Nicole settled into the backseat and enjoyed the view of the city rushing by. The skyline loomed in front of her, with views of Puget Sound in the background. The Olympic Mountains were only partially visible since clouds were beginning to settle in over the prominent peaks. A large ferryboat was crossing the bay, bringing cars and passengers from Bainbridge Island into the city. She noticed the wind picking up, forming whitecaps on the choppy water.

Nicole arrived at Sea-Tac Airport in plenty of time to catch her international flight. The throng of travelers in the terminal looked to be manageable as she guided her luggage to the business-class check-in line. Her slender frame and striking good looks often solicited offers of help from fellow passengers, but she was stronger than she looked and competently lifted the bags onto the belt. After check-in, she made her way through the annoying security screening process and headed to her gate.

Once on board, Nicole settled into her customary aisle seat in business class for the ten-hour flight to Stockholm, and began to review the latest information on the Global Climate Forum. She was engaged in the briefing papers and was not paying attention until the engines powered up for take-off. She gazed out the window to see the buildings and the fertile, green landscape quickly disappear below. The plane gained altitude and moved into the hazy clouds.

The flight attendants got up from their seats and began rattling around in the galley, beginning to prepare the drink cart for the long flight to Stockholm. Nicole could hear their light-hearted chatter in the background and reached for her headphones to block the constant engine noise.

Boom! Without a warning, an explosive blast shook the plane! The deafening sound was accompanied by a blinding flash of light. Nicole instinctively ducked down and covered her head for protection, her adrenaline racing. Terrified passengers screamed in panic, and then everyone fell silent. The plane was no longer gaining altitude.

The flight attendants slammed the drink cart back into its compartment in the galley, rushed to their jump seats, and quickly fastened their safety harnesses.

The quiet Asian businessman next to Nicole pointed a shaky finger to the aisle floor and whispered in a terrified voice, "It came from there—from the baggage hold."

Nicole looked at the steel-blue and gray pattern on the carpeted floor and thought, *The baggage hold would mean it was a bomb!* Her heart raced, and her senses told her it would only be a moment until the plane would be going down in flames. She felt powerless, strapped in her seat with nothing to do but watch the catastrophe unfold.

The plane abruptly lurched upward for a few seconds and then dropped violently downward. Everything seemed to be in slow motion, even though it was happening swiftly in real time.

The pilot took the plane into a steep ascent, looking for an altitude with less turbulence. Nicole thought at least the pilot was able to increase power to change altitudes, so the plane was holding together. It crossed her mind that it could be a thunderstorm and not a terrorist attack, which would have a better chance of survival.

Finally, the plane stabilized.

After what felt like an eternity, the pilot's voice crackled over the intercom. "This is your captain speaking. On takeoff, we encountered an unusual electrical storm. The plane is designed to withstand a lighting strike in an event such as this, so please remain calm. Although part of the electrical system has been affected, the plane is functioning normally. It's standard procedure to check out all systems after a direct hit, so we are returning to the airport. We will be arriving back at Sea-Tac in a few minutes."

Getting hit by lighting when flying out of Seattle on what looked like a normal day? It seemed crazy, although extreme weather, including increased lighting strikes, were becoming more common every year. Nicole recalled how planes had gone down in recent years due to the more severe and quick-forming thunderheads. It had been reported that aircraft, even traveling at high altitudes, had been broken apart by over one-hundred-mile-per-hour updraft winds. Some of the debris had been strewn over hundreds of miles.

The pilot's matter-of-fact voice came back on the speaker, "We will be doing a routine landing, but emergency vehicles will be out on the runway. Do not be concerned; this is standard procedure. We will be at the gate shortly."

Nicole looked around and could see the impact of the incident on the passengers' faces. The seconds of terror and minutes of uncertainty had taken their toll on peoples' nerves, and they gazed out in space with adrenaline-glazed eyes.

The plane descended at a rapid but steady rate. As it approached the runway, all the flashing red lights of the emergency vehicles further heightened the passengers' already overloaded senses. In a few more seconds, the wheels solidly touched down on the runway. Nicole let out a sign of relief.

When the plane finally rolled to a stop at the gate, a firm voice came over the intercom. "Please remain in your seats and ring your call buttons if you need any assistance."

After it was determined everyone was okay, the stunned passengers were told to take their time and walk slowly off the plane. Before Nicole left her seat, she leaned over to look outside of the window and could see the ground crew systematically examining the outside of the airplane.

As she unsteadily walked up the ramp, all she could think of was how unpredictable the world had become.

While she waited in line for a ticket agent, Nicole overheard two of the agents talking. "This is the third plane hit by lightning coming out of Seattle this month!" She recognized that it was more important than ever to get on the next available flight to Stockholm.

Chapter Three

Senate Offices—Washington DC

The senator sat in his formal office, nervously shuffling papers on the massive antique desk, impatiently waiting for his cell phone to ring. He knew he ought to be attending the meeting of the defense subcommittee that he cochaired, but he was waiting for a specific call. It was one that only he could answer. But it was disconcerting that he did not even know the identity of the gentleman who was calling him.

Eighteen months ago, the senator needed funds to turn around his failing reelection campaign. The public was in an anti-incumbent frame of mind, and his ratings were dropping like a rock in the polls. The campaign was looking hopeless, and he had exhausted all of the traditional political avenues to raise money.

In desperation, he began making contacts with acquaintances to get advice. One of them was an old friend who was well connected in the petroleum industry. He told the senator that he might know another way to acquire some funds, but it would all have to be kept quiet.

The friend phoned back the next day and told the senator that someone would contact him that evening to discuss potential funding. He told the senator to personally take the call, be honest, and *not* ask any personal questions. He would not say any more.

As promised, a cordial man who did not identify himself called that evening and asked if he was talking to Senator Clarkston. Then he proceeded to ask the senator several questions about his views on the global economy. The senator took his friend's advice and did not mince words.

First, the man asked him about the report that the United Nations had recently come out with showing how conflicts are caused by weather-related incidences. It basically said that farmers and herders who used to live in peace were supposedly fighting over basic necessities, such as food and water. The senator made it clear that he thought it was ridiculous to blame human conflicts on the weather.

The mysterious caller asked about his views on global warming and the reported association with extreme weather conditions, such as record floods in Europe, monsoons in Southern Asia, and tornadoes and hurricanes in the United States. Again the senator had answered truthfully, "It's all hogwash, but it is essential that I appear concerned for the benefit of the party and the younger people in my state." He went on to tell the man, "Gone are the days when a politician could be honest about things and survive an election."

The last question was about the melting ice cap that was opening access to vast, previously inaccessible resources. The senator immediately said, "US oil corporations should have first claiming rights to the Arctic. My constituency in Texas will depend on it."

The man on the phone had concluded, "If you get the money, I would expect some small favors that would line up with your political beliefs. Would you be willing to help out?"

The senator didn't hesitate. "Yes that makes sense, especially if I agree with the position."

"Then welcome to the team. I'll be in contact."

Over the next forty-eight hours, a stream of donations was made to the senator's campaign fund. In total, it amounted to over twenty-five million dollars. It was enough money to run TV spots and do a media blitz that turned the election around.

The senator had no further contact with his wealthy beneficiary, until yesterday, when a messenger delivered a package. Inside, there was a single, aromatic Cuban cigar, and a note: "You will be receiving a phone call at 4:00 p.m. A small favor is needed."

The senator startled when his private cell phone rang. He reached to answer, noticing that the caller ID was blocked. "This is Senator Clarkston."

"I know. Listen to my directions. If you do well, you will continue to be rewarded. If not, well ..." The pleasant voice from the first phone call had taken on a menacing tone.

"I understand," responded the senator. It had been clear from the very beginning, especially when the senator saw how much money had been given to his campaign—if he didn't comply with the caller's request, he knew his career would be over.

"We need you to hold a welcome reception at a climate forum in Stockholm."

"What? I thought you were going to ask me to do things that supported my politics."

The voice on the other end of the line became angry. "That is exactly what you will be doing! You said yourself it was important to *look* supportive of the environment, and the event will serve that purpose, *so that is what you are going to do!*"

The senator bristled at being told what to do, but he had no other choice. He was at the mercy of this powerful blackmailer and forced to comply with his directions.

Chapter Four

St. Petersburg

In the northern part of St. Petersburg, Dosha was racing to an appointment that had been set up by her company. Her sad little Ukraine-made Zaz car lurched unwillingly forward, sputtering as she navigated through the city's early morning traffic.

Dumb car, she thought as she gained speed slowly. *I'll never make it to the meeting on time.*

She had taken the car to the repair shop countless times before. She longed to have one of the more reliable foreign cars favored by young Russians. However, such a purchase was not in her budget, so the Zaz was her primary mode of transportation.

Dosha was a registered tour guide who had met all the strict criteria set by the Russian government. She had spent five years in school studying art and architecture at the university, and another year studying for the certification exam. There wasn't a block in the city about which she couldn't give a detailed political history.

Dosha was sought after by the most prestigious tour agencies in Europe to give their wealthy clients a memorable cultural experience in St. Petersburg. She had an upbeat attitude, the ability to quote literature, and a command of the scholarly details that rivaled even the most educated Cambridge retirees. Her short, dark red hair could easily be spotted by her clients when following her around the city. Although below average in height, she walked with confidence, so people usually perceived her as taller than she was. Her bright smile could disarm even the most difficult tourist.

One of Dosha's valuable traits was her cleverness at answering politically sensitive questions often asked by the Western tourists. She could tactfully explain the controversial policies of the Russian government and had acquired many witty stories and jokes to ward off political conflicts. When asked about working conditions in Communist

Russia, she would quip, "So long as the bosses pretended to pay us, we pretended to work."

Dosha had been raised by her maternal grandmother, a traditional Soviet citizen, who to this day longed for the security of the former Communist state. Despite being raised in a strict environment, the young Dosha frequently angered her teachers by being overenthusiastic in class and asking too many questions. Her grandmother punished her harshly but could not dampen her creative spirit.

As she coached her car over one of the eight drawbridges that crossed the Niva River, she thought about how the circumstances of her next assignment were a bit strange. Yesterday, she had been summoned to her boss's office. He had stressed the importance of making a good impression and wanted her to make *every* effort to cooperate with some man named Oliver Odin.

This forewarning was disturbing. Her boss had never concerned himself with anything she had done before, so why now? She had never shied away from challenging groups because they appealed to her adventurous spirit and she always learned something interesting about human behavior. There had been many difficult assignments over the years, from uptight Moscow government officials to unruly Americans just looking for a good time, but she had handled them all and he had left her alone. So what was the big deal about this one?

Chapter Five

Kennedy Airport – NY

Several hours later, Nicole boarded a flight that connected through JFK. The traumatic incident on the plane had put her in a reflective mood. She knew personal life was taking a backseat to the increase in demands from work. Her boyfriend of two years, Sam, was running thin on patience. He had been asking, "Where is the work-life balance everyone talks about?"

The subject had come to a heated discussion the night before when they were having a nice dinner at a neighborhood restaurant in lower Queen Anne Hill. She told him how long she would be gone on this next business trip to northern Europe.

Sam groaned, "Two weeks? You have been working ten-hour days and just returned from Asia two weeks ago!"

"I admit it. I've been busy. But there've been a lot of disasters lately and it's my job to get aid to people!"

"Well, you certainly haven't had the need to spend time with me."

Or maybe I haven't wanted to, Nicole said to herself, thinking about the sailboat that Sam had recently purchased. He was constantly asking her to take extensive time off from work to go on long trips with him.

She continued to push deeper into the truth of the matter, "Perhaps you need someone who isn't as committed to their job as I am?"

Sam slowly picked up his martini glass and took a couple of sips while contemplating an answer. "Maybe you're right."

The rest of the meal was finished in silence with only limited conversation in a cool, cordial manner. It was inevitable. They were going their separate ways and probably had been heading that way for a long time. Momentum had been keeping them together, and probably not much more. Nicole had picked at her meal with little appetite left, knowing that everything was going to change.

Her experiences with long-term relationships had not been positive. She found that boyfriends said they loved and admired her, but their actions showed they were usually on the lookout for someone not complicated, to boost their ego. She had developed the sense that she needed to protect herself, and as a result was distrusting, always ready to flee. And now Sam was complaining about her travel schedule.

It was a year ago when Nicole was working at her job as a Corporate Responsibility Officer at a global athletic company, when she received a phone call from Carl Everson, asking to meet for a cup of coffee. This was *the* Carl Everson who had retired at age thirty-five after founding one of the largest social networking sites in the world.

Nicole had agreed to meet Carl at a coffee house at the bustling Pike Place Market overlooking the waterfront. The day would forever stand out in her mind. She remembered the rich aroma of coffee beans mixing with the scent of baked cinnamon rolls wafting from the bakery next door. The shouts of the fishmongers in the distance could be clearly heard as she listened to this wealthy man talk about his passion for doing good in the world.

After the first espresso, he confided, "The foundation is consuming my life. It is more demanding than starting my company ever was. I am looking to leave the day-to-day operations to someone I can trust because there is a lot at stake."

"I can understand that. When I came out of college, my first job was in New York City, at a financial institution that specialized in bringing privately owned companies public. An eighty-hour work week was common, and in trying to do an outstanding job, I was putting in even more hours."

"So what brought you to Seattle?"

"I started looking for an opportunity where people had some time to have a life outside of the workplace. I was lucky to land a finance position, but I was still looking for that perfect job where you get up in the morning and it feels like you have a purpose."

Carl raised an eyebrow.

"So when an opportunity opened up in the company's newly formed Corporate Responsibility Office, I applied for it, and here I am."

Nicole drank her cappuccino and settled back casually in her chair, looking expectantly at Carl.

Carl began, "I am looking for a person with excellent business acumen and extensive experience in social responsibility. That combination is hard to find. My associates are either socially challenged or don't understand business. I was floundering until I saw your speech on starting micro businesses in third-world countries. It was very convincing." An hour later, they found themselves still talking about the problems of the world and the role the Everson Foundation.

Carl called a month later to ask Nicole if she would be up for the job of the executive director for his foundation. She simply said, "I would be humbled by the opportunity." Three months later, she moved to the Everson Foundation and never looked back. Just as Carl had described, the job turned out to be intense, with excessive amounts of travel. Success was measured on how many lives you saved. It was as simple as that.

As soon as the flight arrived at JFK International Airport, Nicole checked her messages. There was a voice mail from Carl Everson, saying, "Please call me. I have some things to talk to you about."

She walked down the busy concourse, punching in Carl's speed dial and dodging the multicultural mass of people swarming to catch their international flights. It was rare for Carl to call at all, so she was anxious to find out what he wanted.

He answered right away. "Hi, Nicole. It has been an interesting twenty-four hours."

"What do you mean?" She could tell by his tone that this wasn't going to be an easy conversation.

Nicole took refuge next to a large pillar to avoid being bumped by the passengers streaming by. Trying to concentrate, she focused on the black scuff marks on the floor in front of her.

"I had a couple of phone calls from board members who are concerned about your trip to the climate forum and the foundation's position on funding for research in alternative energy. They think your approach is too extreme."

Nicole took a deep sigh. "And what do you think?"

"You know I'm with you, but you need to slow down and spend more time persuading individual board members to support you."

"Who called you?"

"They made me promise confidentiality."

Nicole was frustrated by their lack of confidence, but she felt compelled to reassure Carl. "I'll deal with it."

"There is one more thing. Senator Clarkston from Texas personally called me to make sure you accept an invitation to the reception he is giving in Stockholm for VIPs. I think it's important that you be there."

"Senator Clarkston at the Climate Forum? Now that is interesting! I'm surprised I didn't hear about it sooner."

"I got the impression he was inspired to arrange it at the last minute."

"Could you have the office send me the details?"

After the call, Nicole felt stunned. Her own board members had gone around her to talk directly to Carl. That was not good. She froze for a few moments, suddenly inspired to grab a cab into the city. She could lose herself in the crowds, maybe go to a play and skip the trip to Stockholm altogether. Besides, a number of established aid organizations were located in NYC, and everything would be a lot easier. Why go fight a battle that wasn't popular with all the members of the board?

With a heavy heart, Nicole picked up her carry-on bag and slowly began to walk down the long concourse. Passengers streamed around her, often cutting back rudely in front of her, but she did not pick up her pace. Her bag was heavy, her neck ached, and she felt dull to the world. She reached the gate just as they announced the final boarding call for her connecting flight to Stockholm.

Chapter Six

London

A man was standing patiently in the immigration line with his Saudi Arabian passport in hand. It was a busy time when many international flights were landing at Heathrow. In the long lines, those waiting shifted their weight from one foot to the other and glared at anyone in front of them who took too much time with the immigration officer.

The man had black hair and a dark complexion. He was thin but of average height and wore a conservative dark blue suit with a white shirt and striped tie, and carried a leather briefcase. He glanced around and noted that he did not stand out from the rest of the passengers from Dubai. He felt he looked like many of the other young men on a routine business trip from the Middle East to London.

He slowly worked his way to the front of the line, observing that some individuals who looked like him were questioned more thoroughly than others. He began to get nervous but concentrated on not letting it show. He took a slow, deep breath and tightly grasped the handle on his briefcase as he walked up to the passport control officer's window.

The officer took his passport, looked at the picture, and then studied him closely. The man's heart pounded, so he concentrated on breathing evenly while the Passport Control Officer scanned his passport in the computer. When the officer asked him questions, he responded in a friendly tone and looked the man directly in the eyes.

After a few more seconds looking at the computer, the officer stamped the passport and handed it back to him. The passport that had been given to him worked flawlessly. He had made it into the country without incident.

He followed the crowd to baggage claim to wait for his luggage from flight EK 029 from Dubai. People flocked around the baggage carousel, pushing forward to get in position to grab their luggage when it came off the belt.

Nearby he noticed a young woman with tight jeans and a low-cut blouse struggling to get her luggage off the belt. He moved swiftly and deliberately to intervene in picking up her huge bag. The woman thanked him when she took hold of her oversized suitcase with large wheels. She gave the man a smile and a little wave before she turned to walk toward the customs area. For a brief instant, he allowed a small sneer and uttered, "You bitch," under his breath.

Zafir caught the slip in behavior and quickly returned to the professional business demeanor that he should be portraying. He spotted his new, knock-off designer bag and moved in to retrieve it but was pushed aside by a rude man lunging for his suitcase. Zafir did not want to stand out by chasing the bag, so he let it go around the carousel a second time before successfully claiming it.

He hung back a moment to observe the crowd before moving toward customs. He chose to fall in line behind a man in a rumpled sports coat who was looking around nervously. He had not recently shaven, and his bag bulged, looking like it might pop open at any moment. When they reached the front of the line, the customs agent stopped the disheveled man for questioning, but waved through the self-assured young businessman.

Zafir walked out of Heathrow customs with a smug look on his face. He had a triumphant feeling because everything had gone according to the plan. It had almost been too easy, but he knew it was just the beginning.

He maintained his heightened awareness as he navigated through the crowd toward ground transportation. He steered clear of the licensed taxis queue and instead negotiated a fare with a driver who approached him before he reached the taxi line. The driver told him he would give him a very good deal and that his car was close by.

It was meant to be, because Zafir had been told to find a private driver so his whereabouts could not be easily traced. Plus, he recognized the man's Pakistani accent and was interested in what he was doing in London. They walked outside the arrivals area, where they passed many of London's famous black taxis. It was chilly and raining lightly. The taxi driver pulled out an umbrella and held it clumsily over Zafir's head as they trudged past a parking structure. It became obvious that the car was not close at all. The driver kept pointing and repeating, "It's ahead, over there."

Finally they arrived at a flat lot where there was an assortment of aging vehicles. The driver began to profusely apologize, "So sorry—car runs better than looks." They approached a black car that had a couple of dents. The driver took Zafir's "designer" bag, and then opened the back passenger door to reveal burn holes in the upholstery. Zafir also noticed the car had no meter and was almost overwhelmed with a fishy smell, likely left over from the driver's lunch.

However, Zafir didn't mind as long as the illegal taxi could take him discreetly to his destination. He was relieved to be out of the airport, and felt extremely lucky to have found an unlicensed cab so easily. He abruptly instructed the driver, "Go to King's Cross Station."

In broken English, the driver asked him, "Where from?"

Zafir said nothing. He removed his tie and loosened his tight shirt collar because he had been instructed to look more casual at his next destination. He looked out the window and observed the drab industrial buildings and terraced, working-class flats going by.

Without prompting, the driver began to tell his own life story. "As a boy, I lived in Pakistan. Life was good, but father was member of Pakistan People's Party that wanted democracy for country. Father was arrested when military regime took over. Oldest son had to flee country to make money for family."

Zafir listened to the story with amusement. He deduced that the family was once quite wealthy and connected to a corrupt regime. That is why this man was allowed to work as a taxi driver in London, because he was sympathetic to the West.

When they approached King's Cross Station, the driver concluded, "Someday get asylum, return home. Now have little money."

Zafir had no sympathy for the man's sad story. Every day millions of people were starving while rich Westerners continued to profit. It was this man's own fault that he had to flee his own country and serve the wealthy.

Chapter Seven

The Interview

The windows of Dosha's little car were wide open so the wind blew freely through her short, tousled hair. Since St. Petersburg had so few days of good weather, Dosha made a point of relishing every moment. This was the time of year of the famous Russian white nights, when the sun set after ten and twilight lasted all night long.

The Russian people forced themselves to stay awake around the clock, probably to savor the painfully short summer and prepare themselves for the long, bitter cold winters. Young couples flocked to the romantic city to get married. Families picnicked along the river banks, and Russian citizens pushed their bodies beyond normal limits to take advantage of the light. It seemed that all the citizens of St. Petersburg had more energy and drank more vodka than the rest of the year combined. It was if they had been granted a reprieve for the harsh winters they had to endure.

As she drove by city hall, Dosha saw the young brides and groomsmen already lined up at city hall so as not to miss their designated time slot. This time of year there were at least four or five wedding parties waiting outside of city hall for the short ceremony to make the marriage official.

When she approached the designated meeting place, Dosha slowed to look for an open parking space in which to squeeze her dilapidated little car. A brand-new Lexus and a BMW impatiently honked and then accelerated around her, obviously in a big hurry.

Expensive foreign cars were becoming more and more common in the city. They were usually the premier choice of slick-looking men in their late twenties and thirties, most often entrepreneurs associated with organized crime. Although Dosha frequently had to explain to her clients that even though fraud, corruption, and financial embezzlement were common, the mafia usually left the general public alone. It wasn't as brutal or organized as most foreigners had heard or imagined.

She spotted a small parking space close to the canal. It was located near some disheveled-looking men who had obviously been sleeping off their hangovers from the famous Russian vodka. As her car noisily came to a halt, they scowled and groaned, got to their knees, and began to rise with the commotion of the new day. Slowly, the men with paunch bellies and dark circles under their eyes began to shuffle along. *What a shame*, Dosha thought, since statistics showed these men would probably be lucky if they lived into their fifties.

She could barely squeeze her car into the little space, but she somehow managed. Getting out of the car, she quickly headed across the street to avoid contact with the grumbling men as they lumbered down the street. She was running a couple of minutes late so she walked briskly toward the square where the meeting was supposed to take place.

As she approached the equestrian statue of Nicholas I in the middle of the square, she noticed a man striding deliberately toward her from across the street. He must have been waiting in the shadow of a building and had spotted her as the logical person to be his contact. When he came closer, she guessed he was somewhere in his late thirties with dark hair slightly gray at the temples. He had a lean, well-muscled build and was wearing a crisp black shirt, black slacks, and sleek leather shoes. She could make out a very determined expression on the ruggedly handsome face. He came to an abrupt halt in front of her with a questioning look on his face.

"Hello, I'm Dosha from Novicoff Travel Group. I presume you are Oliver?"

The only reaction was a slight nod.

"I understand that you are briefing me on a special tour that will be on an excursion from Stockholm to St. Petersburg?" she asked tentatively.

"That is correct."

Not very verbal, she noted when a long pause ensued. To fill the silence, she said, "Shall we get an espresso at the Hotel Astoria to review the itinerary?" pointing in the direction of the hotel.

"Yes, of course."

They turned to go across the cobbled-stoned plaza toward the famous hotel only a half a block away.

"Have you been to St. Petersburg before?" she asked.

"Yes, many times, but only for a day or two for business."

As they walked, Dosha listened carefully and tried to identify Oliver's accent. What was it? American with some Aussie and maybe a tinge of German thrown in? She could normally figure out an accent very quickly, but he had obviously lived in many places so it was difficult to pinpoint.

There was another long silence, so Dosha started into her tour guide narrative. "The Hotel Astoria held a special place in Russia's history and was a symbol of pride for the citizens of St. Petersburg. It was rumored that during WWII, Hitler had picked this hotel for his victory party because he believed he would inevitably defeat the Russians. He intended to claim St. Petersburg for his own, and for that reason he refrained from bombing the city. Now the hotel is a frequent choice for international professionals to meet to conduct business."

They took a seat in the relatively empty café, where they had a wonderful view of the Saint Isaac's Cathedral. Dosha knew this location well because it was a regular stopping point on her city tours. It was a popular site because the Russian aristocracy had spent large sums of money to bring the best European artisans to work on the cathedral. It also had a colorful past because during the Soviet era, it was turned into the Museum of Atheism, and in WWII, the golden domes were painted gray to avoid the attention of enemy aircraft.

Oliver was not looking at the cathedral. Instead, his attention was fixed on Dosha. He noted her modern appearance with short, red hair that was fashionably cut. Her green, tailored shirt brought out the glint in her green eyes.

"How long have you been leading tours in St. Petersburg?" he finally asked.

"Four years, with tour groups of almost every nationality."

"How many languages do you speak?"

"Four fluently: Russian of course, English, German, French, and a working bit of others. Why do you ask?"

He suddenly leaned forward and cracked a brief smile. "I guess I'm interrogating too much. I should be briefing you, but it has been a long week."

Oliver had no time to waste in evaluating Dosha for the job ahead of her. He did not plan on telling her about the potential dangers of the assignment. There would be time later after he had collected more information to see if she was the right candidate.

Oliver explained, "The tour group will consist of eighty people, including politicians, senior management of public and private corporations, and many gifted scientists who specialize in environmental research."

He went through some more specifics regarding the attendee list while Dosha listened attentively to their bios.

When he was finished, Dosha commented, "It's an interesting group of people. I will have to research the dismal Russian environmental practices because I'm sure they will ask."

Oliver went on, "Your job will be to keep them interested in the tour agenda."

"Well, I guarantee that I'm one of the more entertaining Russian tour guides that you will be able to find."

Oliver recognized that Dosha had a lot of spirit and confidence, so she could probably handle even the most difficult group. She also seemed forthright, so he would be able to work with her on security issues.

"Your job will be to keep me informed of any unusual behavior or incidents that involve any of the travelers. By the way, we'll be flying you to Stockholm to assume the tour guide responsibility from the beginning of the cruise. Also, there is a planned stop in Helsinki that you should be aware of. You might want to brush up on the sights in the city."

Dosha was excited. "I'll start preparing right away. There is a rich history of sunken ships and precious cargoes at the bottom of the Baltic Sea. Many are just being discovered now because the Soviets used to worry that military secrets would be exposed. This will be a fascinating trip!"

Oliver just smiled and said, "It will be interesting for a lot of reasons." He motioned to the server for the bill. "I'll be in contact regarding any new information."

After the meeting, Oliver left directly for the airport to fly to Moscow. He was scheduled to meet with the Russian Federal Security Service to discuss intelligence information about the transmissions that had been intercepted. Oliver was also curious to find out what they knew about the upcoming climate forum in Stockholm. If they were willing to cooperate, the Russians were a good source of information, particularly on all their northern European neighbors on the Baltic Sea.

Chapter Eight

Stockholm Arrival

The taxi dropped Nicole off in front of the ultra modern Nordic Lights Hotel. She walked into the lobby, where there was an interesting interplay of colored lights against the stark, black, cube-shaped furniture. It was obvious that the hotel had been conceived as a showcase of modern Swedish design to attract the hip, young business traveler.

At the small bar, there was an interview going on between a middle-aged businessman with thick glasses and a young woman who was trying to act more experienced than she looked. Behind the bar, images were flashing on a muted TV of what looked like yet another mudslide that had devastated a village somewhere in India. Mothers, fathers, sisters, and brothers were digging frantically with their hands, trying to save their loved ones.

Two men sat down at the bar, ordered a couple of beers, and asked the bartender to change the channel to a football match. These disasters had become so common that most people just ignored the broadcasts. Catastrophic human suffering had become a routine news event.

At the front desk, a vivacious young desk clerk smiled. "Welcome to the Nordic Lights Hotel. How was your flight?"

"Not bad after we finally got going," Nicole said as she handed the slim, Swedish blonde an American Express card.

She pulled up the reservation and said, "Ah yes, you have a suite on the conference level."

Nicole had booked the suite because she wanted to personally meet a few scientists to discuss proposals for funding. She had also left open some time slots to meet with those who stood out during the Climate Forum. It was important because many brilliant scientists were not very adept at selling their ideas, so promising research often went unfunded.

"There are several messages and a couple of deliveries waiting for you. The packages have already been brought to your room."

Nicole immediately thought it must be the usual favors given by people trying to get money for their various programs. She had discovered that representing a foundation with deep pockets made one very popular. Maybe people were just trying to be nice, but she was always suspicious.

"Here are your messages."

There were four messages: two from the foundation office, one from Senator Clarkston inviting her to the reception that Carl had told her about, and a manila envelope with "Nicole Hunter" written in bold letters.

Nicole finally reached the room and opened the door to be greeted by bouquets of flowers, chocolates, and a bottle of champagne. The mood lights above the bed illuminated a soothing blue glow. It was nice to be in the hotel room after a grueling long-distance flight. She opened the manila envelope that had been given her at the front desk and pulled out several grainy black and white photos. The first photo was of three men entering a modern skyscraper. They were photographed from the back, were dressed in conservative suits, and were carrying briefcases.

The second photo showed a group of six people seated around a large table in a dark room. It was if the picture had been taken behind some sort of screen, so it was hard to make out. Everyone was in shadow, as if they were purposely hiding their identity. The location seemed unusual as the room had irregular stone walls and appeared to be lit with candles.

The last one was the most disturbing because it was the most personal. Nicole recognized the circumstances immediately. It was a photograph of a lunch in a downtown Seattle sushi restaurant. She was meeting with a couple of the board members to discuss the new strategic vision for the foundation. The photo must have been taken discreetly from a table nearby, or maybe by one of the wait staff, because everyone in attendance was easy to identify.

Nicole's first thought was that the photos were some kind of joke. What could they possibly mean, and why were they sent to her hotel? She was puzzled, unsure if this was information she was supposed to have, or some kind of threat that needed quick action.

She examined the manila envelope and realized it must have been hand-delivered because there was no postage or return address. If there hadn't been a personal photo in the envelope, she would have ignored the whole thing. She could not fathom the connection between the photos. As a starting point, she decided to call the front desk to see who had made the anonymous delivery.

The day clerk who had been on duty in morning was not there, but the woman at the front desk was helpful and said she would make a few calls.

A little later, the woman phoned back. She said the day clerk had only vaguely remembered the delivery person as a quiet young man, and could not recall him wearing a uniform or having any identification. The woman politely inquired if hotel security should be contacted, to which Nicole declined.

She hung up and then called a colleague who was the security liaison officer at the foundation. Sydney specialized in background checks on the legitimacy of the individuals and international groups applying for grants. She would know what to do.

"Hi, Sydney, how goes the battle?"

"Oh, the usual. Are you calling from Stockholm?"

"Yes, I finally made it. Some photos were waiting for me when I checked in at the hotel. Could you help me figure out what they mean?"

"Sure."

Nicole went on to briefly describe each of the photos and explained what little she knew about the person who delivered them.

In a concerned tone, Sydney said, "You shouldn't just blow them off. You never know what the connection could be to you or the foundation."

"But I can't think of any reason why they were sent to me."

"Could you scan the photos and send to me so I can do some research and find out if there is anything behind it? I have a few contacts who specialize in international security. They might be able to help. "

"Okay. I'll take them to the hotel's business office right away."

"Perfect."

Nicole hesitated for a second and then decided to ask a favor. "There is one other thing that I want to talk to you about. Carl Everson called me to tell me that a couple of the board members are not happy with my decision to attend the Climate Forum. If you hear anything, I would appreciate if you would let me know. I need to figure out what I'm dealing with."

"I can do that, and by the way," she added, quickly changing the subject, "there is a great techno DJ playing at Club Kharma, probably not too far from your hotel. You really need to get a life and check it out."

"You are more right than you know."

Sydney's boyfriend was a musician in Seattle, and she was a devout follower of the Seattle techno music scene. She dressed in a unique style all her own. Her overdyed black hair, dark eye makeup, dark painted fingernails, and unusual choice of attire often caught people by surprise. Most people would not guess that she graduated magna cum lade with a double major in international affairs and criminology at a prominent university. Nicole liked the fact that she was unbiased and loyal and very motivated to get all the facts before coming to a logical conclusion.

Sydney said, "I'll get back to you as soon as I've looked at the photos and spoken with my contacts."

With the conversation completed, Nicole felt like she could focus on other things.

She decided to make a phone call to Sam to tell him that she had arrived safely after a scare on the flight out of Seattle. She wanted to gauge his mood and reaction. It would be the first time she would talk to him since having the argument at the restaurant before she left on the trip.

The phone rang a few times, and then she heard him say, "Hello?" Nicole could hear loud music and voices in the background.

"Hi! It's me. I thought I would check in. What's going on?"

"Nothing, I'm just having drinks with my friends at the club."

Nicole noticed that Sam was slurring his words a little. She could also hear high-pitched laughter in the background and realized that most of the "friends" were female.

"Do you have a minute to talk?"

He avoided the question and said in a sarcastic voice, "Where in the world are you and who you saving this time?"

"Never mind. I thought you might be interested in how the trip went."

"No, not really. I'm telling a very funny story to my new best friends."

Nicole realized this conversation was going to be the confirmation of the end of their relationship and went directly to the point. "I think that both of us know this is not working and it's time to call it quits."

There was a sharp intake of breath, and he seemed to sober up for a moment. He said, "Wait, let's not rush."

"I really don't see any point in dragging this all out. It is best to have a clean break."

"Nicole ..."

She hung up the phone and sat down on the bed. It was not a surprise, since this relationship had taken the same course as all the others. It was fun and hopeful for the first year but started going downhill the second year. She knew it would just be a matter of time before it turned ugly, so it was best to break it off before the rehashed arguments began.

It had been a lousy day. Nicole lay down on the bed and closed her eyes to try to relieve the headache that had descended on her.

Chapter Nine

The London Cell

The taxi driver dropped off Zafir at King's Cross Station in northeast central London. The light rain had developed into a steady downpour. He sought refuge under the arched roof of the busy railway station and surveyed his surroundings. The scurrying people seemed to all blend together, with their heads down and overcoats buttoned up snugly. The air smelled of traffic fumes and wet cement. How different this place was from where he grew up, where it was always warm and the colors were vivid, with pungent aromas assaulting the senses.

Zafir assessed the scene in all directions, trying to determine if anyone was following him. He didn't notice anyone suspicious, but just in case, he walked out of the station through a different entrance than he came in. He crossed the street, walked a ways, and looked around again. He was damp and chilled but maintained his alertness. Finally, he went back to the railway station and located another unlicensed cab driver to take him to Newham in East London.

This borough of London was located about five miles east of the River Thames, so Zafir sat back and watched the foreign, gray city go by. He knew that his contacts attended the University of East London and were majoring in Computing and Technology. They were known for both their intelligence and extremism, and in a short time he would be conferring with one of the most advanced underground terrorist cells in the world.

The driver dropped him off in the warehouse district on Romford Road. It took a few moments to get his bearings. He immediately saw that many of the people walking by and in the shops looked like himself: dark, Middle Eastern. He instantly felt more comfortable than any time since arriving in London.

He had been e-mailed instructions to go two blocks north, over the rail tracks to Forest Lane Road. There, he had been told to walk up and down the road until someone came to meet him. As Zafir walked down the lane, he thought about how far he had come from the slum that he and his mother lived in. He was now well educated and had the power to change the corrupt world that had injured them so grievously. If his mother had still been alive, he was convinced that she would be very proud of her son.

He had been so preoccupied remembering his past that he didn't notice a man sliding from behind a warehouse delivery door. The man stepped into his path and demanded, "Halt." He carried an AK-47 assault rifle that was aimed at Zafir from only a couple feet away.

"I am Zafir and you should have been told I was coming."

The young man with the AK-47 pointed the weapon away from him. "We've been waiting for you," he said in English but with a definite Pakistani accent.

"I have come a long way and it is a pleasure to be here," Zafir proudly stated.

"Come with me, and we will find you a place to rest and meet the others."

Zafir followed the man into the dark warehouse. Inside were shipping boxes stacked high, almost to the ceiling. The two men weaved a path between the palettes of boxes, turning right, left, and then right again. The first rows of huge boxes said "Made in China" and had many numbers on them. The man with the AK-47 said, "This is the business that finances our real purpose."

Zafir asked, "What business is that?"

"We import counterfeit merchandise labeled with popular logos and sell them in the flea markets in Eastern Europe. Famous brands always sell well, even if the quality is not so good."

He went over to one of the large boxes, opened the top, pulled out one of the items, and threw it to Zafir.

"That looks like it might fit you."

It was a t-shirt that had a large Nike logo on the front.

"Counterfeit brands are a very profitable business, and if we get caught, the government just confiscates the property. Some of the inventory comes from real factories where workers skim off the top by making overruns of popular products and then ship them out the back door. Other products are made by copying the originals with cheaper materials."

They continued toward the back of the warehouse until a crack of light from an open door became visible. Zafir could hear muffled voices drifting toward them. Inside were two men working at computer terminals, and one more was heating a vial of caustic-smelling liquid over a burner. The entire left side of the room looked like a chemistry lab, with glass tubes, metal racks, and monitoring equipment.

Along the back wall, white plastic containers were stacked and labeled with serial numbers. The men looked up from their work and nodded to him as he entered their workspace. They had clearly been expecting him.

"Sit down, my friend. We have much to tell you. My name is Husnan, and we are here to help you succeed."

"Thank you; your reputation is greatly respected," said Zafir with admiration in his voice.

"As is yours. I understand you have masterminded attacks on oil companies by bringing down their company's computer systems."

Embarrassed by the compliment, Zafir said, "You are too kind. I have just been able to create enough instability in the market to affect the price of oil for a day or two."

Husnan smiled. "But that brings havoc and instability to the institution."

Zafir thought about how far he had come since he had been recruited from a state-run orphanage outside of Jidda. It had been a scorching day, and the dry wind blew sand into his face as they left the crumbling building. He had entered a transport vehicle where a young man, just a couple of years older than himself, put a blindfold on him. The young man didn't say a word, but Zafir accepted this act because he so desperately wanted to leave the orphanage behind. There could be nothing worse than being locked up, literally wasting away with little food.

Zafir had been brought to a remote training camp with other unwanted boys who were collected from the streets and poorly run orphanages. From the very beginning, he stood out from the others because he was driven and had an uncanny ability to pick up new languages. Camp leaders eventually found it useful to bring him along to assist in business transactions, such as acquiring explosives and firearms.

Zafir had stayed in the background, listening to the chatter of the dealers. As the deals approached closure, the sellers often bragged amongst themselves, thinking no one could understand them. Then he would inconspicuously pass the information on and would often save the camp from paying too high a price or buying defective weapons.

At the age of fourteen, he was sent to a smaller cell to take advantage of his exceptional intelligence. There he felt he was more fully utilized because this cell was technologically advanced and had access to an extensive information technology network.

Now, Zafir was working with the London cell, and it was the highlight of his young life. He could not help but admire the cyber terrorists who were leading the way in the new world. The cell's contacts were far-reaching, and the network had taken years of meticulous planning to build. Their ability to hack into secure websites was well-known and admired by the other cells. They had demonstrated their skill in creating viruses that could bring down major systems and extract secret information from classified government sites, all without being detected.

Zafir knew these men had been educated in the UK and had a good understanding of the Western world. They were a new breed of terrorist, because instead of blowing themselves up, they wanted to be around to increase their knowledge to use even more leading-edge, technical approaches for radical change.

Husnan began, "We have been able to plant several key parasitic backdoor security holes in targeted systems, enabling us to obtain classified and precise information for the mission."

Zafir inquired, "How have the backdoor programs been installed?"

"We have programmers at universities who contract projects for governments and major private companies. They have created the security breaches for us. We access the gaps when we need them."

Zafir was impressed. He had hacked many systems, but it was usually done on a more haphazard basis, primarily using a Trojan with a payload.

Husnan explained proudly, "The chemistry lab is a new and vital addition to our cell. We have had a recent infusion of cash, from a private sponsor, so we have the funds to start developing chemical weapons. In fact, the black market in poisons and other toxins is booming, and they have become much more valuable than traditional weapons."

Zafir commented, "It is a blessing to have such a benevolent sponsor."

Next to speak was the mechanical engineer. "I am providing you with detailed schematics of the target. Study carefully and commit as much information to memory as possible."

Zafir smiled, knowing that would not be a problem.

Lastly, the chemist spoke. He could not contain his excitement as he held up a small vial of liquid. "Here is a valuable sample obtained for us by our sponsor. Someday we hope to manufacture it ourselves."

He gave Zafir complete instructions for its use and emphasized its volatile properties. He finished by saying, "If you succeed, we will have weapons at our disposal that will change history."

With the combination of the members' hacking skills and the cell's new mission to manufacture chemical weapons, Zafir could not help but be impressed.

The briefing and final preparations lasted for several hours, until it was time to leave for the flight to Stockholm. He had been provided a credible cover, a work permit, and official documents to support it.

Finally, he was given the small vial of liquid. It had been sealed in a small, sample-size cologne bottle and then hidden in a shaving kit along with travel-size shampoo and other toiletries. All the other tools needed to perform the assignment had been smuggled onto the ship over the past year and were hidden where Zafir could easily access them.

He left the warehouse that night, inspired, with a purpose that he had not felt in a long time. He knew in his soul that it was time for his mother's death to be avenged.

The man with the AK-47 accompanied Zafir to the end of the block and motioned him to continue down the dark street. Zafir pulled up his collar against the damp chill, secured the small kit containing the vial of liquid, and then began to retrace his journey back to Heathrow.

To be careful, he walked many blocks beyond the point where he had originally been dropped off. He was in a good mood because he felt he had gained the confidence of the esteemed terrorist group and he was proud to be have been assigned such a critically important mission.

It was late, and the streets were bare, with only an occasional, lone passerby. There were not any taxis to be found. The ones he did see had passengers in them, so he just kept walking. Eventually he had no choice but to draw attention to himself by grabbing a cab when another passenger got out. The driver looked at him in the rear-view mirror while he called in his current location and the airport destination to the dispatcher. Zafir sunk down low in the seat, trying to become invisible.

He arrived at the airport with little time to spare to get through security and catch the late-night flight to Stockholm.

Chapter Ten

Intelligence

On the flight from Moscow to Stockholm, Oliver sat in business class and reviewed the file on known terrorists active in the northern European region. The Russian Foreign Intelligence Service had been very open and even helpful in sharing this information, knowing it would be to their benefit for Oliver to intercede.

He noticed that the ties between organized crime syndicates and terrorists on jihad missions were becoming increasingly intertwined. Several names on the list were known to him from his intelligence work on illegal weapons. The black marketers would feed the weapons for the attacks, resulting in business dealings and dependency between underworld capitalists and religious zealots.

While he drank a glass of wine and snacked on almonds, Oliver wondered if that was why he had been assigned to this unusual case. Originally, he had argued with the director of the Global Security Alliance, "My skills in tactical intelligence and precision targeting will be wasted on this assignment."

The director answered, "The experts at the Alliance have recommended you."

"But I am more knowledgeable about weapon sales to transnational terrorist organizations."

"You will go where the Global Alliance determines you are the most valuable."

Oliver countered, "Instead of working to resolve a dangerous arms deal, I will be doing routine security for a group of bureaucrats who have a track record of not making decisions."

The director decisively told Oliver, "It's time to expand your horizons," and then walked out of the room.

Oliver knew he had developed a reputation for producing results in seizing large caches of illegal weapons and cutting off the most dangerous black market suppliers: those who sell to the highest bidder. But now he had been called in because there had been an increase in intelligence chatter hinting at something big happening in northern Europe. It was an ambiguous assignment, one that he was not looking forward to.

As the sun was setting out his business-class window, Oliver turned on the overhead light and opened another file containing the Security Alliance's intelligence reports. He reviewed the second, more complete communication that had been intercepted by an airborne device passing over a known terrorist camp at low altitudes.

He was familiar with this surveillance technology in tracking the movement of shipments of weapons across borders. It had radar reflective panels attached to it and special light panels that hid it in broad daylight so it was virtually undetectable. The device was able to transmit video and sound to minute detail, and was even effective in getting information out of hilly areas where satellites had difficulty transmitting.

From his dealings in the weapons trade, Oliver knew that many successful extremist factions had broken down into smaller groups, some with only five or six people to direct and control precision strikes. These groups ran independently but could inflict damage on a horrifying but limited scale. Now, it was becoming apparent that more intricate and coordinated communication systems were beginning to develop between these cells. This likely meant that bigger and more systematic terrorist attacks could be on the horizon.

Oliver adjusted his seat back to a more comfortable position and attentively studied the analysis. The linguists at the Security Alliance had meticulously examined the intercepted messages. After much debate, they reported the core translation as "battered earth," with the reference to a more precise coordinates, Stockholm, including a brief reference to a ship.

After more scrutiny, they concluded that the most probable target was the Climate Forum taking place in Stockholm. Next, they investigated the people and circumstances around the forum and discovered that a select group of people would also be attending a private Baltic Sea cruise. At that point, the combined events were given a high level threat status.

Oliver arrived early in the morning in Stockholm. He checked into a drab, functional hotel near the airport. He showered, had a quick breakfast, and then headed back to the airport to get up-to-speed on how the intelligence work was proceeding. It was important that he get to the

Passport Control Office to oversee the calibration of the visa information on travelers beginning to enter Sweden.

Key diplomats, business leaders, scientists, and concerned citizens of the world had started to arrive in Stockholm. The Swedish government was cooperating with Oliver on running a program to match terrorists on international watch lists. He added the information from Moscow to the international database to cross-match passport entries into Stockholm over the last three months.

As the computer processed the data, Oliver paused to look out over the long lines of people going through passport control. He was looking through the one-way window in the sterile security office with metal furniture and white walls. A group of loud and jovial middle-aged Americans stood out, probably having consumed too much liquor on their flight to Stockholm.

In another queue, there was a group of school-age children in uniform being led by a stern-looking school teacher. They were followed by a British tour group who appeared to be concerned about sticking close together. To add to the confusion were tourists and business people from every corner of the globe dressed in both traditional and modern attire.

So many people coming from so many different places, Oliver thought wearily. The line of people in passport control only confirmed how complex this assignment was and how impossible it would be to find a lead to trace the intercepted intelligence. Maybe it was all a hoax.

He knew he could do better work when he could focus on a single target, with good surveillance prior to getting involved, but it was not his choice. He grimaced as he thought back to the agency chief giving him orders to "expand his horizons."

At that moment, his cell phone alerted him that he had received a text message. It read, "Call Jake - important."

Jake was one of the agency's analysts who worked in gathering intelligence on high-profile cases. Oliver had worked with him for many years. He had a talent in monitoring massive amounts of information and finding the connecting threads. His knack for sorting out the important information from all the background noise was impressive.

Oliver placed a call right away to see what was up.

Once his assistant pulled him out of a meeting, Jake greeted Oliver and said, "Hey, I thought this might be important so I wanted to contact you. I received a call from Sydney McIntyre, who is a security advisor for the Everson Foundation. Her colleague arrived in Stockholm to attend the Global Climate Forum and received some threatening photos."

"What is the Everson Foundation?" asked Oliver.

"It's a charitable foundation in the States that is quite powerful due to its financial resources."

"Hmmm … and the photos?"

"Sydney told me that one was shot in the Middle East, one at some kind of heated international meeting, and another with people from the Everson Foundation. We are working to identify the locations and people right now. I'll get back to you with more information when we have it."

Oliver thought for a moment. "It may be a long shot but I suppose is the only lead we have that corresponds with our intelligence."

"There is one other thing. The group she is with will be continuing on a cruise following the Climate Forum, some sort of think tank. It sounds like a fit with the intelligence we received. I'll text you the contact information."

"Thanks, Jake. Let me know if any other leads come up."

Oliver hung up and turned to the computer terminal to look at the output. The list of known terrorists and alias names did not reveal anything significant. More interesting was the list of people who came up with unusual travel itineraries prior to their arrival in Stockholm.

Oliver called the number given to him by Jake to follow up on the threatening photos received by the Everson Foundation Director.

"Hello, Sydney; this is Oliver Odin."

"I've been waiting for your call."

Oliver explained, "We are on alert for any unusual activity in Stockholm right now. The photos could be a threat, and they should be investigated. I am at the airport in Stockholm and heading into the city. Could you arrange a meeting with your director as soon as possible?"

"Yes, of course. I'll contact the director right away."

Chapter Eleven

The Connection

A couple of hours later, Oliver walked into the Nordic Lights Hotel. He had the front desk call the room number of the director of the Everson Foundation and went to the lobby bar to wait. The bar was empty so it would be an acceptable place to have a private conversation.

While waiting, Oliver studied the computer printouts that he had received from the Swedish Immigration Service. The criteria would identify anyone who came from a country that was known for terrorist activity but had also visited at least three other high-risk countries in the last year. Oliver knew this was an indication of funding from an unknown source, or very mobile travelers with no apparent business affiliation. The legitimate business people would be cross-checked with company records, and the "students or not identified" put in a different category.

Oliver was engrossed in the names on the list and the countries they had visited, when he saw someone heading his way out of the corner of his eye. He turned to greet the person and quickly realized that the director was not the male he had assumed but a beautiful woman with penetrating eyes and a disarming smile.

The front desk had pointed to the man working on his laptop in the lobby bar. Nicole hoped this meeting would not take too long because she had another appointment following this one. She walked toward the man, who seemed to sense her approach. He turned and stood up to greet her.

"Hello, I'm Nicole Hunter from the Everson Foundation." He looked a little surprised, like she had caught him off-guard.

"Uh, I'm Oliver Odin. Thanks for meeting me on such short notice."

"Well, my security manager didn't give me any choice. She was insistent that I meet with you."

Nicole sat down in the comfortable lounge chair and ordered a cappuccino to fight off the effects of a sleepless night. In order to hurry things along, she handed the manila envelope to Oliver and said, "These are the photos that were left for me at the front desk."

Oliver carefully looked over the outside of envelope and then pulled out the photos, looking at each one briefly. Then he put down the envelope and turned his attention back to Nicole. "Tell me about the Everson Foundation and explain to me what you do."

He listened attentively as Nicole gave him a brief synopsis. His only reaction was raising an eyebrow when she told him the amount of money that passed through the foundation coffers.

Then she asked, "So what exactly is it that *you* do?"

"I am a specialized agent with the Global Security Alliance. I normally work with the illegal weapons trade."

As Oliver continued on, Nicole began to realize he was not the bureaucratic security officer that she had expected. This was a man who dealt with the dark world of greed and deception on a grand scale. It was his job to stop those who no one else could, even if it meant risking his life.

Nicole couldn't help but ask a personal question. "What motivates you to do such a dangerous job?"

He looked straight at her and said, "Let's focus on the assignment."

Nicole was intrigued by his evasive answer.

Abruptly, he turned his attention back to the photos and methodically began to ask questions about each one. "Do you recognize the men walking into the building or the location where the pictures were taken?"

"No, I don't know anything about the first two photos, but I immediately recognized the one taken at the restaurant in Seattle."

"Tell me about that one."

"My budget director and I were meeting with two of the foundation's board members. The board was in town for a briefing on global warming and its impact of the human condition. This was a new direction for the foundation's money and not all the board members were in favor of it. We were meeting with two of the biggest dissenters at lunch when the picture was taken."

Oliver asked, "Who are they and what do they do?"

"This one is Jamal Nasir, who sits on boards for numerous global corporations. The other one is Jean Cutter, who is a university professor and a former corporate lawyer. They are both highly regarded in their work, but they are old school and not very progressive about environmental issues. They prefer the foundation to give aid to people after tragedies have already happened. I want to take a more proactive role, such as educating people and improving the environment, instead of giving money to countries after a huge crisis has occurred. We are pouring money down a black hole and simply cannot keep up with the need. There have been too many natural disasters, warlords, and warring factions to effectively save people from physical harm, starvation, and brutality!"

At that moment, Nicole realized she had been going on and on about her work. Oliver had stopped writing and was gazing at her with keen interest.

She stopped. "Sorry, sometimes I get too passionate."

"I don't think someone could be too passionate about a job like yours," he offered.

Nicole was surprised by the gentleness of the comment. She suddenly didn't know what say, so she asked Oliver, "What do you think about these?" pointing to the photos.

"I think the people who sent them to you may see your foundation as a threat to their cause. Can you tell me about the role of the Everson Foundation in political, social, and economic affairs in the Middle East?"

"There is no connection that I know of."

"We are working on identifying the people and places from the copies that were sent to us by your security manager, Sydney McIntyre. So far, we know that the building in the background of the first photo is the Abraj Atta' Awuenya Towers in Ridha, Saudi Arabia. It is headquarters for many businesses related to energy, mainly gas and oil."

"In Saudi Arabia?"

"Maybe someone could be unhappy about your interest in the Climate Forum? Of course, that is just a conjecture at this point."

Nicole said, "I deal with corporate politics and inept agencies, not fanatical groups."

Oliver furrowed his brow and looked concerned. "Well, you may have wandered into new territory."

"Oh great, that's just what the foundation needs," she said dejectedly.

"We have intelligence that puts us on alert in Stockholm during the dates of the Climate Forum, along with references to a ship. This all may be a coincidence, but it signals a warning."

"That is interesting, because we have invited an elite group of people to attend a think tank symposium on a cruise on the Baltic Sea following the Climate Forum."

Oliver looked at Nicole with heightened interest. "I think it will be best if I go to the Climate Forum to monitor what is going on."

"The general assembly begins tomorrow. Most of the speakers for that session will be presenting their previously submitted papers. My main focus will be on private meetings with more current research."

"Since this threat may be directed at you and your foundation, I'll also need access to your private meetings."

"I suppose I can arrange for 'an analyst' to come along with me so you can attend the whole thing."

"That would work."

"The first official social event takes place tonight when Senator James Clarkston throws a cocktail party for the US delegates. Do you need access to that as well?" Nicole asked.

"Who will be there?"

"My guess is that it will be mostly politicians and business people. James Clarkston is a powerful, conservative senator from Texas. I think he is trying to be politically astute for the younger voters in Texas, but his major financial support comes from huge global energy companies. I must say that I was surprised when I heard he was hosting a cocktail party at the Climate Forum."

"That does seem unusual."

"There must be a back-story that I'm not aware of," admitted Nicole.

"It sounds like something I need to check out."

"We probably need to elevate you from a lowly analyst to a benefactor to attend the social event. Can you come up with a story on why you are donating lots of money to the foundation?"

"No problem," stated Oliver.

"Great; can you be here at eight? We can go together and I can introduce you to the other guests."

It crossed Nicole's mind that Oliver was a remarkable man, and attending the reception might actually be more fun than she had originally thought. It almost sounded like a date, but of course it was only a security assignment. She looked at her watch and realized she was late for her next meeting. "I've got to run, but I'll see you tonight. Thanks so much for checking this all out."

The two scientists in her next meeting had spent the last ten years of their lives working on developing an alternative fuel. David Cason was tall and lanky with unruly blonde hair, and wore a wrinkled shirt. He had an infectious, boyish grin that gave him an immediate likability.

Chen Wu was shorter and neatly dressed, with closely cropped hair. He appeared more serious than David, with intelligent and inquisitive eyes that shone through his dark-rimmed glasses. Nicole smiled as she thought what a mismatched pair they made.

When they began to speak, Nicole realized they were very compatible, because they were both modest scientists who cared deeply about their work. They completed each other's sentences and deferred the attention to one another, frequently giving each other the credit. It seemed they had a lot of respect for each other.

David said, "I started working on the project when I was an undergraduate student. I carried it on to my graduate studies, where I met this brilliant guy," pointing at Chen and flashing a smile. "We teamed up, and from then on, all of our free time has been spent in the university lab, working on the breakthrough."

Chen explained, "We contacted your foundation because we need help with funding to test the procedure outside of the lab. So far, everyone seems to be more interested in having us sign legal documents than talking to us about our work. We need a partner to help us."

Nicole thought their dedication and intelligence were impressive, and their motivation was for the greater good, not for money or fame. She asked them to provide documentation on their project so the probability of success could be established by independent scientists. Potentially, this might be a breakthrough that would alter the dire predictions of global climate change.

They did not hesitate. David rummaged through a worn backpack and handed over disks that contained research files. Nicole promised she would give it due diligence and get back to them as soon as the foundation had reviewed it.

She really liked these guys and hoped their work lived up to their reputation. It reminded her why she liked her job so much: she had the ability to cut through the bureaucracy and get things done.

Chapter Twelve

The Reception

Oliver showed up in the lobby promptly at eight in a sharp-looking black suit. Before they left for the reception, Nicole and Oliver spent some time over a glass of wine discussing his cover for the Climate Forum. Oliver had done research on a wealthy family living in the Cayman Islands who had made their fortune in rare gems. He would assume the role of youngest son, who handled all the philanthropy for the family's estate. The story was that he was making a large donation to the foundation and was in Stockholm to personally decide where the money should go. Nicole thought it was a good cover because it played to Oliver's international accent and polished demeanor.

They walked to the reception being held at the nearby Nordic Sea Hotel, the sister hotel of the Nordic Lights Hotel. People were arriving, mostly dressed in cocktail attire. They followed the stream of people, passing large aquarium tanks filled with exotic fish. Outside the banquet room door was a reception line that consisted of Senator James Clarkston and his Washington DC delegation.

Senator Clarkston said with a charming Southern drawl, "So happy to see you, Nicole. I'm glad you could make it. So who is your friend?"

"Thank you, senator. This is—"

Oliver quickly interceded and smoothly introduced himself as Jonathan Walton from the Cayman Islands.

Senator Clarkston's interest was piqued. "One of my favorite places to visit. Let's talk later."

Inside the room there were elaborately carved reindeer ice-sculptures on a long table surrounded by northern Swedish delicacies. The food was laid out on beautiful ice platters with unique foliage arrangements in the middle. The deer sculptures looked as if they were grazing in a small forest.

A smiling hostess greeted them, served champagne, and gave them an invitation to visit the world-famous Ice Bar. Their designated time was nine o'clock, and she explained it was the highlight of the reception. Each group would be rotating through the famous Swedish Ice Bar at forty-five-minute intervals. She emphasized it was a must-see.

Nicole and Oliver wandered over to the extravagant spread of food and read the descriptions of the Swedish delicacies: Bleak roe with almond potato pancake, forest mushrooms with peppered lingonberries, gin-spiced reindeer with vanilla-flavored juice and Arrack-marinated cloudberries.

Nicole left Oliver sampling the cuisine and scanning the people in attendance. When she crossed the room, she noticed a small group of political types near the bar who were getting loud. One of the men who stood out was a short, stocky man with a martini in one hand and a cigar in the other. For some reason, he looked vaguely familiar, but she couldn't place him. Maybe she had seen him at a fundraiser. He was red in the face and talking emphatically to a pretty woman in the group who appeared to be annoyed by his advances.

Nicole changed directions and went over to visit the scientists and environmentalists who had grouped together. As she came closer, she realized that the two scientists that she had met with earlier, David and Chen, were among the group. She was surprised to see the two of them at a cocktail party with Senator Clarkston because they had seemed to be scientists with few resources and no political affiliation.

Nicole inquired, "Hi, guys! What are you doing here?"

David joked, "We couldn't pass up a free meal." Chen didn't say a word and seemed to avoid Nicole's gaze.

To the broader group, she asked, "Is there going to be anything interesting presented at the opening tomorrow?"

One of the more vocal environmentalists said, "The forum itself is going to be rather ordinary—mostly a presentation of the work already published."

Keeping his voice low, David leaned over to Nicole and said, "The more breakthrough projects will be discussed on the excursion to St. Petersburg. We'll be able to synergize with the other scientists."

She was pleased to hear this since the Everson Foundation was arranging the collaborative cruise on the Baltic Sea.

At nine sharp, Nicole and Oliver headed to the Ice Bar entrance for the tour. Senator Clarkston and his aide accompanied the group, which was also comprised of Washington DC environmental policy-makers and some scientists.

The bar attendants outfitted the group with oversized silver parkas shaped like capes, complete with hoods and attached gloves. The group looked like it was getting ready for an expedition to the North Pole, providing humorous fodder for the intoxicated guests.

A woman in the DC delegation said loudly, "We don't need parkas; we've got Absolut insulation." The immediate group all laughed hysterically.

A drunken man next to her quipped, "You look like an ice queen."

She flippantly responded, "And you're an idiot in a snow suit."

After the partygoers finally managed to wrestle their parkas on, the group passed through the first door and arrived in the air lock chamber, separating the warm hotel from the arctic environment.

The attendant paused in the crowded chamber to tell them the Ice Bar was harvested from the Torne River, on the border of Finland and Sweden, where the famous Ice Hotel in Jukkasjarvi was located. The bar was kept at a crisp twenty-three degrees Fahrenheit year round so the group could only be in the bar for forty minutes due to the frigid conditions. Even the bartenders and the wait staff were required to rotate out of the cold environment at that time.

As they passed through the second door, a blast of cold air hit them. They stepped into a surreal room completely made of crystal ice. Light refracted through the ice blocks and created a pasty blue reflection on human faces. Everyone's silver parkas took on an eerie, unearthly glow, and it felt as if they had entered an alien environment.

The impact of the cold temperature hit Nicole, and she realized that forty minutes would be a long time to be in this environment. She walked over to the bar, made out of a thick slab of ice, and ordered a fun vodka drink from the bartender, who was dressed in a sleek black outfit with a wild furry, silver hat. He wore insulated gloves while he pulled out a square glass, made entirely out of ice, and expertly poured from unusually shaped bottles.

When Nicole picked up the ice glass, she had to grasp it tightly so that it would not slip out of her gloved hand. She laughed at the frivolity going on around her. She could see that the guests were in high spirits, accentuated by the arctic environment and the free-flowing alcohol.

After talking to several of the environmental policy guests, Nicole could see that Senator Clarkston had excused himself and was moving toward her. She had been introduced to him once before at a fundraiser in Washington DC, but she never really liked the man. He came across pompous and always seemed to be working some angle or another.

He came to her and gave her a hug. "Are you enjoying yourself?"

"Oh yes. This is quite the experience; thanks for inviting me."

"Well, you are an important little lady!" he said in a booming politician's voice that sounded condescending.

He took hold of Nicole's arm and directed her toward one of the ice tables. "Have you met the scientists that are working on that breakthrough hydrogen fuel project?"

"Actually, I have—" but the senator interrupted to make introductions.

"Nicole, this is David and Chen. They are the best and the brightest young alternative fuel scientists in the nation."

They raised their ice glasses, and David playfully said, "Hi, Nicole. Long time, no see."

With a look of surprise, the senator said, "So you know each other?"

"We have been very interested in their work for over a year and have recently had some discussions."

"Oh really? I didn't know that."

At that moment, the senator's aide tapped the senator on the shoulder and whispered something in his ear.

The senator said, "Excuse me. I have to go talk to some new guests who have just arrived. I hope you have a good time," and headed directly to the exit door.

Nicole turned to David and Chen. "I'm curious. How do you know Senator Clarkston?"

Oliver had been casually moving around the group in the Ice Bar while taking in the whole scene. No one seemed to notice that he was observing, more than participating, in the social activities inside the Ice Bar. He had watched Nicole talk to the bartender and mingle among the guests. She was animated and having a good time. As he tracked her movements, he found himself thinking that she was an interesting woman. He reminded himself that he needed to focus on all the guests in the room.

He saw the senator scan the room to seek out Nicole and then usher her over to an ice table occupied by a couple of young men. It wasn't long until he saw the senator's aide come over to apparently tell him that he needed to be somewhere else. The two of them hurriedly left, going out the door, back to the air chamber. Soon after, the aide came back into the room with his hood up on his parka. He was headed in the direction of the table where Nicole and the scientists sat.

Oliver suddenly felt all his senses go on alert. What was bothering him about this man? The aide moved in a very deliberate fashion as opposed to the short, choppy strides when he left with the senator. His hood was fully draped over his head, like he didn't want to be seen. Oliver circled around some guests to get a better view. Only the lower part of his face was visible beneath the hood. He looked closer at his pinched nose and taut lips. This was *not* the senator's aide.

Oliver swiftly moved diagonally across the frozen room to intercept the man. Partway there, he saw a glint from a weapon as the intruder reached under his silver cape. Oliver made a dive for the man just as bursts of gunfire lit up the room and sent shockwaves through the ice.

Chapter Thirteen

On the Ice

It was cold and quiet. Nicole rolled over and felt a sharp pain in her left arm. There was a small river of dark red fluid with sparkling glints of ice floating in it. She looked to see the source and was horrified to see that David was lying oddly against a wall of ice blocks and his blood was forming a pool next to her. She saw Oliver bending over another body and he was working feverishly to keep him alive.

The formerly smooth ice was now splintered and fractured. Jagged cracks ran irregularly through the walls in a fascinating pattern. The ice had transformed from a pure reflective surface to a shattered one that Nicole could not take her eyes off of. She could feel her mind floating, wanting to block out everything and go to sleep in this arctic environment.

From far off she heard, "Nicole, Nicole, say something, Nicole."

She realized she was having difficulty understanding the words. Was it Oliver speaking? He seemed to be in a cold blur, very far away. She fought hard to bring everything back into focus.

Oliver implored, "Nicole, listen to me. You're okay."

She managed to say, "What happened?"

"A man pulled out a gun. You've been shot in the arm. The impact knocked you to the floor."

It all seemed like a bad dream. Nicole tried to focus. "What are you doing?"

"I'm trying to stop the blood flow from this man's wounds."

Nicole looked at the body on the floor and saw that it was Chen.

She whispered, "Is David dead?"

"He didn't have a chance."

"I was just talking to him," Nicole numbly uttered.

Oliver clenched his jaw while he put pressure on Chen's wounds.

"I saw the gun too late so David died."

Nicole weakly asked, "What happened to the guests?" The change from the jubilant party to a morgue-like atmosphere in the Ice Bar was too difficult to comprehend.

"You were unconscious. They panicked and almost trampled each other to get out."

Suddenly the door burst open to disturb the unearthly quiet. Police exploded into the Ice Bar, followed by medical personnel carrying life-saving equipment.

Oliver yelled, "Over here! I need help!"

Two of the men ran to where Oliver was applying pressure to Chen's wounds. "On the count of three, we will take over. One, two, three—change!"

A rescuer went over to take David's pulse to see if there were any signs of life. The man listened for a few moments and then closed David's eyelids to hide his dead stare.

From where she lay, Nicole could see that Chen's face was white and he wasn't moving at all. Then she heard someone say, "He has a faint pulse." They put an oxygen mask on him and started working feverishly to save him.

Having left Chen in the hands of the emergency crew, Oliver came straight to Nicole. She watched him approach her deliberately. He had a handsome square face with a strong jaw line and defined cheekbones. His dark eyes were narrowed in concern, and he ran his hand through his longish hair. His white shirt was covered in Chen's blood, and his black slacks hid more of the dark, sticky fluid.

He hovered over her and took her gloved hand. She could feel his protectiveness surrounding her. He said, "Nicole, you are in shock, but these people will take good care of you. I need to find out who did this." Then he was gone. Looking down, she noticed that an extra parka had been put over her. She now realized that Oliver had come to her first before helping Chen.

A competent young man worked on bandaging Nicole's arm while she was transfixed by the scene around her. Someone covered up David with a blanket but did not move him. They would probably wait until the crime scene had been thoroughly analyzed. Chen was carefully lifted onto a gurney and then wheeled out.

At that moment, Nicole could not feel any physical pain but only extreme sadness. These were two brilliant scientists who had the capacity to change the world, gunned down. It was too overwhelming to comprehend.

A few hours later, Nicole was lying in a hospital bed. The modern hospital had the familiar blend of antiseptic cleaner, cafeteria food, and drug smells. She had been listening to the various sounds of hushed voices and the constant beeping of some monitoring device next door. Gurneys, wheelchairs, and other medical equipment were wheeled by her door and continued on to some unknown destination down the hygienic corridor. Finally, she heard the approach of soft steps that stopped just outside her door. The chart was taken out, and the pages flipped through slowly. She had been waiting for what seemed like forever for the physician to arrive because she planned to convince him that she did not need to stay.

Nicole had been shot in the arm but it was not a severe wound, entering and exiting without breaking any bones. Another shot had grazed her temple, but it was not serious, and she needed to get back to her hotel to get ready for the Climate Forum. The loss of blood only made her a little light-headed and her arm slightly painful.

She made an attempt to convince the physician that she did not need to stay, but he was not hearing it. In a strong Swedish accent, the doctor was trying to reason with her, "You're in shock and need to rest."

Her cell phone rang, and she picked it up to avoid the doctor's lecture. He wrote something on the chart and left.

"Nicole, are you all right?" asked a very concerned Sydney.

"David was killed, and Chen is still in surgery. We still don't know if he will live," Nicole said with her voice rising in frustration.

Calmly, Sydney said, "Yes, I know. Oliver called while you were being taken to the hospital."

"Sydney, who would do such a thing?"

"I don't know, but we will find out. The report from the agency is that Oliver tried to stop the intruder from firing. When he went for the gun, he likely saved your life and possibly Chen's, but unfortunately David was sitting on the end so he was not so lucky."

"It all happened so fast. I was talking and then suddenly I was lying on the floor."

"Oliver is now working with the Swedish police on tracing the weapon and going over all the details of the shooting. We'll find out more in the next hour or two," assured Sydney.

Nicole insisted, "I just need to get out of the hospital."

"Let's discuss when you should fly back to Seattle. I'll have the arrangements made."

"No, I intend to stay in Stockholm. It's important that I stay for the Climate Forum. I can't give up now."

"Nicole, we already have the global media looking for stories. The murder at the Ice Bar will give them a sensational start for the opening of the forum. I'm afraid it won't be long until everyone sees your picture on almost every major news station in the world, and they will want an interview from you."

"I can handle it from Stockholm. If you set it up, I'll do some phone interviews for the top news programs."

A nurse came into the room and gave Nicole an impatient look. "I have to go. Let me know if you find out anything."

She asked the nurse, "Is there any news on Chen?"

"He's out of surgery. He is in critical but stable condition."

Nicole relaxed a little. "It's good that he made it through surgery."

The nurse changed the IV and bandages while talking. "So far he has been lucky. The quick response to stop the bleeding, combined with the cold environment, slowed down the flow of blood and gave him a fighting chance. Normally, he would have bled out."

Nicole was beginning to feel very relaxed. Her guess was that the doctor had given her something so she would calm down and stay in the hospital.

Oliver was in the crime lab at police headquarters in Central Stockholm. He had his head in his hands and was silently cursing himself for not stopping the shooter before he killed someone. He was just able to reach the intruder's arm and knock the gun away as they crashed to the floor, but the murderer rebounded quickly and slipped away as the guests screamed and ran for the door. The witnesses in the bar could only describe the man as being dressed like everyone else in the room.

The crime scene investigators were still combing the Ice Bar for evidence, but the only good lead was the weapon itself. Oliver had immediately recognized it as a Russian-made Makarov, one of the more frequently encountered handguns in the weapons trade. This particular version had high impulse and held a ten-round magazine and was currently being used in countries such as Iraq and Afghanistan, along with many other places in the world. It was so common that it would be hard to trace unless there were fingerprints or some traces of DNA. Oliver knew the gun's origin would lead some people to believe it was terrorist activity, but the nature of the crime did not seem to fit the profile.

One thing that Oliver was sure of was that Nicole was also an intended victim. He remembered the shooter aiming directly at her before he knocked the gun off target. Something else that bothered him was the timeframe between the senator leaving the bar and the shooter coming in. They should have passed in the bar lobby, but the senator and his aide both claimed they did not see anyone when they exited the bar and removed their capes in the dressing area. The Swedish police were continuing to question the staff and guests, but so far there were no firm leads. The only thing that was certain was that this was a well-planned hit by an accomplished assassin.

Oliver decided it would be more useful to go to the hospital because Chen had made it through surgery and was still alive. Hopefully, he could reveal more about his relationship with the senator and answer how he came to be invited to the reception.

It was also important to check on Nicole and assess the security situation in the hospital. Even though highly trained security guards had been placed outside their rooms, there was a good chance that the professional assassin would return to complete the job.

His first stop was on the sixth floor to check on Chen's condition. As he approached the door to the intensive care unit, the guard stepped in his way. Oliver showed his credentials, and the guard took his time looking at the photo. After answering a few questions, Oliver entered into the observation room where Chen's vital signs were being closely monitored by the intensive care staff.

The critical care nurse explained that he was still in a coma, but there was room for optimism because Chen's pulse was getting a little stronger. She warned that even if his recovery continued to go well, it would take some time to know the full extent of his injuries.

Nicole heard a knock, which roused her from a nap. Oliver came through the open doorway. "Hey, you; how are you doing?" He sounded like he was trying to be positive but had a weary tone in his voice.

"I'm okay. I just need to get out of the hospital and get back to work, but the doctor won't release me until tomorrow. Maybe I should just walk out. What could they do to stop me?"

"Relax. I think the world can live without you for one day. Take it from me: it's better to rest and rebuild those red blood cells you lost. You'll have more energy. I know from experience."

"What experience?" Nicole asked. "Have you been shot?"

"Yes, a couple of times, but I'll have to tell you about it over dinner sometime." Oliver had said it before he realized what he was saying.

"I'll take you up on that. When?" she couldn't help but say.

"How about tomorrow night? We can celebrate your release from the hospital."

She smiled and motioned to her surroundings. "Oh, I don't know … as you can see I'm pretty busy right now and I'm not sure I have anything to wear with my bandages."

Oliver cracked a rare smile. "Think of it as a new fashion statement. Besides, I'm always a sucker for wounded women."

"I guess I can't refuse such a special invitation."

"Then it's set. Tomorrow at eight."

The anticipation of the upcoming date was put on hold while Oliver took time to explain what little information they had on the assailant and the weapon as Nicole drowsily listened.

He said, "The police are interviewing witnesses who could have seen the shooter outside the bar and in the lobby of the hotel. They think it could be a terrorist attack, but I kind of doubt it. The person would have had to have a lot of inside information to execute the plan."

Nicole thought for a moment. "It is so hard to think who would be motivated to do such a thing."

He quietly said, "I'm also doing a deep search on Senator Clarkston and his contacts."

"This is crazy. It is a Climate Forum, not a politically charged event."

"I would normally agree, but the worldwide media has focused on this meeting, and the Swedish police have their hands full," explained Oliver. "People have been gathering outside of the Stockholm International Fairs complex to show their support for a global environmental agenda. When the forum opens tomorrow, there could be tens of thousands; we don't know."

"Maybe it will finally provide the catalyst for the change we need," Nicole emphasized as she tugged on the blanket.

"Yes, but at what expense? There could be people with different motives mixed in the crowd."

Nicole was fighting to stay alert.

"You need to rest. I'm going back to the crime lab to do some work. I'll see you tomorrow."

"Wait, Oliver. Sydney told me that you saved my life and Chen's … thank you!"

"It's my job," he said as he studied the cracks in the floor.

While drifting off, Nicole noticed how Oliver put his hands in his pockets and took them back out again a couple times before quickly turning to leave.

Forum Eve

The global news networks featured the killing of the prominent, environmental scientist on the eve of the Climate Forum. It was reported that he was on the verge of a dramatic, alternative energy breakthrough when he was cut down by an assassin's bullet.

Most people believed that it was another act of brutal terrorism. But those who specialized in high-level intelligence quietly questioned that conclusion. They found it likely that others could benefit from the crime and were not convinced by the terrorism claim.

In the end, the incident became a catalyst to fuel an outcry from concerned citizens around the globe. Environmentalists began streaming into Stockholm. At the International Fairs Complex, the number of people outside of the conference swelled to overwhelming numbers. Many were carrying signs to protest their disgust at the inability of world leaders to come to any solutions. It was a volatile and emotionally charged scene as the Climate Forum got underway.

Chapter Fourteen

Day One

Spending the first day of the forum in the hospital was not what Nicole had planned. The medical team kept interrupting to take her vital signs, and the constant beeping from the monitoring device next door had started to drive her crazy. She could feel the hours slipping by when she could be at the forum networking. The only redeeming factor was that she had privileged access on her computer to the papers that were being presented the first day.

During the night, she had forwarded her cell phone calls to the public relations department at the foundation. In the morning, she contacted them to decide which calls to return and which ones the foundation could handle. There were many calls that came from people wishing her a speedy recovery and a safe journey home.

One of the messages was from Sam. It simply said, "I heard you were shot. You'll probably be famous now."

It hadn't even occurred to her that he might call, and it was a very cold message that only reconfirmed to Nicole that it was time to move on.

A large share of the calls came from the new media. They all said it was urgent that she should call them back immediately, but she was very selective about the calls she returned and then contacted the foundation to handle the rest.

In addition to the information-seekers and the well-wishers, there were also several threats. Most of them were agitated anti-environmentalists who left long, lecturing messages. But one in particular was more disturbing than the others. The caller had left a monotone, matter-of-fact message saying, "This is only the beginning. Go home to Seattle *now*!"

Nicole stopped everything she was doing, got up out of bed, and walked over to the small window overlooking the hospital courtyard. She asked herself, was she taking too big of a risk? Should she just give up and book a flight home?

After staring out the window for a while, she decided it wasn't in her nature to back down. It was as if the caller was taunting her. It only made her mad and intensified her feelings that her work was important.

As the day went on, the news media increased their efforts to gain access to her hospital room but were turned away by the guard. In the afternoon, a photographer tried to sneak into Nicole's room wearing a white medical coat, but security intervened just as he came through the door.

Later, the guard told her, "Security was added to cover the stairwell and elevator."

"Do you think that's necessary?"

"It was ordered by Oliver Oldin, so we have complied."

Nicole realized that he was probably the one responsible for assigning the guard to her room in the first place.

As it turned out, Oliver showed up before the dinner engagement because of the necessity for Nicole to be escorted out of the hospital upon her release. Members of the media were waiting downstairs in force. They were determined to film the hospital release of a wounded survivor of the Ice Bar murder, knowing that it would produce excellent ratings.

Oliver did not like the media attention that Nicole was getting and maintained it was a dangerous situation that needed be avoided altogether. Without her knowledge, he arranged for an alternative route to be taken out of the hospital. He insisted on taking her down a back elevator, out through a side door in the kitchen, to a waiting private car.

It was like a scene in a bad movie where the president's life had been threatened and the Secret Service were hustling him out of harm's way. They made it down to the side entrance and reached the waiting car, when several journalists came around the corner.

Oliver barked orders. "Let's go and keep moving; do not stop." He put his arm around Nicole's shoulder as if to shield her from anything that might happen. The waiting car accelerated toward them, and Nicole was guided inside by Oliver as it was moving. Oliver slammed the door shut and said, "You are safe now."

The driver gained speed just as the journalists started pressing against the car and yelling questions through the glass. Luckily, they came from the back so the path in front of the car was clear. Oliver looked out the back window for any cars trailing them, but the press was on foot, and by the time they retrieved their support vans, the car had turned the corner and escaped.

He settled back and calmly said, "I hope you don't mind, but I took the liberty of changing hotels so you can have some peace."

Nicole hesitated. "Oh, I don't know. I would need to stop by the hotel to get my luggage."

"It's all been taken care of. We'll just go to the new place where you can settle in," he said.

"So you have the connections to barge into my room and pack up all my stuff?"

"Yes, I guess so," he offered somewhat apologetically.

"And you put a security guard outside my door at the hospital without discussing it with me?"

"It was necessary," said Oliver flatly.

"Hmmm … I would prefer to know what is going on. So where are you taking me now?"

"It's a small flat on the outskirts of the city … not too far away. I've arranged to have a nice dinner brought in so you can rest."

Nicole had to admit that it sounded pretty nice, even if Oliver had been a little forward in changing hotels and making the dinner plans.

They arrived at a private residence in a very nice area outside of Stockholm. "Wow, how did you find this place? It is definitely a step up from staying at a hotel."

Oliver didn't say anything. Instead, he hopped out of the car and politely opened the door. With Nicole's arm bandaged and in a sling, she didn't protest the help. They walked through a small garden area, took an elevator up to the second floor, and entered an ultra-modern apartment decorated in Scandinavian décor. It had two bedrooms, a living room with a bar, a formal eating area, and a gourmet kitchen. The only complaint Nicole could come up with was that it lacked windows toward the beautiful garden that they had passed through on the way in.

"It's a nice place. Have you been here before?"

Again, Oliver ignored the question and stated, "The hospital also provided a nurse since you were in such a big hurry to get out of there."

"I don't need a nurse!" Nicole protested.

"It is the only way that we could get you out of the hospital without an international incident, so accept it."

She thought to herself that Oliver was used to being in charge, because he had been dictating her life since the shooting. Part of her resented the intrusion, but the other part was grateful for the help. She realized she was probably being a little over sensitive because of her recent breakup with Sam.

It had only been a short time since leaving the hospital, but Nicole was becoming very tired. She didn't have the energy that she had expected, and even though she didn't want to admit it, she was satisfied to settle into the apartment. Oliver talked quietly to the nurse and then excused himself. He said he would be back at eight for dinner.

Oliver thought that transferring Nicole to the safe house had gone as well as could be expected. The nurse at the safe house was a trained agent who would watch out for Nicole's safety, as well as her health.

Oliver was now sitting at a secure, video-conferencing facility in downtown Stockholm. He had dialed into a detailed briefing of the latest intelligence coming in from key agencies around the world. No group had yet claimed responsibility for the Ice Bar shooting.

The five intelligence experts on the call debated as to whether the shooting was connected to the intelligence that led Oliver to Stockholm in the first place. Since the shooter walked into the room and headed directly to the three people, the situation pointed more toward an independent crime than a terrorist act. They reasoned that a terrorist's intention would be to blow up the whole Ice Bar, if not the entire hotel.

The experts reported that crime specialists were continuing to interview the guests, bar staff, and hotel workers. They were also in the process of conducting background checks that included political connections and financial dealings of those in attendance.

The initial findings included some conflicting political interests on the part of Senator Clarkston. It seemed that the senator was adept at supporting both sides of an issue when it worked to his advantage. The records from his different phone lines showed that he was in contact with his major oil constituents on a weekly basis, and generally had a very complex network of acquaintances. But none of this information would be inconsistent with a big time wheeler-dealer politician like Senator Clarkston.

Oliver had hoped there would be a quick resolution so that he could concentrate on the threats that still shadowed over the forum, but there was no immediate suspect. The silver cape, which made the shooter indistinguishable from all the other guests, had not been found. He must have taken take it off, carried it away, or returned it to the rack with the others.

The crime lab was working to test all the capes that were at the bar to see if they could find gunpowder residue on the one that the killer wore. If they could find the cape, they may have a chance to find a strand of hair or other DNA evidence to run through the international crime databases.

Oliver's cell phone rang, and he recognized the hospital number. The resident in charge told him that Chen had regained a low level of consciousness and could speak a few words at a time. The doctor warned that Chen was disoriented and confused but would likely continue to improve over time. This was the best news Oliver had heard all day. He would stop by to see Chen at the hospital before going to dinner with Nicole at the safe house.

Oliver arrived at the hospital and hurried to the elevator to go to the intensive care unit. The all-too-familiar smell of antiseptic, drugs, blood, and sick and dying people engulfed him as he walked down the hall. How long had it been since he was a patient himself? Maybe two or three years?

He put his hand over the thick, deep scar on the left side of his chest. It was a constant reminder of the bullet that had nearly taken his life. Was he imagining it or was it harder to breathe, just as it was when the bullet had collapsed his lung?

Oliver stopped briefly to talk to the security guard on duty to get an update, but all was quiet. He entered the intensive care unit. Chen was very still, but he did not have the oxygen mask on, and he had regained a little color in his face. Oliver said, "Chen, *Chen*." Chen's eyelids fluttered and opened wearily.

Oliver bent down close to his face and said, "I'm here to ask you some questions so we can catch the person who did this to you. Can you hear me?"

Chen gave an almost imperceptible nod that he understood.

Oliver went straight to the point because he knew he didn't have much time. "Did you see the person who shot you?"

Chen shook his head slightly from side to side.

"Why were you at the senator's reception? Do you have a connection with him?"

Chen softly whispered, "Money."

"Was Senator Clarkston going to sell the alternative fuel to the oil companies?"

"Research failed ..." Chen trailed off and Oliver couldn't hear anything else that he said.

Oliver picked up his jacket and said to Chen, who had already fallen asleep, "I'll let you rest, but I'll be back tomorrow."

Chapter Fifteen

The Quay

Dosha arrived at the Stockholm airport and took a taxi to Stadsgarden, where the *Sea Bridge* cruise ship was moored. She was thrilled to be in Stockholm and couldn't stop smiling as she peered out the window at all the fantastic Scandinavian architecture on her journey to the dock.

The tour was scheduled to begin the day after tomorrow. Guests would arrive in the late afternoon, with a cocktail reception and captain's dinner scheduled for that evening. Dosha had been told that the tour was comprised of a small group of VIPs from the Climate Forum and that the goal of the symposium was to create synergy between the best and the brightest. Her job was to make sure they were also entertained with the history and sites of the Baltic region when not engaged in the strategic meeting. Dosha had confidence that she would be the perfect guide for this prominent group of people.

She arrived at the busy dock where the ship was still being serviced and going through a rigorous inspection by officials. From a distance, she could see that it was small by cruise ship standards, but was elegant, with polished wood and gleaming brass railings.

A group of men in khaki uniforms were setting up a security checkpoint with a metal detector at the end of the gangplank. She approached one of the men who appeared to be supervising the others.

She showed her credentials while saying in English, "Hello, I'm Dosha, the tour guide on the ship."

He was plainly irritated and impatiently said, "The ship arrived late from the last tour, so it is not ready to board. You can leave your bag here and come back in a couple of hours."

She dropped her bag at the man's feet and dialed Oliver's number to tell him she had arrived in Stockholm. His voice mail answered, so she left a message. She had no knowledge that Oliver was embroiled in the Ice Bar assassination that she had seen on the news.

Dosha strolled on the walkway along the quay and felt a sense of freedom. It was rare when she had the opportunity to visit a place by herself, without people trailing behind asking questions. She soaked in the wonderful view of Stockholm city across the river. At that moment, she felt like she was one of the luckiest people on earth. She had a job that allowed her to travel, and she often worked with smart, important people.

As she contemplated her good fortune, she headed directly for Gamla Stan, better known as Stockholm's Old Town. She was very excited to see the thirteenth-century town with cobbled streets and medieval alleyways. It was still early, so the throngs of tourists had not yet arrived en masse. She walked fast to see the final resting place of the Swedish royalty at the Knights Church and the clock tower of Storkyrkan, and made a special effort to see the Nobel Museum.

She finally stopped to rest in the sun at a charming outdoor café and ordered a coffee that was peppered with cinnamon and cardamom. Dosha looked at her watch and sighed. Her two hours of exploration had gone by so quickly, and it was now time to get back to work and check in at the cruise ship. She walked down the hill, enjoying every moment of the view and the people she saw along the way.

Zafir was working on polishing the brass railings on board the *Sea Bridge*, but he was closely observing everything going on around him. He was dressed in the standard blue jumpsuit that crewmembers wore when servicing the ship in port.

He had reported to work the day before with a formal contract that guaranteed him a job for six months, with the opportunity for an extension if he performed well. It had been easy because everything had been well planned by the London cell in advance. They arranged for the job and provided him with all the recommendations and legal documentation that he needed, so all he had to do was show up.

His main duties would be working as a server in the dining room for the privileged guests, but when they were not on board, he performed other custodial tasks. So far, everyone Zafir had met came from poor, third-world countries where the job on a cruise ship offered them a chance for a better life. Many of the workers had children they hadn't seen in over a year, but they regularly sent money home to pay for their clothes and education. Zafir found it ironic that the cruise line recruited workers from poor countries to keep the wages low. How appropriate to have to cater to the wealthy but only be able to earn a subsistence living.

Zafir noticed the young woman walking toward the ship from quite a distance away. Dressed in a green shirt and black pants, she had a spring in her step and was happily taking in the environment around her. He could not take his eyes off her short red hair and friendly expression and was surprised when she headed directly to the ship. When she passed through security, she must have said something funny to the men, because he heard them all laugh loudly.

He continued to watch her every move as she cleared security and literally bounced up the gangway. Now she was only a few yards away, and he heard her ask where the head steward could be found. The man pointed down the deck in his direction. She came his way, smiled at him, and brushed by him on her way to see the head steward.

Zafir felt a thrill at the brief touch. Her directness and brazen dress was totally inappropriate, yet for some strange reason he found himself intrigued by her.

Climate Forum

By the end of the first day, scientists concluded presenting their damning evidence that again made clear the impact of global warming. But instead of showing pictures of glaciers melting and temperatures rising, they substantiated the correlation between the changing climate and the rising toll on human life. They confirmed that climate change was fueling the violent and unpredictable storms that had become more deadly each year. The facts showed that the planet was in distress and that civilization was in trouble. In conclusion, each of the keynote speakers made a passionate plea for change.

Updates were being streamed from the forum to a live Internet feed. The time was past where global leaders could meet to establish long-term goals that were ultimately ignored or not met. The debate between wealthy nations and poor nations was over. The devastation was too great. It was apparent to all in attendance that action needed to be taken now.

Those who had not tuned into the Climate Forum broadcast were alerted by breaking news from their local new stations. By the end of the first day, most of the civilized world was debating the information and trying to affix blame.

Chapter Sixteen

Safe House

Oliver stopped by the hotel to take a shower and change into a steel-blue sweater and black jeans. He was looking forward to a relaxing dinner engagement, and he had good news to tell Nicole about Chen regaining consciousness. His driver waited while he stopped at a quaint wine shop that had been recommended by the concierge.

He wandered around the wooden racks featuring different varieties of wines, feeling at home in this environment and enjoying the process of selecting a nice wine. He eventually decided on a Chilean wine that was a blend of Carmenere and Cabernet Sauvignon, not outrageously expensive but definitely worth the price. He hoped that Nicole was feeling better and would enjoy the private dinner that he had gone out of his way to arrange. He found himself uncharacteristically enthused about the evening.

It was early evening, and Nicole had spent a couple of hours talking to the various news media. Most reporters were fishing for inside information on the killing, but she relentlessly communicated that David's life was an incredible loss to the world.

The apartment was well equipped with a state-of-the-art communication system so it was very easy to work and monitor the live video feed from the Climate Forum. There had been no surprises on the first day of presentations, so Nicole felt that she had not missed any critical new research.

The bigger surprise was when she switched over to the news and witnessed the throngs of people outside of the International Fairs complex. The crowd was chanting and waving signs, demanding action for global environmental change. It continued to grow and was getting more contentious as the day went on.

There were many graphic posters. One showed a body of a person who had tragically drowned in a tsunami and had been impaled on a tree branch. Another sign showed the bodies of school children who had been buried in a catastrophic mud slide at their village school. The message was clear: the people wanted change and it would be hard for the bureaucrats to ignore the pressure.

A news reporter talked about the escalation of super-storms and the resulting devastation. The station ran footage from around the world to illustrate the magnitude of the problem. An aerial shot showed a forested area where the trees fell like match sticks and were all lying in the same direction.

They switched to Guangzhou, China, where the people on the street were wearing face masks because carbon monoxide had reached toxic levels. The reporter had a mask around his neck, but during the short broadcast you could see his red eyes begin to burn. The newscast finished with a commentary that this was not a problem for one country or even one hundred countries. It was global in scale.

When Nicole walked around the apartment, she realized this was a special place intended for important people who needed instant access to the outside world. She was just beginning to discover all the electronic equipment that was hidden in various pieces of furniture. There was a large screen that dropped down from the ceiling at the touch of a button and had a video conferencing system to go with it. She noticed several discreet cameras and inadvertently pushed some buttons, causing a computer console to pop up.

The nurse was very knowledgeable about how everything worked, but she was not forthcoming on explaining *why* the apartment was so well equipped. It seemed odd that a nurse was so adept at operating the electronic communications systems, and it was obvious that she had been here before.

The apartment was decorated with very expensive art pieces and fine furnishings. The front room had pale yellow, buttery leather furniture and geometric designed wool rugs on polished hard wood floors. The kitchen had black granite countertops, rich wooden cabinets, and chrome appliances. There were sculptures of human figures and faces made out of colored glass in the entry hall and in the dining area.

In the living room, there was a series of three colorful paintings that were hung together to form a larger work of art that covered the entire wall. Nicole concluded that all the artwork were originals that must have cost a small fortune to acquire.

She heard pots and pans banging in the kitchen, so she went to investigate. The nurse had inconspicuously let a chef in the house, and he was preparing to cook dinner in his white apron and hat. He was a tall, blonde man who looked too fit to be a chef. He was surrounded by colorful, fresh produce and was slicing and dicing on a large cutting board.

As he chopped onions at an unbelievable speed, he talked with a heavy Swedish accent. "I'm the executive chef from a restaurant a few blocks away. I'm here to cook you a gourmet, multi-course dinner for two. I hope you're hungry."

Nicole was amazed that such a large man would have such great finger dexterity. "Oh yes, I am. Whatever it is you are making, it smells delicious."

Promptly at eight, Oliver showed up at the house with a bottle of wine. Once again, the nurse let him in before there was any knock on the door. He looked fresh and more relaxed than Nicole had seen him before. He also appeared to be in unusually good spirits.

"I have excellent news for you," he said as he walked over to the liquor cabinet and pulled out a corkscrew. "Chen has regained consciousness and was able to say a few words. The doctors are fairly confident that he will continue to improve."

Nicole's face lit up. "That's great! I'm so relieved that he is better. I need to go see him as soon as possible!"

"I don't want to get your hopes up too high. I was only able to talk to him for a few moments before he slipped back into unconsciousness. He will be sedated for the rest of the night."

"Was he able to tell you anything?" Nicole asked in earnest.

Oliver expertly uncorked the bottle while he talked. "He is not very lucid but he did not seem to recognize the shooter. He also mumbled something about failed research."

"That is interesting, because they told me they were on track for a major breakthrough. I'll call Sydney to have her delve deeper into their research."

Oliver leisurely poured two glasses of wine. "I have already been in contact with her, and you need to relax." He offered Nicole one of the glasses. "Let's toast to David's life and Chen's recovery!"

"Yes, to David and Chen." The wine was smooth and pleasing to the palate. The server came out with an almond mushroom pate as they sipped the wine.

"So, Oliver, what is this place? It is certainly not an ordinary apartment."

"I wanted to talk to you about that. I didn't want to alarm you when you were first hurt, but I'm sure the killer was also aiming for you. We decided it was best to put you in a safe house and give Chen extra protection at the hospital."

Nicole quickly put down her wine. "What? That doesn't make any sense. I received some crank calls while in the hospital, but why would anyone want to kill me?"

"Honestly, we don't have a lot of leads, so we need to be very cautious until we find out. By tomorrow we should have more details."

Nicole had been on alert mode for the last twenty-four hours and wanted to block all of it out for the time being. Oliver had been a godsend from the beginning and had managed the situation with speed and intelligence. She looked over at him and said, "Are you always this attentive to the women you are protecting?"

He laughed and said, "I hunt down a lot of gun dealers and financiers, and they are not as good-looking as you."

"Oh sure. An international agent like you must have a girlfriend in every city."

The nurse abruptly came into the living room and asked if there was anything else that they needed. Her shift was over and the security agents would be monitoring the house overnight.

Oliver said, "Thank you for your services; we'll take it from here." Then he turned to Nicole and confessed, "That was Marie, who is both a nurse and a security agent assigned to the safe house."

"I figured out after the first twenty minutes that she wasn't an ordinary nurse!"

He laughed sheepishly. "I guess I'd better start being more honest with you."

"A very good idea!" Nicole agreed.

"But I thought you would be the stubborn and unreasonable type."

Nicole held the stem of the wine glass and turned it from side to side, watching the light change in the purplish-hued liquid. Oliver had unknowingly struck a sensitive chord. She finally said, "That is probably a good observation, but I can be flexible when things are fully explained."

Oliver changed the subject. "I hope you like the dinner. It's from a nice neighborhood restaurant, not too far away from here."

Here she was, with an attractive man who had literally saved her life. The wine and company made her forget all the trauma of the day and worries of the world. It felt like she was in the safest place on earth. Wonderful smells began to come from the kitchen, and soon the chef came into the room and announced that dinner was being served in the dining room. The table had been set with fine china, silver, and candles. The chef told them they would be starting with cauliflower soup with pecarino romano cheese and truffle oil. He disappeared back into the kitchen and returned with the steaming bowls of soup.

With each course came a new bottle of wine that was expertly paired with the food. Luckily it was Nicole's left arm that had been hit, so she was able to eat somewhat gracefully. They could have been in one of the best restaurants in Stockholm, but instead they were in a secure apartment.

Nicole had begun to feel the relaxing effects of the wine, and opportunistically, Oliver began to ask more personal questions. "Have you always been so driven to change the world?"

She laughed. "Oh no, when I was little, I worried about everything! In early grade school, my mother had to push me on the school bus every morning because I didn't want to go. The bus driver closed the doors while I cried. I had to take this awful medicine to calm my stomach."

"You're kidding, right? I thought you were born confident."

Nicole fiddled with her fork while formulating an answer. "I'm not kidding, and I probably still work daily to overcome those childhood traits."

It must have been the wine, but Nicole found herself talking to Oliver like he was a long-lost friend. He was a good listener and only added encouraging comments, probably to keep her talking.

"So I've been rambling on. Why did you become an agent?"

"I'll just say that it was in my blood."

Nicole thought, *There it is again the short, evasive response to a personal question.* She followed up, "Tell me how you got shot. You promised to tell me over dinner."

Oliver bent over slightly, picked some invisible lint off his black pants, and straightened a pant leg. Nicole waited, saying nothing. Finally, he sat up straight. "Yes, I've been shot a few times but only one time was life-threatening."

Nicole's expression softened as she looked at Oliver, realizing how difficult it was for him to talk about it.

"I was closing in on a major arms dealer in Bangkok. There was a fellow agent working with me on the case who had done some of the surveillance work. We were supposed to meet at a local restaurant on a side street. I remember it well: exotic potted plants in front and a wooden balcony above. There was a handwritten menu tacked to a blue sign out front."

Oliver smoothed the same pant leg that he had straightened a few moments before. He looked straight ahead, away from Nicole.

"I strolled into the place. It was empty, like it hadn't been open in a long time, so I proceeded up the stairs. All I saw was a pretty little girl and her young mother, looking terrified. I told them I wouldn't hurt them. Then I saw the man with the gun emerge from around the corner behind them. He was using them as a human shield."

Nicole could hear the intense emotion in Oliver's voice. It was something she had not heard before.

"I leapt for the balcony and felt the shot sear through my chest."

Nicole softly asked, "Where was the other agent?"

"That's what stays with me to this day. He had met a woman in Patpong, the red light district the night before, and didn't complete the surveillance. It was a tough lesson that you can only depend on yourself."

"I sincerely hope that isn't true."

The chef came into the dining room to discuss dessert. They both groaned at the idea of more food but couldn't resist savoring the last bottle of wine. As they talked, the chef packed up his cooking utensils and said good night on his last trip out.

At that point, Nicole joked, "Are we alone, or are there cameras watching every move we make?"

Oliver laughed and said, "They will see what I want them to see," and then he walked over to a console that was hidden in a drawer. He pushed a couple of keys on the console and said, "Now, we are alone."

"So the person on security detail is wondering what is going on in the apartment?"

"Something like that, but I am a trustworthy soul."

"Right, I've heard that one before!"

"I have a high security clearance with most major governments in the civilized world ... so yes, I am *extremely* trustworthy."

Nicole protested, "Governments and women are two different things."

At that moment, he came close, brushing back Nicole's hair with his hand and looking her in the eyes. His appeal was overwhelming. He slowly came closer and brushed his lips ever so slowly against Nicole's in a light kiss and said, "I'm serious."

Instead of resisting, Nicole found herself enjoying his presence. He was strong and all consuming.

As Oliver pulled back from the exploratory kiss, he suddenly looked concerned. He ran his hand through his hair and abruptly said, "This has been an incredible evening, but I must go work on the security and intelligence for the case."

Before she could say anything, he stood up and went over to the control console to reengage the cameras.

"Tomorrow we can go see Chen," Oliver said as a factual statement and headed straight for the door.

"You don't need to worry about me. I can take care of myself," Nicole replied somewhat defensively.

With an edge to his voice, he said, "Maybe you can take care of yourself in your business world, but this is a new game, with people out to kill you."

She simply repeated, "I can take care of myself."

Oliver left the house and walked to the waiting town car parked outside. He was not expected for another hour, so he startled the dozing driver when he tapped on the window. Oliver simply told him that something had come up and he needed to leave.

As he settled into the backseat for the drive back to the hotel, he thought how poorly he had handled the evening. He knew that to do his work, he had to be in complete control. He had trained himself to be calculating in both his professional life and his personal life. There was no room for error, and he moved from place to place on a moment's notice. All relationships had to be considered short-term propositions, knowing that he would always be moving on.

It was true that over the years he had developed a certain satisfaction with this arrangement. It was convenient and suited his personality. But when Oliver had looked down at Nicole and saw a beautiful woman who looked very vulnerable with her arm in a sling, he suddenly felt a major twinge of guilt. It was his job to work *every* minute to keep her alive. What was he trying to do, seduce her? He knew that it would not work to get personally involved with her.

Oliver began to think that one of the most difficult parts of this assignment would be figuring out how to stay emotionally detached from Nicole. She was extremely bright and accomplished but also had a very engaging personality. This was a unique woman who did not fall into any usual category. She had a very direct approach and she did not play the games that preoccupied many of the other worldly women he had been with.

He would have to work harder at being more distant. It was part of the job, and he was good at it. But as the car sped away, it took all his willpower to not ask the driver turn around and take him back to the safe house.

Chapter Seventeen

The Sea Bridge

On board the ship, Zafir was in contact with the London terrorist cell on a daily basis. He had access to a computer terminal intended for employees to keep in touch with their family and friends. It was connected by satellite so was a fairly reliable source of communication when out to sea. An innocuous e-mail address had been established to look like it originated in Saudi Arabia, where Zafir's family would likely reside.

In reality, all of his e-mails were being routed through several different countries before being forwarded to the London cell. They had worked out a coded vocabulary so it looked like he was a family man simply inquiring about mundane things such as his children or his wife's health. In his first e-mail, he reported that he had arrived safely and that everything was just fine.

The operative who Zafir replaced had been working on the ship for two tours of duty, each six months long, and was now scheduled for a home leave. He had joined the cruise in India and had followed the ship on exotic tours throughout the world until they reached the Baltic Sea. His assignment was to be a reliable worker and learn all he could about the inner workings of the cruise ship, including how they determined terminal locations, docking/departure procedures, safety procedures, etc.

He was also given the task of setting up a tool kit in preparation for Zafir's arrival. The contents were specialized, so he had to collect them very slowly in ports where the items could be purchased on the black market. Each small component was brought on the ship one at a time to avoid suspicion. After everything had been acquired, he placed the tools in a small sport bag that was hidden in a safe location to be accessed at a later date.

When Zafir boarded the ship, he was issued two uniforms and told to report to orientation that afternoon. He was given a detailed map on how to find the crew quarters that he would share with five other deckhands. The route would take him through an unmarked door, down three sets of narrow stairs, and through a small corridor where the ship's staff was housed.

As he walked down the first flight of stairs to the lower deck, he began to sweat and become increasingly anxious. His hands trembled as he grasped the rail and forced himself to keep descending to the lower depths of the ship. He could sense that he was going deeper and deeper into the dark water. When he at last reached the crew quarters, he collapsed on the bunk bed, closed his eyes, and pretended that he was in the warm sun back in Jidda.

Even though he did not feel well, Zafir eventually forced himself to look around. He figured the faster he settled in, the sooner he could go up on deck. The shared living quarters consisted of three bunk beds in one room, with a small community bathroom off the corridor. He had his own place to sleep, a small closet to hang his uniforms, and two drawers beneath for his personal items. Everything else was communal.

Zafir did not mention his problem in his communication to the London cell because he had to conquer the fear. Since the London cell had so meticulously planned the mission to signal a new era in terrorism, he had to succeed. His fear was simply a weakness that needed to be overcome. To do otherwise would be a catastrophic failure that would not be tolerated.

He thought back to the time when he began the strict religious, physical, and educational training program taught to him by the men who had saved him from the orphanage. He remembered how he was transformed from a skinny kid to a well-conditioned soldier, taught to kill, even though it didn't come easily to him. He kept telling himself that he could overcome anything and continually admonished himself for being childish and fearful.

But the debilitating anxiety continued, and he felt that he was becoming a madman. He became obsessed with seeing the light of day on deck, or a porthole to get a glimpse of land, where people were walking and riding bikes along the shoreline. When he ascended the stairs, the relief was instant; his nerves would calm and he could function again.

The next day Zafir began to think that in spite of his problem, he was blending in well with the other workers on the ship. His job duties were not difficult, and his English was superior to many of the others. He had attended two training sessions that covered the rules and regulations for the service staff. He learned that when the guests were on board, the main hallways were to be avoided, unless a specific interaction was required. The common workers routinely used the service elevators and corridors so they were invisible to the privileged guests. It was no different than how the royal family had treated his mother back at home, and only reinforced his perceptions of the elite.

Dosha found the jovial ship's steward and was given a personal tour of the ship. She was told the expedition vessel was built in Italy and was one of the finest small cruise ships in the world. The walls were made out of teak wood that was burnished to bring out the fine grain. There was gleaming brass trim everywhere, including the banisters, light fixtures, and picture frames on the original artwork displayed on the walls in the corridors and various rooms. The floor had mosaic tile designs in the reception area and travertine stone as far as she could see. It felt more like a privately owned yacht than a cruise ship.

Beyond the reception area was the lounge, which was also used for meetings and lectures. The lounge had large windows to offer an expansive view for the passengers who did not want to venture to the outside decks.

The steward made a point to tell Dosha, "The ship is equipped with all the latest electronic features, including a large drop-down screen and computer hook-ups for your presentations."

Dosha said, "It's perfect."

From the reception area, they took the sweeping staircase that spiraled down to the elegant dining room on the Magellan deck below.

The steward explained, "Most meals are served here, but when the weather is good, meals are also available on the more informal sun deck."

Next, they took the elevator to the deck above the reception area to the cocktail lounge. It had a bar stocked with exotic-shaped liquor bottles and space for a band next to the small dance floor.

Dosha observed, "I bet the guests have some fun times here."

Past the cocktail lounge was a library that had books on the history, art, and geography of the places where the ship traveled. It also had several computers that were connected to the outside world by satellite, available for use by the guests.

Dosha marveled about the deluxe accommodations on the ship, where all staterooms had sitting areas, large picture windows, and good-sized bathrooms. The built-in wardrobes, chests of drawers, and desks looked like expensive, fine furniture. The staterooms on the top deck were normally for the wealthiest passengers. They were even more spacious and had sliding doors that lead to their own private balconies.

The steward finished the tour by showing Dosha to her own stateroom. "It is a bit smaller than some of the others and has only a porthole to look out of, but it has all the same furnishings as the most luxurious stateroom." He pointed out, "It is located down the corridor from the doctor's quarters where the physician will be attending patients. This cabin was intended for speakers and other support guests who accompany tours on the ship."

"Thank you; it's wonderful."

"I think you will enjoy it. Many distinguished guests have stayed here."

Dosha said, "I feel honored to be in this room," realizing that she had stumbled on an opportunity of a lifetime.

"Let me know if you need anything," finished the steward.

She unpacked her things quickly and went up on deck to have a look around. Across the bay, she saw ship's masts protruding from the top of a building. "Ah, yes the Vasa Museum," Dosha said to herself. She had brushed up on Stockholm's sights for the tour.

She started into the verbal description she would give her clients. "The *Vasa* was intended to be the greatest war ship of all time. In the seventeenth century, the Swedish king personally dictated the measurements, and no one dared to argue with him. The ship is several stories high and carved elaborately with demons, knights, warriors, mermaids, and other strange animal shapes that were designed to scare the enemy."

Dosha closed her eyes for a moment as she recalled the story. "On the *Vasa's* maiden voyage, a sudden squall came up and the sea water began to enter the open gun ports that had just fired a celebratory round. The top-heavy *Vasa* war ship was doomed, and in the first nautical mile, the tragic *Vasa* capsized and sank."

As she practiced her talk, Dosha became aware of someone staring at her. She looked over to see one of the crew looking her way with intense, dark eyes. She smiled at the man and returned to her narrative. "The interesting thing about the seventeenth-century wooden *Vasa* was that it was persevered so well. Since the Baltic Sea consists of mostly fresh to brackish water, it did not have the worms that normally eat through a wooden ship. The ship had been built of oak, which has a high amount of iron to help preserve it. The end result was that it was a major archeological find, and it is now the most visited museum in Sweden."

She looked up again, and the man was still there with his piercing stare.

Her cell phone rang. "Hi, Dosha; this is Oliver. There are some new developments that I need to talk to you about."

"I'm listening."

"There was an assassination in Stockholm that involved many of the people who will be on board the cruise. I want you to know that there are risks that we did not know about when I talked to you in St. Petersburg."

Dosha said, "I've lived in Russia my whole life where I have had many challenges. I'm not about to be scared off by something like this."

Oliver gave it another try. "This could be very dangerous, and we don't have enough information at this time. We could fly you back to St. Petersburg tonight and forget the idea of leading the tour. I want to make sure that you know the circumstances."

Dosha retorted, "This is a good opportunity for me so I intend to work this cruise. Please tell me what is going on and let me decide."

Oliver relented. "In the last twenty-four hours I've come to believe that the group we want you to lead is in danger. We don't know who is after them, so your life could be in jeopardy too. I want to be honest with you and give you a chance to back out. I can fill the job with an agent pretending to be a guide."

"I doubt that. They would be a poor guide."

"I suppose they would be a very bad substitute for you. I agree that it is more important to be authentic at your job than be a skilled agent. You are bright and observant so we could give you a little training in the security area. If you are game, you would be a real asset on the cruise."

When he was done, Dosha said, "Interesting. I had no idea that environmental issues would be a reason to kill someone."

Oliver concurred, "Neither did I."

Dosha paused. She looked around the glamorous cruise ship and realized she was willing to risk a great deal for this opportunity. "This assignment is too remarkable to back out now."

"If you are willing, we'll make it work. I'll see you on board the ship."

For the next couple of hours, Dosha wandered around the cruise ship and introduced herself to the crew members. She immediately noticed what a diverse group of people they were and enjoyed talking to them about their backgrounds. Their stories were as different as their nationalities, but they all had a common theme. The service workers saw their jobs as a way to better their families' lives as well as their own. As she walked around meeting people, she looked for the man who had stared at her on the deck, but he was not to be found.

Chapter Eighteen

Solutions for the Dilemma

The second day of the Climate Forum was dedicated to the scientists who were working on breakthrough technology to solve the earth's treacherous prognosis. The first speaker was scheduled to discuss more advanced techniques to massively expand the harvesting of geothermal power. So far, the attempts to tap into the volcanic activity below the earth's surface had never reached a critical mass and supplied only a small percentage of energy needs. Other presentations would talk about advances in bio-fuel, coal conversion to liquid fuel, and the practicality of cold fusion. Attendees were hoping to hear about *big* breakthroughs in any of these areas.

Nicole arrived early at the International Fairs Complex intending to get there before the news media could set up and look for people to interview. Her plan was to get in the gate before anyone realized she was there.

As she came close to the complex, she could see that the Swedish police were already out in force. The blue and yellow police vans were lined up along the perimeter road. In addition, the equestrian unit was saddling up to get in position to maintain crowd control.

Nicole stepped out of the taxi and picked her way through the crowd that was building for the second day. As she cleared the first gate, she noticed two men trailing her. She was certain that Oliver was behind it, so she went up to the men and said, "Hello. I assume Oliver has assigned you to protect me?"

They were surprised, and one said, "Yes, that's correct."

As Nicole turned the other direction to go to the opening session, she saw Oliver coming toward her. "Good morning. I just checked out the venue for the opening session. It's going to be a very large meeting in a chaotic and uncontrolled environment. It would be a mistake for you to attend."

She glared at him. "Don't you think I should decide that?"

Oliver tried to change tactics and gloss over the situation. "How about we go visit Chen and see how he is doing? You can catch up on the live feed of the forum tonight."

Nicole was angry with Oliver, and it wasn't just about the security issue. They had a wonderful dinner the night before, but when Oliver suddenly bolted, all she could think was, *here we go again.* She had just finished a turbulent relationship with Sam and wasn't ready for another. She knew she was being a bit unreasonable but needed some time and space to think things through.

It was true that she wanted to visit Chen to see how he was doing, and if he was conscious she could ask him more questions about the viability of the work they had been doing. "I'll leave the forum to go visit Chen, but we need to discuss the security arrangement going forward."

To make peace, Oliver conceded, "Okay, you have a point. Let's go visit Chen."

On the way out, Oliver stopped to talk to the captain of the Swedish police who had been assigned to head up the security detail at the Climate Forum. They had collected a few handguns and pocketknives as the people passed through the metal detectors on the way into the forum, but nothing unexpected.

The officer in charge was much more concerned about the crowd outside. Since the media had arrived, they had become more agitated and demonstrative. The officer said their main priority was to focus on crowd control and cool the tempers of the growing masses of people.

When they left through the side gate, the crowd was building to a high-pitched fervor. A man with a megaphone was shouting, "World leaders are attending the forum, but they are only here for their personal, political gain. Meanwhile, climate disasters are killing people around the world while politicians and business leaders pretend to care just to further their careers. In order to avert the human suffering that is in progress, we need immediate action!"

The man with the megaphone raised his right arm in the air. "Are you with me?'

Many in the crowd answered, "Yes!"

He raised his arm again and asked with more power, "Are you with me?"

This time the entire crowd responded, "Yes!"

He continued, "Right now, tornadoes are ripping through northern Florida, with forty-five hundred people presumed dead, many of them children. In Italy, it is raining nonstop with massive slides and flooding, with over nine thousand people dead, and the death toll is rising. In Kenya, people are dying by the millions from starvation due to unprecedented drought conditions and a shortage of grain." He demanded, *"When will this stop?* Our leaders need to feel the pain and take responsibility instead of making hollow political speeches. The truth is that they are contributing to the problem and incapable of solving it!"

The man would pause for effect, like a preacher at a revival. He was skilled at bringing the crowd's emotions to the surface. In a short time, he succeeded in whipping the crowd into an uncontrollable frenzy.

He started a chant, *"They don't care. They don't care,"* and the crowd joined in.

It ignited action, and the people surged forward, pressing against the cyclone gates surrounding the International Fairs Complex. The speaker seized the moment and continued to provoke the masses of people by saying, "And when will *you* help solve these problems?"

People started jostling one another, and Nicole was bumped aside, driven into a cyclone fence. She winced in pain and tried to regain her balance. Immediately, one of the security guards stepped in front of her and blocked the aggressive crowd, pushing back to gain some space. The crowd was surging forward. Oliver grabbed Nicole from behind and propelled her toward a waiting car.

The crowd's anger and resolve continued to build. Several people climbed on the cyclone fencing and shouted for others to join them. They were all caught up in the emotions of the moment. More and more people joined the assault on the protective perimeter.

With the sheer weight of the protestors climbing the fence, the temporary barricade folded to the ground, making it possible for people to scramble over the top. They picked themselves up, not noticing the scrapes and cuts that they had sustained. They regrouped and began to race toward the main chamber of the Climate Forum.

Watching from the safety of the car, Nicole and Oliver could see the emotionally charged protestors being pursued by the Swedish police as they ran through the conference center, knocking down garbage cans and registration tables. The police met them in full riot gear and tried to peacefully block the demonstrators from breaking into the chamber hall, but a few were able to break away.

Later that night, Nicole saw the footage on TV documenting the conflict from inside the lecture hall. The speaker was discussing the viability of wind and wave power when the cameras turned to a commotion coming from outside. Protestors burst through the doors, yelling and screaming as the riot police chased them. The intruders were quickly subdued with clubs, handcuffed, and dragged outside.

The newscasters enhanced the coverage through personal interviews with the people in attendance. The result was that the politicians and business leaders found themselves pushed into discussing new developments. The Climate Forum was the top news story around the globe for two nights in a row, and the stakes continued to get higher and higher.

Chapter Nineteen

Research Trials

The hospital, which had been chaotic the day before, was quiet and peaceful. Family members were shuffling in to visit relatives who were sick or recovering from an illness or operation. The news media was no longer intruding on the human drama in the wards but had shifted their attention to the International Fairs conference site.

As Nicole walked through the entrance, her thoughts went back to the gravity of what had happened. She looked straight ahead, clenched her jaw tightly, and tried to maintain her composure.

Oliver felt her tension and asked, "Are you all right?"

"No, not really ... I guess I'm angry."

"At what?" Oliver prodded.

"That someone who was working so hard to improve the world's condition could be shot down in cold blood."

Oliver nodded and said with determination, "I understand. That's why I must find the killer."

Nicole and Oliver checked in at the nursing station and were told that Chen had had a quiet and restful night. His blood oxygen level had increased and he was able to stay conscious for longer periods of time. The security guard outside the room reported there had been no unusual activity, only the doctors and nurses visiting Chen's room. As they went through the doorway, Oliver said, "Chen looks better. He has more color in his face than when I last saw him."

At the sound of their voices, Chen opened his eyes and whispered weakly, "Nicole, it that you? I'm so happy to see you."

Nicole went over and gave him a one-armed hug, being careful to not disturb his IVs and all the monitoring equipment. "It's so great to see you. I hear that you are doing much better!" Then she turned toward Oliver. "I believe you have met Oliver Odin, who is working on the case. He was at the reception in the Ice Bar when you were shot, and he was the one who kept you alive until the emergency vehicles arrived."

Chen looked puzzled, so Oliver chimed in. "I was in the crowd at the reception, and at the hospital when you were barely conscious, but you probably don't remember."

Nicole took the lead, "We are so sorry about David. It's a tragedy. Do you have any idea of why someone would do this?"

Chen shook his head solemnly. He had a distant, painful look in his eyes, "I don't know …"

Nicole encouraged him a little more. "Was anything unusual going on with the synthetic fuel research?"

Chen began to talk urgently, in a hoarse whisper. "Our study was on track … we were having great results … ran last experiment before the conference … it was a disaster."

"You didn't mention that to me before, when we met."

With a lot of effort, he said, "Some kind of contaminant … probably an anomaly … low-energy nuclear experiments not producing excessive heat … could change everything."

Nicole put her hand on Chen's arm. "If it's too difficult, we can talk about it later."

But Chen insisted on continuing. "Hydrogen, most abundant element on earth could safely ..." but his voice got weaker as the effort to talk tired him.

Oliver and Nicole looked at each other in concern. They stood silent for a while to give him some time to rest, and then Oliver calmly asked, "Chen, how did you wind up at Senator Clarkston's reception?"

Chen roused himself to answer, "Sent support for our work … check for fifteen thousand dollars. He said no strings attached … wanted to support alternative fuel." Chen took a few more breaths of oxygen and continued. "His petroleum partners wanted to increase green energy focus … sent invitation to attend the reception at the Climate Forum … felt obligated to go."

Oliver asked, "So you have a good idea of what went wrong with the last research trial?"

"No time to analyze … contamination of the nuclear transmutation … need to trace back to source."

Nicole thought for a moment and asked, "Would it be possible to have an independent lab confirm the results of your last experiment? We could help you determine the contaminant."

Oliver added, "Maybe someone tried to guarantee its failure. There is the possibility that it could be tied to the shooting."

Chen's eyes began filling up with tears of grief. His face was weary with exhaustion. "I'm so sorry. David is gone. I need help. How can I continue? He was ... great scientist ... best friend."

There was no possible way to console Chen. Nicole and Oliver could only share in his pain. Understandably, he could not comprehend why David had died and he had been spared. As young college students at Stanford University, they dreamed of developing a viable alternative fuel that could change the course of the world. They had come ever so close before the dream was shattered in the Ice Bar. It would be a long journey for Chen to come to terms with David's murder.

Chen had worked hard to communicate and became fatigued in the process. He was a little calmer now, but needed more rest, so Oliver and Nicole excused themselves, saying they needed to get back to work. They stopped at the nursing station and found out that Chen's parents were en route to Stockholm and should be arriving in the next few hours. That information made Nicole feel a little better about leaving Chen alone in the hospital.

She turned to Oliver. "We need to find out who did this, no matter what the cost."

Oliver was distracted and did not respond.

Nicole looked away, thinking back to her relationship with Sam. She flashed back to a situation where she was excitedly explaining a microcredit plan that had been targeted to women in a refugee camp near Kenya's Sudan border. But like most times when she talked about her work, Sam was not interested and had tuned her out. He had not responded, and she had felt invisible and ignored. Was Oliver doing the same thing, or was she being too quick to judge his lack of response as a sign of aloofness?

Nicole took a more direct approach. "Oliver, what are you thinking?"

"Oh sorry, I was just mentally processing the information that Chen gave us. It is a real possibility that the experiment could have been sabotaged by someone who would not benefit from an alternative fuel breakthrough."

"The foundation works with the best in the world in all kinds of research, so we can work on finding the appropriate scientists. This is big, so I don't think we'll have a problem getting scientists to take on the assignment, in addition to their own research."

Oliver looked directly at her and said, "I sometimes forget how resourceful and well-connected you are. I'm usually left to my own devices to solve problems."

"I've figured that out. I'll make a few phone calls and see how we can get someone to review the trials immediately."

"We also need to have a crime scene investigator examine the physical evidence of Chen and David's last trial. It shouldn't only be tested for the viability of the formulas and processes, but also for the tampering of materials."

Nicole thought for a second. "There must be a video conferencing system in the hospital so that Chen can brief the scientists. Can you locate the crime investigator?"

Oliver pretended to scratch his chin in mock puzzlement, "Oh I don't know; I just might be able to manage that."

"Good. I need to meet the organizers of the consortium that will take place on board the ship to facilitate a plan on the actionable items." With that said, Nicole put her good arm in the air and hailed a passing cab. She swiftly got in and left Oliver looking at the back of the taxi disappearing around the corner.

Nicole was initially pleased with herself as the taxi headed toward Central Stockholm. Oliver had started making assumptions about her job and did not understand the importance of what needed to be accomplished in the next week. She recognized that it was only for her own psyche, but she needed to stand up to Oliver to let him know that he was not always in control.

Nicole was grateful that he had intervened at the Ice Bar, but it was time to move on. Leaving in the taxi sent Oliver a clear message about her purpose and intent. If he did not want to work with her on an agreed-upon strategy, then it might be best to part ways. *Besides*, she thought, *it'll just be easier this way*, without wanting to admit why.

It was a short ride back to the Nordic Lights Hotel, where she had meetings set up for the evening. It was time to get her life back to normal and continue her work. She paid the driver and stepped out of the taxi onto the curb.

A motor cycle approached at a high speed. *Suddenly a wave of terror hit her.* She dropped down behind the taxi to avoid a gunshot, but the motorcycle sped by. In an instant, she stood back up and carefully looked to see if anything appeared unusual on the street. There was nothing, but she was still shaking. Her body must be in self-defense mode, brought on by the recent trauma. She walked unsteadily into the hotel, having been shaken to the core by the imagined threat.

Oliver cursed under his breath when Nicole blatantly defied the assigned security detail and escaped in the taxi. But what could he do? He couldn't chase her and force her to have the protection that he knew she needed. It had become obvious that he would have to use different tactics when it came to working with Nicole. She would not follow his direction unless she agreed with the plan, even if it was in her best interest. He had to admit that she did have some good points about the big picture, but it would be a high-risk proposition for her safety. The next part of the journey was going to be a challenge, since he was used to calling the shots.

Oliver decided it would be best to have another highly skilled agent assigned to the next phase of the trip. That would allow him to pursue important leads, and the new agent could take on the extremely frustrating job of protecting the guests. He placed a call into headquarters and arranged an experienced agent to meet him at the quay where the *Sea Bridge* was docked.

Chapter Twenty

Floating Think Tank

The next morning the headlines around the world announced the violent protests at the Climate Forum. The confrontation with the police had continued to escalate, resulting in serious injuries. Over nine hundred arrests were made.

Nicole listened to various reports and searched the Internet for information about the actual presentations given at the forum. She wasn't surprised that most of the reports were not favorable. It was generally viewed by reporters and bloggers that the work presented was a confirmation of what was already known, and that nothing significant had been accomplished. This meant that the role of the Everson Foundation needed to be even stronger to pull together the different factions that could develop an innovative but realistic strategy.

As she had expected, the more critical meeting was going to take place during the Baltic Sea cruise. In addition, a visit to the *Valkyrie*, a scientific ship working on a vitally important environmental project, had been arranged to be part of the trip. Nicole had met the managing director of the Baltic Sea Retrieval Project, Max Lindberg, six months ago at a conference. Nicole found Max to be an inspirational and effective leader, and they had been collaborating on the idea of putting the project on the itinerary ever since. Both sides would benefit.

Nicole put in a call to Sydney at the foundation, who was now her primary source of information. She gave her a brief update of the lack of success at the Climate Forum.

Sydney responded, "Yeah, I have been monitoring different news organizations, and none of it has been positive."

"That means the meeting on the ship is more important than ever! I think everything is set, but I need to give Max one more call to make sure his team is ready for us. By the way, are there any developments in the case?"

"The big news is that you dumped your protection and went your own way."

"True, but they were smothering me and stifling every move I made, so it was impossible to get anything done."

"Hmmm, I'm so surprised that you would do that," Sydney said sarcastically.

"Seriously, what is going on?" Nicole asked again.

"Senator Clarkston was brought into Swedish police headquarters for further questioning. He had to be arrested at his Stockholm hotel because he refused to come in voluntarily and made quite a scene. The Swedish police were pretty disgusted with the senator due to his lack of cooperation. They let several members of international security agencies participate in the questioning. Under pressure, he quickly broke down and admitted to some financial problems, but could not explain the shooting."

"Hmmm … I'm not surprised. He seems more like a white collar crime kind of guy."

"Security analysts have delved into his finances and have found some irregularities in his campaign funds and dealings with international energy companies."

"What kind of irregularities?"

"Mostly financial dealings so far, like an off-shore equity loan that had no record of payments for his new penthouse in Washington DC, and untraceable donations to his campaign. Obviously, there was some improper influencing going on, and the loan appeared to have been set up by a non-existent bank that transferred money from an off-shore account. They are trying to determine the source of the funds, and so far have only been able to trace them back to a bank in the Cayman Islands."

"So is there a tie between Senator Clarkston and the shooter?" Nicole asked.

"Nothing definite yet, but the current theory is that someone might have been blackmailing the senator to set up the reception at the Ice Bar in Stockholm … but that is just a theory so far."

"So he was probably duped into putting on the whole affair?"

"That would be my guess," said Sydney.

"Well, that would explain why he was suddenly so interested in environmental issues."

After talking with Sydney, Nicole put in a call to Max Lindberg to confirm the arrangements for the stop at the *Valkyrie.*

"Hi, Max. How have you been?"

"I'm in DC working on funding to expand the project, but budgets are tight so it is not going all that well."

"That's too bad. It's a tough time, but I am excited for the group to see the incredible work your team has been doing."

"Me too! I'm flying back to Stockholm this afternoon and will be arriving on the *Valkyrie* the morning before your group arrives.

Nicole was always amazed how much commitment and energy Max constantly put out. She had come to believe that he was one of the best role models she had ever known.

"So everything is set for our arrival?" asked Nicole.

"Yes, we are looking forward to showing off our progress."

Nicole said, "It will be incredible, and I can't wait to see you."

The *Sea Bridge* was scheduled to depart from the dock at 5:00 p.m. Most of the delegates had arrived at the port early and were in a festive mood as they checked in and gave their passports to the head steward for security control. They were very pleased with the luxurious accommodations and more than happy to be leaving Stockholm.

There were also some new guests who had joined the cruise. These were individuals who did not attend the forum due to a variety of reasons. Some of these were scientists who were not ready to publish their work or did not want the public spotlight. Others had great influence or financial connections that could bring dynamic change. But the reality was that all the attendees had been carefully hand-picked and screened to create a dynamic and creative think tank.

The participants walked around the decks, clustered in small groups, talking about what had happened in Stockholm and nervously discussing the public's newfound increased interest in their work. Most were distraught about the murder of David because people admired him and had a high regard for his work.

They discussed how there had been much less pressure when no one was paying attention to the environmental issues they were trying to resolve. Now, every move they made was documented and reported on, an uncomfortable life for a group of people who had been previously ignored.

Oliver arrived at a quiet bar located not too far away from the dock where the *Sea Bridge* was tied up. The clientele seemed to consist mostly of tired tourists seeking a place of refuge to recharge themselves. He took a seat in a corner, away from the thirsty tourists, and positioned himself so he could observe anyone who came through the door. Promptly, at two, a gentleman in his early sixties ambled in. He had probably been fit when he was younger, but age had softened him around the edges.

He came directly over to Oliver, stuck out his hand, and in a low, raspy voice, said, "I'm Marcos. Nice to meet you."

"I see you had no trouble finding the place and locating me."

Marcos laughed, "It's easy to spot you young agents. You guys dress well and have those expensive haircuts."

Oliver chuckled. "So much for my undercover look. It appears I'll have to work on it." He thought to himself, *This guy is a real classic.*

Marcos sat down, pulled out a cigarette, and lit it. He looked around and said, "Okay, what's up?

"I need an agent to take over the safety concerns on the cruise so I can focus on the bigger picture and distance myself from the personal security issues."

Marcos raised an eyebrow. "*Personal* security issues?"

"Well I mean ..." Oliver stumbled for a moment. He avoided the question by briefing Marcos on the details of the shooting and the subsequent investigation. Then he finished by saying, "I believe that Nicole Hunter could have been the primary target. You need to make sure that you keep a close eye on her."

Marcos smiled. "I understand your concern. I assure you that my record is solid and I will do a good job of protecting all the passengers on the cruise."

"Thanks."

The two of them headed to the quay where the *Sea Bridge* was docked to talk to the captain about the route the ship would be taking and the safety practices in place. They showed their credentials to the security screeners, boarded the luxury cruise ship, and made their way to the bridge. They found the captain reviewing some charts on a computer screen.

Introductions were made and Marcos asked, "Can you give us an overview of the planned trip?"

"This is a customized voyage. We will only be making two stops before cruising to St. Petersburg. Our usual cruises are much longer, lasting at least ten days and stopping at many other locations. The first port of call will be Helsinki, Finland, where the passengers can disembark if they chose to do so. The second stop will be a rendezvous with a ship at an unknown location in the Baltic Sea."

"A ship at an unknown location?" questioned Marcos.

"That must be the scientific ship that was on the agenda," answered Oliver.

The captain offered, "I have been told that I will be given the coordinates of the ship's location when we leave Helsinki and not before because of the sensitive nature of its mission."

Oliver made a mental note to get further information about the stop.

"After leaving the scientific ship, we will head back out to open water and simply cruise around to allow significant time for the guests to work. Then we will head to St. Petersburg, where the guests will disembark."

Marcos asked, "What security procedures do you have on board?"

"Not many. The bridge is open to passengers during the cruise except when the ship is docking or doing other maneuvers."

Oliver stated, "We will need to change that policy for this trip and make the bridge off-limits for security purposes."

"We pride ourselves on having good relationships with our passengers, but if you think it is necessary then we will comply with your request."

Marcos gruffly said, "It's necessary."

As the captain went on, it quickly became apparent that he had a dry wit about him and liked to talk about himself. He was quite short but had a large ego for such a little man. He joked, "The only reason I am a ship's captain is because my eyesight was too poor to be an airline pilot." He had a dark leathery tan, with embedded lines in his forehead and around his mouth. He looked like he was chronically squinting and smiling. "I'm a Brit, you know, but I've spent most of my professional life as a captain based out of Australia. Then a few years ago I took a promotion to this more prestigious cruise line. Now I live in a luxurious condominium on beautiful Miami Beach."

"It sounds like the good life," agreed Marcos.

The captain confided, "Most of the time, but my girlfriend in Miami isn't happy with how much time I spend at sea."

"Yeah, I know about that problem," chimed in Oliver.

The captain laughed loudly and said, "But I like the arrangement because it allows me to get away from my very pretty, but very possessive girlfriend. It's one of the benefits of being a sea captain."

Oliver began to think the captain would never stop talking about himself, so he said, "Tell us about the ship's navigation system."

He began, "The GPS system, navigation system, and the sonar equipment are all the most up-to-date equipment available." The captain became animated when he spoke about his ship and pointed to the equipment as he talked about its advanced capabilities.

It was time to end the visit, so Oliver said, "We have reason to believe the cruise could have some potential security issues so we will be in close contact if anything develops that you should know about." Oliver and Marcos thanked the captain for his time and left to check in to their cabins.

Chapter Twenty-One

Arrival

Nicole was running a little late and arrived at the dock just a few minutes before the ship was scheduled to sail. Since her arm was in the sling, she paid the taxi driver a little extra to bring her luggage to security and put it on the belt for screening. She showed her passport to the officer, passed through the metal detector, and started up the metal plank to the ship. She walked slowly, taking in all the sights and sounds of the impressive ship.

The *Sea Bridge* was not the common large, touristy cruise ship, but more of a boutique one. She looked up and saw many guests gazing down at her as she walked up the gangway.

On deck, she was greeted by a smiling young woman with incredible dark red hair and a charming Russian accent.

Dosha introduced herself and said, "I'm your tour guide for the Baltic Sea excursion. I believe you are Nicole, since you are the last name that is not checked off on my roster and you are the only one with their arm in a sling—a dead giveaway, I think."

She smiled. "Yes, I'm Nicole Hunter. It is nice to meet you."

Dosha continued on with a worried frown on her face. "I'm so sorry about the incident at the Ice Bar. It is very tragic. I saw it on the news and Oliver told me a little about it. I hope you're doing okay."

"I'm fine, just a little tired. So you know Oliver?"

"Not very well. He was the one who talked to me about the job opportunity on the ship. He was in St. Petersburg on some business and took time to interview me for the position."

"Are you some kind of operative or agent? It seems that everyone connected with Oliver does some sort of espionage work."

Dosha grinned. "No, I'm an ordinary tour guide from St. Petersburg. So Oliver is some kind of agent? He didn't tell me that. He only said that my job might be more dangerous than he originally thought, but I told him I wanted to stay on."

"Since you are on the cruise and have already met Oliver, I doubt that you are ordinary in any way. Hopefully, Oliver is wrong and the cruise turns out to be very safe and productive. It's nice to meet you, and I'm glad that you will be coming with us."

Nicole had felt an instant camaraderie with Dosha. She seemed honest and straight-forward and did not take long to get to the heart of the matter.

Dosha emphasized, "You are a brave person to continue on with your work after what has happened. I'm sure I would not have had the courage. If I can help you in any way, please let me know."

"Thank you. I might take you up on that offer."

Dosha motioned to the left as she said, "The opening session will be held through that door, in the conference area, in an hour and a half. Here is the packet that includes the updated agenda and some highlights of the tour. You will want to get settled and have a rest before the session starts. Your luggage has been taken to your room."

"Thanks for your help. I'll see you soon."

The guests on the deck applauded as the busy crew cast the lines away from the dock. The powerful thrusters started, and the ship headed out to sea. Everyone was happy to begin a new chapter of a trip that so far had been incredibly troubling.

The quiet engines powered the luxury cruise ship out of the port to a gentle sea. It was a balmy evening with the summer sun filtering through a white haze, likely caused by the industrial waste from the industries around the Baltic. The smog amplified the sun's circumference and blurred its borders. The water seemed to be a gentle lake instead of notorious angry sea that had untold wreckage sitting on its floor.

Nicole checked in at the reception desk and then proceeded to her room. She closed the door to the stateroom and felt relieved to have made it to the ship safely. She was pleased with the arrangements that the Everson Foundation had made, although it was not public knowledge that they were the hosts.

Nicole's arm had a dull ache, her head was pounding, and she was feeling a bit nauseated. She knew that she had been under an extreme amount of stress, and the trauma of the past few days came screaming down on her. For some unknown reason, she grabbed her cell phone to make a call to Seattle while the ship was still close enough to Stockholm to get a signal. There seemed to be urgency in her mind to make the call, like time would run out.

She dialed Sam's number and waited anxiously for him to pick up. The call went straight to his voice mail. She asked herself, *what the hell am I doing? He probably saw my number and purposely did not answer, or was out on a date.* She felt she must be reaching for some obscure security where none existed. She began to tell herself, Let it go. Let it go … and move on. She was good at that.

Nicole lay down on the bed, under the safety of the bed covers, to briefly escape the worries of the world. But she could not stop thinking about everything that had happened. She found herself working every angle to try to figure out the deadly puzzle that was going on. But it was an impossible task and she soon crawled out of bed, making a conscious decision to go on the offensive and try not to overthink everything.

On the way to the opening session, Nicole went by the hotel manager's office to check in and say hello. He was the only one on the ship who knew that the arrangements for the cruise were made by the Everson Foundation. Everyone else had simply been told that it was an extension of the Climate Forum.

She knocked on the hotel manager's door. An older man wearing a classic navy blue sports jacket with a nautical emblem on his pocket opened the door. "What can I do for you?"

"Hi, I'm Nicole Hunter from the Everson Foundation and I wanted to stop by to make sure that everything is going smoothly."

In a very charming British accent, the man said, "I have been expecting you. Your foundation has been very helpful in providing me with all of the information that I needed. Everyone has checked in except for two scientists who were sharing a room. After listening to the news, I believe that they will not be coming. Am I correct?"

"Yes, sadly so," Nicole confirmed. "Chen is still in the hospital, and I believe David's body is being flown home for burial right now. It is all so tragic because they were both great guys and brilliant scientists. We had high hopes for their research."

"Well then, we will have to arrange a memorial service sometime during the cruise. Would that be appropriate?"

"I think that would be wonderful. We could all benefit from a tribute to a great man. I'm glad I stopped by. Please let me know if you need anything else."

The opening session was just getting underway as Nicole quietly entered the room. She sat in an empty leather chair in the back and turned her attention to the speaker. The shipboard consortium had been set up to be run by professional facilitators who could help organize and drive the participants to action. Their job was not to let the sessions get bogged down with too much information or be monopolized by a few vocal people with personal agendas. The facilitators had the professional skills to keep the meeting focused and would politely cut-off someone to redirect the conversation. Nicole knew this would be the only way to accomplish the aggressive goals that had been set for the meeting.

The lead facilitator was explaining to the group, "The agenda consists of a series of brainstorming sessions that will determine the match-ups for presenting specific concepts later in the cruise. Then we will have a day off in Helsinki, Finland, for sightseeing, and the following day we will rendezvous with a highly specialized scientific ship working on a high-priority environmental operation."

A buzz ran through the group and hands immediately shot up, asking for more detailed information. "Could you explain the scientific ship's mission?"

The facilitator was a man in his fifties who had an impressive, full voice, much like a newscaster or talk show host. "The scientists and crew on the scientific ship *Valkyrie* have been working for two years to first map and then retrieve the chemical weapons that were dumped at sea at the end of World War II. As we know, these weapons were cruelly designed for the mass killings of large groups of people."

Many in the audience nodded solemnly.

"At the end of the war, the Baltic Sea provided a convenient dumping ground for countries trying to dispose of the nerve gas. The sea was viewed as the ultimate burial ground, and the dumping was completed long before anyone was concerned about environmental issues. The canisters were placed on old ships and sunk, or simply dispersed randomly along the bottom and drifted with the currents."

The facilitator paused, creating more anticipation. Many in the audience leaned forward as he continued, "Since the Baltic Sea is a stagnant and shallow body of water, it turned out to be a terrible place to dump weapons, with a high risk for ecological destruction. Over time, the metal casings disintegrated and slowly leached nerve gas into the Baltic Sea, causing grave danger to humans and the aquatic environment. There had been several discoveries of fish with mutated internal organs and increasing cases of human poisoning."

Someone interrupted, "And a good chance for genetic abnormalities in humans, right?"

"There is no question that even one or two molecules would bring damage to the human genetic code and put future generations in peril. An international coalition was finally formed to locate and safely contain the leaking weapons before it was too late."

The facilitator stopped, took a sip of water, and scanned his notes before continuing.

"The research ship recently transitioned from a mapping expedition to an active recovery operation. The dangerous job of collecting the canisters from the sea bed has been underway for a month. It has been a painstakingly slow process because each canister has to be handled with extreme delicacy. The first cache has been retrieved and will soon be transported for safe storage until a procedure to render the chemicals harmless is approved. Any missteps could cause an environmental disaster of huge proportions."

The guests' eyes were riveted on the speaker, and many were taking notes as the facilitator explained, "When docked with the scientific ship, the environmental scientists on the *Sea Bridge* will review the work procedures for recovery and storage. However, the main focus would be to assist in the methodology to render the chemical weapons safe."

The facilitator leaned forward, took a deep breath, and put both hands on the podium for emphasis. "The chemical weapons must then be effectively neutralized to avoid creating another bio hazard for future generations. It is a race against time to save the sea and surrounding coast from becoming a virtual wasteland."

To avoid a flood of questions, he finished by saying, "So that is all the background information I can give you, but there will be a more in-depth briefing from one of your colleagues who specializes in this area when we get closer."

Dosha was the next presenter, and she knew following the last professional presentation would be hard. She wanted to tantalize the guests with images of important sites they would see on the cruise. She moved to the podium, took a deep breath, and gave everyone a big smile. "Hello, my name is Dosha, and I would like to introduce you to the exciting history of the Baltic Sea and the countries that surround it." After a couple of slides, she paused to look out at the group. She could tell by their attentiveness that they were also interested in her talk. Granted she was only a tour guide, but she felt that her first presentation was going pretty well.

Oliver was standing off to the side, so Nicole did not see him when she walked into the room and sat down. In the last twelve hours, he had done his research and knew just about everything there was to know about Nicole. He knew where she had worked and for how long, how much money she made, who her friends were and all her grades since high school. He even knew how many parking tickets she had, and all the places she had travelled out of the country. He stared at her knowing that if she knew that he had checked up on her background, she would be furious with him. But he knew it didn't matter, and he continued to stare.

Chapter Twenty-Two

Disagreement

For the first work session of the morning, the guests were divided into four smaller groups located in different areas on the ship. One of the groups was given the task of solving the extreme weather conditions that had developed in the past five years. The goal was not to forecast the trajectory of the intensity of the storms, but rather to brainstorm solutions for curbing the conditions that caused the extreme weather.

Nicole decided to sit in on the creative ideation session taking place in the lounge. By mid-morning, the group had little yellow sticky notes plastered all over the walls and windows. The participants had developed some interesting ideas and would now group them for similarities. Everyone seemed to be motivated, and things were going well, so Nicole wandered off to the library where another group was working.

When she walked in, it was obvious that something was going on. She could feel the tension in the group and could see the annoyance on the participants' faces. A heated discussion seemed to be escalating, and even the professional moderator looked a little flustered.

In a raised voice, a man was saying, "It is not the role of an oil company to save the world! We have to make a profit, just like anybody else."

"So who is going to take responsibility if you don't?" demanded a scientist in a blue, short-sleeved shirt.

"We have devoted huge sums of money to alternative energy to supplement carbon-based energy."

The scientist held his own. "But look at the profits that your company continues to make and you only devote a very small percentage to the research and development of new energy. In fact, your company has pulled back and is only doing research and development on bio-fuels, even though your advertising implies you are beyond oil."

"You don't understand the scale and size of the amount of energy this country uses! All those bullshit alternative oil projects add up to nothing."

Another woman entered into the discussion. "So why do you imply that your company is interested in renewable fuels when it really isn't?"

The angry man shouted, "You're all full of shit! I don't need to put up with this idealistic crap," and stomped out of the room.

Individual conversations broke out in the room, and the moderator said, "Let's take a fifteen-minute break and we'll begin the next phase of the session."

Nicole was pretty sure the man who walked out of the meeting was the VP of Research and Development for Unified Energy, a major global oil company. He had been touted as a supporter of environmental causes in an industry where support was more show than reality.

Since she was not prone to letting things slide, she followed him out of the room. His fast pace reflected his anger.

"Excuse me," Nicole said to catch his attention.

He kept walking, so she repeated even louder, "*Excuse me.*"

He whirled around and rudely asked, "What now?"

"Pardon me, but I would like to introduce myself. I'm Nicole Hunter, from the Everson Foundation. I would like to talk to you about the meeting you were just in."

He hesitated with a pained expression on his face, trying to decide whether to engage or not. He finally blurted out, "Nobody wants to hear that a company has shareholders and we have to make a profit."

"I agree that some well-meaning people find that hard to understand. Do you think it is possible to develop a model where we solve some of the environmental issues and business can still benefit?"

He grumbled, "I suppose it's possible, but highly improbable."

Nicole pressed on, "Well, we have the best and the brightest people on this ship to work on it. We need to leave the old arguments and entrenched positions behind to have a chance."

"Then tell that to those people in that group; all they want to do is argue and blame big business," he flatly stated.

"As soon as we are done talking, that is exactly where I intend to go next."

He looked at Nicole with curiosity and then put out his hand. "I'm Jack Silverton, VP of R & D for Unified Energy."

"It's nice to meet you, Jack. Do you have a few minutes to strategize on how to make the group more effective?"

He shrugged his shoulders. "I suppose it wouldn't hurt."

After being asked his opinion on how to improve the group, Jack began to channel his anger in a more constructive manner. Nicole had used this technique with many belligerent people. Involve them, ask their opinion, and suddenly they become more congenial and actually start to be problem solvers instead of troublemakers.

"My boss keeps pressing me on this conference. He is calling me daily, wanting to know what is going on and what I am going to do about it. I think my job depends on what I do, and I am pretty sure I'm going to get fired," Jack revealed.

"Why do you think that?" Nicole asked.

"I don't know; I just don't understand what he wants from me and I can't seem to do anything right."

Nicole was familiar with his boss, an arrogant CEO who thought he had all the answers. Jack was feeling abused and sorry for himself, which likely drove some of his caustic behavior in the group.

He added, "My boss is coming to St. Petersburg for a meeting, and I'm certain he is going to fire me. Why else would he be here?"

She tried to be encouraging and offered, "Maybe he is here to discuss some of the issues about the pipeline under the Baltic Sea."

"I doubt it," he mumbled.

Nicole asked, "Will you come back to the group tomorrow, after I have talked to them to resolve any issues on that end?"

"As long as you tell them to be more realistic, I guess I could give it another try."

"Great. Then I'll see you at the next brainstorming session."

At the end of each day, a debriefing session had been scheduled with all of the facilitators. Nicole knew they would look at the dynamics and results of each group and make corrections to improve the process. Hopefully, they could get this group on track so they could tackle more creative issues.

David's memorial service had been planned for the following day when the *Sea Bridge* docked in Helsinki. Since Nicole was there at David's death, she felt it was important to personally announce the special event. At the end of the afternoon work session, she walked confidently to the front of the room and stated, "A special memorial service has been planned to celebrate the life of a truly great environmental scientist, David Cason. The service has been arranged for tomorrow afternoon and will be held at the famous Rock Church. Our purpose is to honor our own hero whose life was taken away prematurely."

Nicole had received another bit of good news earlier in the day, but had been saving it for this moment. Her serious voice changed to a more lighthearted tone. "I have also been told that Chen has gained significant strength and is insisting on joining us on the cruise."

There were sharp intakes of breath and audible expressions of joy from the group.

"He will need some assistance, but the doctors have cleared him for travel. He will be flying into Helsinki and will attend the service for David. He will then board the *Sea Bridge* to contribute to the success of this esteemed group."

The group rose simultaneously in a standing ovation to celebrate the news. There were tears in many of the audience's eyes. It had been a positive day with a hopeful future.

Oliver had waited in the background, while several of the guests mingled with Nicole, expressing their happiness at Chen's recovery. When everyone finally dispersed, Nicole saw him walking directly toward her. They had been tactfully avoiding each other since boarding the ship. He said, "Nicole, do you have a minute? I have some new information."

"Hi, Oliver. Is everything going okay?" Nicole said in a friendly tone. She had been feeling a little guilty about her impulsive decision to abandon him on the street.

Oliver raised both eyebrows and looked at her a bit confused.

She tried to joke, "I bet not many people have ditched the security detail of Oliver Odin."

He retorted, "Never—that is, of course, unless I let them."

Nicole bit her lip and gave Oliver a hint of a smile.

Not sure what else to say, Oliver resorted to the latest developments. "The authorities have found the silver parka worn by the killer at the Ice Bar. It had gun powder residue on it and was hanging with all the other capes on the coat rack."

"That is good news!"

"The forensics lab also discovered several strands of hair that are being run through DNA analysis. The parka was cleaned the week before the shooting, but was still worn by a variety of people. We should have the results soon."

"I hope they are able to come up with something conclusive."

Oliver hesitated. "There is something else. Uh, we have found a connection between your board of directors at the Everson Foundation and Senator Clarkston. Jean Cutter who was in one of the photos has met with the senator on a couple of occasions."

Nicole thought for a few seconds. "That is not surprising in itself since they both deal with large conglomerates and could easily cross paths."

"Yes, but it is an uncanny coincidence."

Nicole said protectively, "It would be devastating if there was any connection between the Everson Foundation and the crime. Everson is one of the most ethical and well respected foundations in the world."

Oliver maintained, "Like every other organization, the Everson Foundation must police itself to maintain its integrity."

"Yes, that's true, but this would be a terrible blow to the credibility of the philanthropic community and our ability to make positive changes. It would be equivalent to something like the president of the American Cross conniving to murder someone who is developing synthetic blood."

Oliver tried to interrupt. "We still have a lot to check out."

Nicole persisted, "I can't believe that Jean Cutter could have anything to do with it. Even though we often did not agree on tactics, it seems absurd that she could be connected to David's murder."

"What didn't you agree on?"

"It was the issue of responding to a crisis after the devastation had occurred versus working to prevent the tragedy in the first place. Jean believes it is God's will when violent storms occur and that humans are not a contributing factor."

"There is corruption everywhere these days, but there is also a chance that someone is trying to discredit the Everson Foundation."

Nicole pulled on a strand of her glossy hair and twisted it in her fingers while she thought. "That is a possibility. Government and big businesses usually do not like foundations with lots of money meddling in world affairs. We don't have a political or monetary agenda, so we make a lot of people nervous since we are independent and may not take their side."

Oliver conceded, "I had no idea how much impact a foundation like yours could have on global issues. Very interesting."

Nicole looked pleased. "That is the nicest thing you have said to me!"

"Thanks, but I'm afraid that many powerful and influential people have recognized the same thing. The power structure is changing in the world and they don't like it. It could be why David was killed."

"I suppose we threaten the status quo since we're pushing for rapid change, but it is hard to understand why people can't see that we have to do it. The acceleration of natural disasters has wiped out a scary number of people, and the pace of destruction is accelerating."

Oliver looked directly at Nicole. "People only know what has worked for them in the past, and they are afraid to lose their power. People go crazy when you threaten their money or power. It's human nature."

"You're right, but should we stop what we are doing and ignore the plight of the earth?"

Oliver didn't immediately answer. She could tell that he was wrestling with her question by the far-off look in his eyes. This was a man whose job was to eradicate evil forces in the world of illegal weapons and drug lords. Everything was black and white. Issues of global climate change were not as easy to classify. Who was right, and who was an alarmist who would profit from dire predictions?

Oliver eventually sighed. "I think you are doing the right thing."

She had to smile. Oliver had come a long way in the last couple of days.

Oliver continued, "Would you consider having a drink with me? We can go over the plans for the next few days and relax a little."

"I think that might be nice."

Might be? Oliver thought to himself, but instead said, "How about a nightcap right after dinner?"

"Sounds good. I'll meet you in the bar."

All during dinner, Oliver glanced over to Nicole's table to see how she was doing. Nicole was having a good time with a quirky-looking guy who seemed to make her laugh constantly. *What could be so entertaining?* wondered Oliver, who then chided himself for continuing to sneak looks throughout the dinner. *At least she accepted my invitation for a drink*, he reminded himself.

Oliver was sitting next to a plump woman who giggled incessantly when he made polite conversation with her. He did not know that she was a famous statistician who had supplied some of the most compelling and credible information on climate change. He tried to be polite and not show his annoyance when the woman latched onto his every word.

He excused himself before the dessert course and mumbled that he had some work to do. The plump woman gave him a sad look as he walked past Nicole's table and left the dining room. He picked up his messages and then went up to the bar to wait for Nicole. He was quite certain that it would take some time before she arrived, so he settled in and ordered a vodka martini. He looked at the messages and didn't see anything interesting so he struck up a conversation with the bartender.

Nicole saw Oliver leave the dinner early and wondered why he was in such a hurry. He brushed by her table, like he was giving her a hint that she should leave. But she didn't want to be rude, so Oliver would just have to wait. Besides, the dinner was good and she was enjoying herself talking to the interesting people at her table.

Nicole was sitting next to Ian Whitehouse, a professor from Oxford, who turned out to be a good conversationalist and also had a great sense of humor. He was tall and thin with dark glasses, and had a captivating British accent. He was a professor of environmental studies at Oxford University and quite young for a professor at such a prestigious university. His expertise was in aquatic chemistry and biogeochemical engineering, both growing fields that had become very popular with the rise in funding for environmental science in recent years.

When asked what he did, the professor explained, "It is my enormous pleasure to teach students from all over the world. They are the best and the brightest, and many are brilliantly creative."

"In what way are they creative?" Nicole prodded.

"Let's see, there was an assignment on how to better communicate the impact of global climate change. A student made a delightful animated movie of a polar bear shaving in preparation for global warming. It was absolutely hilarious, and the point was made."

That led to everyone at the table telling the global warming jokes they knew, which were many. It didn't take long for the six people at the table to be laughing so hard that they were gasping for breath. They probably annoyed everyone around them, but they were having a great time.

When Nicole at last looked around, most of the tables had emptied out. She remembered that she was supposed to meet Oliver and realized that she had probably kept him waiting awhile. That is *if* he had waited. She excused herself from the table, explaining that she had a late meeting to attend. Ian Whitehouse stood up and made a point of shaking her hand and then putting his left hand on top of hers. He said warmly, "It was fantastic meeting you. We must have dinner again, very soon."

Nicole made her way up the stairs to the ship's bar and found Oliver sipping a martini. She touched his shoulder in a friendly gesture and sat beside him on the tall barstool.

"So, you're finally here," said Oliver with a hint of irritation. "Do you know our bartender?"

"Yes, I do. Hi, Ahmin. I'll have my usual."

When Ahmin turned away, Nicole said, "I make a point of knowing the bartenders during any event we put on. They can be an invaluable source of information."

"Now you are talking like an agent. So how was your dinner?"

"It was very entertaining," Nicole responded.

"Yes, I could see that. You seemed to be having a *very* good time."

Nicole wondered if she detected a note of jealousy in his voice, or maybe it was her imagination. She changed the subject. "So, what's going on?"

"I want to go over the security plans for the rest of the cruise with you."

"Okay."

Oliver tersely declared, "I'm leaving the ship in Helsinki to fly to Saudi Arabia. Marcos will be assuming my duties."

She was caught by surprise. "Oh really? So when did you decide this?"

"Since we have new leads that need to be investigated, and it is impossible to do anything on a cruise ship in the middle of the Baltic Sea. I will be in constant communication with Marcos, so I will know everything that is going on. Why, will you miss me?" Oliver said a little sarcastically.

At that point Nicole realized that Oliver had probably had a couple of drinks before she arrived. Although he was not noticeably drunk, he was not himself. "I guess I've become accustomed to your interference in everything I do, so I probably will notice your absence."

"I'm sure Marcos will assume my role quite well."

"I doubt he will be able to replace you. He seems to be quite the gentleman."

"And I'm not?"

"Well, I suppose you can turn on the charm when it's in your best interest."

Oliver just looked at his drink and didn't say another word.

"Well, maybe I got carried away. I appreciate what you have done for me so I need to thank you for everything," she said, lightly touching him on the knee.

Oliver turned from studying his drink to look straight at her. He said, "I appreciate that."

"Seriously, I will miss you. When are you planning to leave?"

"After the memorial service at the Rock Church has concluded. We don't know who might show up; plus it will give me time to brief Marcos."

So there it was: Oliver was leaving for another assignment. Nicole didn't quite understand why, and felt disheartened. She thought maybe she was being oversensitive and her recent breakup with Sam had something to do with it. Anyway, it was clear to her that Marcos could not fill Oliver's shoes. She had become attached to Oliver's direct approach and challenging personality. She would miss him, but she tried to convince herself that now she could devote all her time and energy to making the think tank successful.

Chapter Twenty-Three

Helsinki

The next morning, while most of the guests were still sleeping, the *Sea Bridge* quietly docked in Helsinki. Because the *Sea Bridge* was a small cruise ship, it was able to dock at the popular South Harbor, located right downtown, where ferries from Estonia and other Baltic countries dropped off their passengers.

Within sight of the ships, located between the sea and the city's historical buildings, was the Kauppatori Market. In a couple of hours, the market would come alive with the frenzy of vendors scurrying to set up their booths in time to entice the tourists coming off the cruise ships. The talented artisans made a good living selling Finnish glass, jewelry, knives, furs, hand-woven rugs and other crafts to eager visitors wanting to buy locally made products. Flowers and fresh vegetables added even more color to the vibrant marketplace.

The stop had originally been planned to be a break from the intense mental grind of the symposium and improve creativity. But the plan had been altered to include the memorial service for David to be held in the late afternoon, just prior to the guests returning to the ship.

Nicole woke up early, looked out the window, and saw that the ship had already docked. She grabbed her cell phone and called Sydney in Seattle.

"Hi, Sydney. We've arrived in Helsinki. How is the video for the service coming?"

"I think you'll like it. We were able to obtain a few clips of David in college, goofing around with his friends and working in the lab. We interspersed that footage with images of his vision for the future."

"So it feels appropriate for a celebration of life?" Nicole asked.

"Yes, I think so. The people who saw it here thought it was very inspirational."

"That sounds good. You're the best! Thanks for making this happen so quickly."

"Many people contributed. I just put it all together, uploaded it, and sent it to a video company in Helsinki. They are burning a DVD and bringing it to the church to test out the quality."

"I am headed there to make sure everything is set up."

Sydney warned, "Be careful, Nicole. We still haven't caught David's killer, so you can't be too cautious."

"I'm sure the murderer will not be in Helsinki. That would be crazy. The person would have to be on the ship with us!" Nicole joked.

Sydney paused for a few seconds and firmly said, "That is not out of the realm of possibility, so you must be careful."

"Sydney?"

"Yes," she said.

"Did you know that Oliver was leaving the ship to track down some leads in Saudi Arabia?" Nicole couldn't help but ask.

"I heard the decision was made at the last security briefing. His superiors feel that he is the most capable of pursuing the more dangerous leads," Sydney explained.

"That is good to know. I thought he was giving up because I had given him such a hard time."

"Oliver? From what I hear of his reputation, he is extremely stubborn and doesn't give up on anything."

"Thanks, Sydney. I'll talk to you after the service to let you know how it went."

The Rock Church was hailed as one of the major architectural achievements in the world and was literally built out of a natural rock outcropping that was forty feet above street level. The walls had been blasted from the inside out, to create a circular shape to the church, with the majority located below ground level. Only the dome of the roof was visible from the street, so the whole structure looked like a flying saucer landing on a rock platform.

Nicole walked into the bunkerlike entrance and got her first view inside the unusual church. The walls were all made of stone, with no other decorative elements other than the interesting patterns and textures created by the play of light on the rocks themselves. In contrast, the domed ceiling was made of copper in the center, with hundreds of long slender windows around the perimeter that provided the natural light that gave the church a spiritual and almost unearthly feel.

A lone voice was singing a beautiful and soulful song. Nicole looked around and determined that it came from one of the pastors moving around the front of the church. He was putting music sheets on the grand piano. Even though he was far away, the singing was strong and clear, showcasing the incredible acoustics of the church. She hoped this would be the pastor who was going to give the service for David. His voice was so beautiful that it would bring solace and inspiration to all those who attended.

She located the small media room where a representative from the media company was making adjustments on the sound board.

"Hi, I'm Nicole from the Everson Foundation. You must be from the media company?"

"I'm Jalmar. Would you like to see the video?" he asked with a strong Finnish accent.

"Yes, could you put it on the monitor in here so no one in the church can see it?"

As she watched, David came to life on the screen.

A college friend said, "David was a prankster and an inspiration. He took it upon himself to put up hand-written signs in virtually every corner of the lab to keep the stress level manageable. One read, 'All wisdom can be found on T-shirts' while another said, 'If you don't succeed, redefine success.' We will really miss this quirky, caring guy."

The film then shifted to a more serious side, with a narrator explaining David's achievements and had poignant testimonials from family and friends talking about why they would always remember him.

David's mother ended the video with, "My son was different from the day he was born. He was misunderstood for much of his life because he was smarter than everyone else and cared deeply about humanity. He was meant to accomplish great things, and I hope you remember him because he was a good man."

Nicole wiped away the tears that were streaming down her face. She knew the video would be perfect for the tribute. With red eyes, she went back into the main hall and found several security guards searching the church, scouring it for who knows what. She walked around, taking time to regain her composure.

Back in the shadows, she could see Oliver and Marcos quietly talking. "Hi, guys. Have you found anyone lurking around trying to kill us?" She asked in a slightly sarcastic voice.

"No, at least not so far," answered Oliver.

"Well, Oliver, after the service, you will be free at last," she couldn't help but say.

"How do you figure? I'm still working on the case."

Marcos jumped in, "Don't forget, you still have me to torture."

"I'm sure you will be more accommodating than Oliver."

"Oh, don't be so sure," remarked Marcos.

"See you guys later. I have to go meet Chen."

Nicole returned to the street outside the church because Chen was scheduled to arrive at any moment. He was being transported from the airport in a special van outfitted to carry a wheelchair.

Outside, the clouds had burned off and it was a sunny day with just a little wind to rustle the trees. A road block had been set up, and security guards were diligently checking vehicles as they came close to the church. Everything was relatively quiet, so the press had not gotten wind of the service, which had purposely been kept low-key.

It didn't take long until a white utility van pulled up. The driver talked to one of the guards and then parked directly in front of the rock church. The driver got out and opened the side doors to reveal Chen, who looked pale and vulnerable but much healthier than the last time Nicole saw him at the hospital.

Nicole felt a lump in her throat and was barely able to speak. "Chen, it is so great to see you. How do you feel?"

"Better," he said in a composed voice.

An attendant hooked up his wheelchair to the lift to bring him to street level.

"Thanks so much for meeting me. This is a bit overwhelming, but I felt that I must come," he said as the wheelchair was lowered to the sidewalk.

"Believe me, I understand. It is important that you are here for everyone else. By just being here, you are providing hope and courage."

"How is the symposium going?" Chen inquired.

Nicole thought for a moment and then responded, "Some creative ideas have come up, but so far we have not had any major breakthroughs."

Chen gave a weak smile. "We will have to change that."

"Let's go inside; the guests will begin arriving soon."

They had removed one of the wooden chairs so Chen's wheelchair could be put in its place. He was located next to Nicole in the first row so that he could easily be wheeled to the front of the church to say a few words about his best friend and colleague.

Chen said, "It was a hard decision whether to come here and continue on with our work or go to his home town for his burial. But I think this is what David would have wanted me to do."

Since David's body had been flown back to his parents in the States, the service at the Rock Church would not include a casket and would be strictly a celebration of his life. Chen bit his lip and looked a bit downcast.

Nicole could tell that he needed some reassurance, "Yes, I agree. David would have wanted you here to be with his colleagues and to continue on with his work."

Soon the tour buses arrived and guests began to silently stream into the unique church. The sun was shining in from above, and the cavernous walls were highlighted. By the look on their faces, one could tell they were in awe of the beauty and uniqueness of the surroundings. Dosha had made sure that everyone had been briefed on the history of the church in advance of arriving so that the service would be uninterrupted.

Most of the scientists congregated toward the front of the church and sat in the first few rows, often stopping to say a few words to Chen or to simply touch him on the shoulder. They obviously felt a close camaraderie with the wounded and grieving scientist. The rest of the guests spread out among the birch pews off to the side or behind the group of close-knit scientists.

Ian Whitehouse, the Oxford professor, sat directly behind Nicole, He leaned forward and asked, "How are you holding up?"

"Pretty well. I just want the service to be perfect," she quietly commented.

"Please tell me if I can be of any assistance."

Ian had been very attentive since the friendly conversation they had at dinner. It seemed that Nicole was bumping into him at every turn on the ship. It had become almost awkward and it seemed that Ian may have misinterpreted the good time they had at dinner. She secretly hoped that he wasn't coming on to her because she did not want to deal with it. She was much more concerned with Oliver's impending departure.

The organist took her seat and began to play the subterranean, modern pipe organ. The sound was powerful, resonating throughout the unusual space. It did not surprise Nicole because she knew that they sometimes used the church as a recording studio because of its almost perfect acoustics.

Nicole turned around and glanced at the crowd behind her. Everyone seemed captivated by the Handel concerto that set the mood for the otherwise modern tribute. For some reason, she looked up and could see Oliver in the shadows at the back of the balcony. He was scanning the church for potential threats, and she could feel his state of alertness from where she sat. He must have seen her turn her head, and their eyes made contact for a brief moment. She gave him a hint of a smile, but he did not return the acknowledgment and continued his search, looking for anything out of the ordinary. Nicole felt a pang of disappointment. She was frustrated with herself, feeling that she had left things unfinished with Oliver.

The organ stopped playing, and the minister walked to the pulpit. He spoke in accented English, giving comforting words to his audience. Next, members of the choir sang a beautiful, ethereal song that was haunting in this otherworldly environment.

Then it was time for Chen to speak. Nicole hoped he could gather the strength to deliver his message. The pastor came over and wheeled Chen to the front of the church. There were a few moments of uncomfortable silence as Chen wrestled to get his emotions under control. It seemed like everyone was holding their breath.

Then he began. "David was not only my best friend but also a brilliant scientist who inspired everyone around him to do their best work. He was a funny guy who liked to see his friends laugh, and he never missed an opportunity to tell people they were important and doing a good job. His dream was simple: preserve the precious life that so many of us take for granted."

Chen's voice choked up so he took a few long breaths to calm himself. Then he continued strongly, "I think the best tribute that we could give David would be to use this think tank to come to agreement on a strategy to improve the climate crisis. Nothing short of this would be acceptable for my friend and our colleague who we honor here today. Please join me on the *Sea Bridge* in a collaborative effort to make this a turning point for our battered earth. Let's identify breakthrough solutions and make our work a reality. David would have expected nothing less from all of us here today."

Immediately the video began to play. Seeing David so full of life up on the screen only emphasized the magnitude of everyone's loss. It did a good job of supporting what Chen had just talked about. Nicole felt a little guilty, but she couldn't help secretly hope that it would help inspire those in attendance to finish his work.

The service ended with the organist playing a classic Bach piece, but instead of filing out, people collected in the front of the church. Nicole could hear the emotion in their voices as they talked about the funeral and David's work. They seemed more motivated than ever to put aside their differences and come up with some viable solutions.

She smiled at Chen and whispered, "This is what we needed to move forward. David would be very proud of you."

"Thank you," he quietly said. It had obviously been his intent all along to spur on the participants to work harder and more closely together than ever before.

Many people came to visit with Chen, telling him what an inspiration he was to them. Nicole turned to look up at the balcony one last time, but it was empty. Oliver was nowhere to be seen. He must have left as soon as the service was completed, and she knew at that moment she would really miss him. His presence had made her feel safe, and she wished he was still there.

Finally, the group made their way slowly back to the buses for the short ride to the ship. Nicole climbed in the back of the van to ride with Chen.

She looked at him hopefully. "It was a great tribute for David, wasn't it?"

He signed wearily, "Yes it was, but his true legacy will be the completion of his work. Nicole, you must help me do that," he implored. "It was all I could think of when I was laying there in the hospital. I promised myself that if I lived, I had to finish it."

"Yes, you're right," she emphatically agreed, "We *will* make every effort to make it happen!"

The hotel manager had arranged for a reception and dinner on the sundeck to complete the tribute. The champagne was poured and everyone toasted one last time to the tragic loss of a brilliant man.

Chapter Twenty-Four

Progress

The day after the memorial service, there was a dramatic change in the atmosphere on the ship. The agenda was narrowed down to a few big ideas that could make a real difference, and it had been decided to let the guests choose their focus. By lunchtime, three of the four groups requested that food be brought into the breakout rooms because they did not want to take the time to stop for lunch.

One team was working on the science behind removing carbon from the atmosphere using a photosynthesis model. Several of the scientists were sharing their most confidential research and were working on a plan to combine it into one large project. Nicole's VP friend, Jack, was very excited to be part of this group, because finding a way to remove carbon would exonerate the oil companies from all their promises to develop clean fuels. She was sure he thought this would be a great way to impress his boss and save his job.

Another group was working on hydrogen fusion, with Chen leading the charge. He had briefed all of the scientists on the methodology and results of the experiments that he and David had conducted. Nicole was drawn to this group because she had never seen such a wide open sharing of highly sensitive information. Several of the scientists in the group seemed to click with the work that Chen and David had done, adding their own technical knowledge to the discussion.

Nicole witnessed an eager scientist grab a pen, and he began to write a formula on the white board. Chen absentmindedly adjusted his glasses while he closely watched. When the scientist was finished, he brushed his hands together, backed up, and turned around. Nicole saw Chen break into a grin. He gave the scientist a high five, and the other members of the group began to clap each other on the back and whistle their approval. Nicole became excited experiencing the group's exhilaration.

She knew just enough about cold fusion to know that it was the holy grail of clean energy. It was a low-energy nuclear reaction that could potentially produce excessive heat. The ingredients were simply a metal, such as nickel; hydrogen in the form of water or gas; and something to cause excitation, such as electricity.

Many studies had claimed success in the field, but no one could reproduce the results, causing scientists to explain the successful trials as simply experimental error. The only thing Nicole knew about cold fusion research was that it was a hotly debated topic in the world of project funding because of its huge energy potential. But the problem was that it was not accepted by the scientific community so it lacked credibility. As a result, it was difficult for nonprofits and others to justify giving money to these projects because of the high risk of failure.

But it appeared Chen's team believed they had made a breakthrough. Nicole thought that if there was even a small chance that they were on to something, it would be worth it. She had only limited knowledge of what the group was talking about, but she did know that the best minds in the world were collaborating on it. For her, it made all the sacrifice and heartache of the job worth it, and she must help make it happen.

Chapter Twenty-Five

Preparation

It was late in the evening and Zafir had finished his shift serving dinner and cleaning up the dining room. The ship was relatively quiet because the guests were exhausted from their taxing day of work and collaboration. Most of them had gone directly to their rooms after dinner to regain their energy for the next day. The only sound, besides the hum of the engines, was occasional laughter coming from a hardy few who had gathered in the bar for a night cap.

As he left the dining room, Zafir was feeling guilty. On his first night on the ship he was supposed to have carried out an important task given to him by the London cell, but he had failed to do so. He had reasoned that it would be stupid to make the trip to the cargo hold too early because he was at risk of being exposed. The next day he rationalized that everything was in proper order, so why tempt fate when he really only needed to visit the cargo hold one critical time?

He did not want to admit that he was terrified to operate in the complete darkness under the sea. He had gone so far as to lie to the London cell by communicating that he had been successful. But he couldn't wait any longer, and tonight was the night that he had to go below deck to find the parts and tools left for him by his predecessor. He had simply run out of time. He must gather his wits and conquer his irrational fears.

He tried to be confident when he descended to his bunk room to change his clothes, but he was already breathing hard. He had rehearsed the trip in his mind countless times since his visit to London, but that was before being on the ship. It had all seemed so easy, until his first trip down to his bunk room. Now he must focus on the task at hand and block out where he had to go. He took a few deep breaths, grabbed his small athletic bag, and forced himself to begin the journey that would require him to go down to the lowest level of the ship to reach the cargo access door.

Each step down felt like a death sentence. Zafir gritted his teeth and began to hum, trying to distract himself from the sea that was closing in around him. He felt sick, and it was taking him too long to descend, but he couldn't make his legs move any faster. Finally, he reached the bottom and could see a door marked "Cargo Hold" in front of him.

He unlatched the metal door and stepped into the dark cargo space. He was terrified. He stood still and thought about the strict religious discipline and severe physical training he endured at the camp. The leaders drilled over and over that the mission was the only focus, singling out and ridiculing anyone who showed fear. But in the end, what he remembered most vividly was his mother's soft voice encouraging him to go on.

His hands were sweaty and he felt clumsy, but he managed to turn on a small pen light to get his bearings. The directions were ingrained in his memory, and he carefully picked his way through the metal storage racks toward a wall that had large electrical boxes. He looked for a metal panel that had been marked with the numbers 28941 on a green sticker. Just as it had been described to him, he found the panel on the lower left-hand side.

His hands shook badly as he pulled out a small screwdriver to remove the six screws holding the metal cover in place. It should have been a simple task, but the suffocating air was making it difficult for him to breathe. He felt like an oppressive weight was pressing on his chest. Pausing for a moment, he closed his eyes in an effort to regain his composure and still his trembling hands.

After several unsuccessful attempts, he finally managed to remove the screws and lift the metal covering off the panel. Inside was a simple cardboard box, a little bigger than the size of a normal briefcase, sitting exactly where it was supposed to be.

He opened the box and ran his fingers over the timer and vaporizer unit that looked more like a personal air-conditioner. He could see that the cables had been neatly coiled and the attachment wires and the battery pack were all there. Then he opened the mini-laptop that was no more than six inches wide and attached to the battery pack. He pushed the power button and it came to life, glowing in the dark cargo hold.

The sweat dripped down his face and obscured his vision. He wiped the sweat on his sleeve and continued, reaching into his pocket for the small box that contained the vial of liquid that he had carried on the flight from London. He had transported the nerve gas on board the plane in his shaving kit in his carry-on, since it was within the airline's size limit. Although, it could have been noticed for its unusually secure packing, it had been overlooked by the bored security screeners.

He rubbed his forehead on the sleeve of his left arm, making sure not to jar the box in his right hand. The next step would take a steady hand to place the vial in the chamber of the vaporizer and complete the weapon. He took another deep breath to calm himself, but his attention wandered to his location under the sea, sending his panic level to new heights.

Once again, he deviated from the original plan because of his uncontrollable fear. He was supposed to put the vial in the device and initiate the programming of the timing sequence while still in the cargo hold, leaving only the activation at the site. But he couldn't stand another second in this hell hole under the surface of the sea. His hands were now shaking so badly that he struggled to unzip the athletic bag he had brought with him. He had to get out now.

He put the vial box back in his pocket, roughly grabbed the device and small computer, and shoved them in the athletic bag. There was no time to reattach the panel because he was psychologically suffocating and his whole body was screaming for air. He held the bag tight and scrambled up the stairs two at a time, almost knocking the bag against the wall. He didn't stop until he had reached the open air on the deck.

Zafir drank in the cool air in the strange light of the night and patted the box in his pocket to make sure it was intact. He knew he was not scheduled to be on the deck, and in a few moments he would be found out ... but he could not move. He let his thoughts wander to the happy times in his childhood when he ran free on the streets of Jidda with the other children. The memory of his mother telling him what a clever boy he was came to mind, but he shook his head from side to side, thinking that he was weak and afraid, and maybe not so clever after all.

He finally willed himself to move and start the descent to his shared cabin, where he would hide the athletic bag from his bunkmates. He started toward the stairs that would lead him directly to the workers' quarters, but as he turned the corner, he ran into someone coming the other way.

"Excuse me," he mumbled and looked down to make sure the impact hadn't damaged the fragile contents in the bag.

Dosha recognized the young crewman who had often gazed at her from afar. "Hi, what are you doing out so late at night?"

"Nothing," said Zafir quickly.

Dosha smiled. "You're not enjoying the wonderful sea air? That's why I'm here."

"Oh yes, of course. It is crowded down below," Zafir offered haltingly.

"Have you worked on the ship long?"

Zafir was uncomfortable with this line of questioning, especially with a woman, but he couldn't figure out a way to politely dodge her. He had already been caught where he shouldn't be, and he was trying to casually hide the bag behind him.

"This is my first tour," he said while nervously looking away from Dosha.

"So you are new. How did you get the job?"

"A friend of mine recommended me, so I had to take it. It is a good opportunity for me."

"But won't you miss your family being away for so long?"

Zafir tensed at this question, and without thinking, he blurted out, "My mother died long ago. There is no one else."

Dosha looked at him sympathetically. "Oh that's too bad. My mother also died when I was very young, but I had a grandmother to look out for me. It was all quite tragic."

Zafir cocked his head to the side, looking as if he was listening, so she went on, "One day I found a wooden box in my grandmother's closet that had a program with a photograph of my mother as a young dancer in the corps de ballet with the Kirov Theatre. The box also contained a newspaper article about a young man who was an outspoken proponent of worker's rights in the shipyards of old Leningrad. When my grandmother's friends came over to play cards, I tricked them into telling them about my parents."

Talking to Dosha was unfamiliar territory for Zafir. At home, he was accustomed to a complete separation between the world of a man and that of a woman. Only minimal social interaction was allowed, with a male guardian always present, and a woman's clothing could only reveal her eyes and hands.

The conversation with Dosha felt illicit and dangerous, but he was intrigued by her story and he didn't want her to be suspicious. He rationalized the interaction was necessary to maintain his cover.

"You were smart," Zafir managed to say.

"Not really, they had been 'sipping' on some good Russian vodka when my grandmother went to the kitchen. I innocently asked the ladies if they had seen my mother dance at the Kirov Theatre. They looked at me in surprise and one said, 'Oh, so you know about her? She was a beautiful, talented dancer. She looked just like you.'"

Dosha leaned on the railing and turned her head to look out at the light reflecting off the water. "I had to find out about my father, so I asked the ladies if they knew him. They began to giggle and were very excited to talk about such an exciting topic that was full of indiscretion. By that time, I think they had forgotten I was there. They said my father was a passionate and articulate dissident at the shipyard. He was an attractive combination of danger and charm, irresistible to an impressionable young woman."

Out of the corner of her eye, Dosha could see Zafir stealing some sideways glances at her. "Eventually, my father orchestrated a peaceful demonstration at the shipyard, and shortly afterward he was quietly convicted of treason and sent to a corrective labor camp in Siberia."

Zafir shifted his weight from one foot to the other. He had become absorbed in the story, temporarily forgetting why he was on the main deck.

Dosha went on, "My mother was devastated and went into a deep depression, even refusing to leave her room. Then one frigid Russian morning in January when the Neva River was frozen and the snow was deep, I was born. Not long after, my grandmother woke to find a note saying that my mother had left to find my dad at a family work camp in Siberia. It was no place for a baby. When I was six, my mother wrote to say she would be coming home very soon, but she never did. In the end, I came to the conclusion that my parents had been star-crossed lovers in an unforgiving world."

"So sorry." Zafir looked at Dosha and then quickly turned away, surprised that he really meant it. This intimate conversation was becoming overwhelming. He suddenly said, "I need to go," grabbed the bag, and took the stairs several at a time to flee the situation, saying to himself, *What am I doing? I need to focus.*

Even though he was rattled, he was forced to make a stop before going to the crew quarters. The London cell was expecting a communication from him, and it was overdue, so he had to go to the small room that contained the computer shared by all the staff members. When he entered, there was a crew member using the computer terminal, so he politely waited his turn. After what seemed a long time, the man logged out of his e-mail account and said, "All yours."

Zafir sat down and typed out an e-mail saying that the sea was "calm and clear ahead." Those words would notify them that everything was a go and they should proceed to launch the trawler that was waiting off the coast of Lithuania. It had taken only a couple of minutes to set off a chain of events that would be irreversible. Zafir logged off, shut down the computer, and left the room.

Chapter Twenty-Six

Rendezvous

The scientific ship *Valkyrie* was just a small dot, barely visible on the horizon. Marcos was looking through powerful binoculars as the ship's features slowly became more distinguishable. It was the same color as the sea, so it was quite hidden and did not demand the same attention as the bright white ferries and cruise ships that frequently passed by.

It was an ultra modern ship that had been built for its intended purpose, harvesting and transporting dangerous chemical weapons. The ship sat low in the water and had an almost stealth appearance, which was not easily visible to the casual observer. The top line was sleek and aerodynamic, but in stark contrast, the hull had a bulbous shape to protect the dangerous cargo below.

Marcos turned to the captain and asked, "How long until we rendezvous?"

"It will take twenty minutes to arrive at the destination, but the docking procedure will be much longer because of the sensitive nature of the mission."

Marcos grumbled, "Can't be too careful, I suppose."

He was very anxious to get on board the ship and conduct a thorough security search prior to any guests leaving the *Sea Bridge*.

Nicole was working on her laptop in the library. She periodically looked out the large window and could see the ship was getting closer to the rendezvous with the *Valkyrie*. She was excited because she was sure the guests would benefit from the stop and it would be fun to see Max again.

She had sequestered herself in the corner because she didn't want anyone to look over her shoulder at the information on her computer. Sydney had sent back the photos that were left at the hotel, with enhanced resolution and improved contrast. She also told Nicole that a facial recognition program had been run on the photo taken in the dark room with six people around the table. There had been two hits on the people facing the camera: an Iranian oil minister and a Russian deputy premier. But Nicole had no idea what those people might have to do with her.

There had to be something that she was missing. Why would someone send these photos to her unless there was a message that she was supposed to understand? She studied the photos diligently, but she had no clue what they meant.

Nicole closed the computer and looked out the window again. She couldn't help but think about Oliver and wonder where he was at that moment. *He's probably trying to control someone else's life*, she thought with a smile. Admonishing herself for thinking of Oliver, she forced herself to focus on the upcoming meeting on the *Valkyrie*. It would be fascinating.

One deck below, Zafir was busy serving breakfast to the guests, but he repeatedly glanced though a porthole to watch the scientific ship come into view. He knew this ship well, so he was only looking to confirm that the rendezvous was going as planned. On the flight from London, he had easily memorized the details of the engineering schematic that had been given to him. He etched it in his memory and not only knew the exterior and deck plans, but was also familiar with the ventilation and electrical systems running throughout the ship.

Zafir knew that the new financial backer of the London cell had advised them the *Valkyrie* was an important target with significant longer-term benefits. But actually obtaining the plan had been a major achievement accomplished by one of the clever software programmers at the terrorist cell in London. The programmer had a track record of obtaining sensitive information by hacking into university research programs. Many of the university programs were sponsored by both private and government funds, so they had high security, but with broad access.

The scientists were busy collecting and analyzing data on leading-edge programs and sometimes were not as diligent in security as they were with their research. They did not even think of the potential consequences when the information fell into the wrong hands and was turned against the people it was intended to help.

When serving meals, Zafir had listened carefully to the conversations about the visit to the scientific ship. All the guests were talking excitedly about the day in great detail. He caught snatches of conversations about the delicate nature of the retrieval process and how long it had taken to get the international funding.

He was even able to pick up an agenda for the meeting that someone had inadvertently left on the table at breakfast. The welcome/overview was scheduled to be given by the managing director, Max Lindberg, and then the larger group would be broken down into three smaller groups and rotated to different stations to view the ship's facilities.

The first rotation would be set up to see the salvage operation in progress as the crew brought up the last encased chemical weapons at this site. The next station would show the handling procedures and storage facility specifically built for this dangerous job. The last rotation would show the positions on a map of the remaining sites that needed to be cleared of the rapidly deteriorating casings that were leaking in the Baltic Sea.

Following the tour, an ideation session was planned back on the *Sea Bridge*, to generate ideas for methodology to dispose of the chemicals. A couple hours later, the *Sea Bridge* was scheduled to depart for St. Petersburg.

Chapter Twenty-Seven

Crucial Phase

Zafir had to slip onboard the other ship without being detected. This part of the operation had been left to his discretion because the circumstances were situational and could not be predetermined. It had sounded simple at the time, and although there had been many ideas given on different approaches, it had been left to Zafir's ingenuity to find a way to get on board. The only requirement was that after he accomplished the mission, he would swiftly return to the *Sea Bridge* and contact the London cell to give the go ahead to close in on the target.

The options weighed heavily on Zafir's mind. When the ship began the docking procedure, he began to realize that this was not going to be treated as an ordinary stop on the tour. He felt the omnipresence of the security agent as the ships joined together. He knew that this was the person who would try to stop him from his divine mission. Marcos was watching *everything* and seemed to be waiting in anticipation for something unexpected to happen.

In order to succeed, Zafir needed to gain access to the ship without using weapons or drawing any attention to himself at all. If he was successful, everything would appear normal when the *Sea Bridge* left the scientific ship.

Zafir went down to the kitchen to report in for his afternoon shift. When he arrived, everyone was working on assembling platters of food or packing items in various containers to be taken over to the scientific ship. He was told that a snack and beverages had been planned for the guests upon arrival on deck.

The ship's purser came into the kitchen and asked who would volunteer to take the food over and stay to serve the guests.

Zafir's hand shot into the air. "I would like to help."

The purser pointed at Zafir and three other men, saying, "Let's go. We need to get this food over right away."

"Yes, sir!" Zafir couldn't believe his luck. But he needed to figure out how to pick up the small athletic bag that had been hidden in his room and hide it so he could carry it over to the other ship.

He decided to scout out the situation on his first trip to check out if this would be his best chance to make the transfer. He carried over a platter of shrimp, going by Marcos, who looked him up and down when he passed by. On the way back, he walked quickly, but not fast enough to arouse suspicion. After he turned the corner, he raced to his room to pick up the nylon athletic bag.

He arrived in the kitchen out of breath, but just a few moments later than the others. He tried to be nonchalant as he entered, bending down to put the bag on a lower shelf, close to the door. Luckily, no one seemed to notice.

On this trip, he was given the assignment to transport flat trays of small pastries. But where was he going to hide the bag? Zafir hung back, trying to decide what to do. He frantically looked around and saw a metal cart that could hold the multiple pastry trays and had a drawer for utensils. He took out all the serving pieces and flattened the bag into the drawer. Now he must bring the cart up the elevator and catch up with the group.

When he exited the service elevator door on the main deck, he quickened his pace, realizing that he was conspicuously behind the others. From a short distance, he could see the gangway that he needed to cross with the cart, which would be a bit awkward. At the same time, he also noticed that Marcos was walking in his direction. He forced his eyes forward and proceeded on, knowing that this would be his only chance. If he failed, it would be over.

Then he saw a woman touch the man's shoulder and say a few words to him. He turned in her direction, and at that moment Zafir thanked Allah for the blessing he had bestowed on him. It was appropriate that a woman had distracted the agent from his job. *I am saved*, thought Zafir. He looked straight ahead and pushed the cart deliberately over the bumpy gangway to the *Valkyrie*.

Once on board, he left the cart on the top deck, grabbed a pastry platter, and followed everyone to the galley. He set down the tray and then returned to get another one along with the small bag in the utensil drawer. When he returned, it was no problem storing the athletic bag in a large pot on a metal rack filled with various cooking pans. He was sure they would not be used during the reception. In a fluid movement he turned back to the trays, ready to begin the preparation for the event.

The chef came into the kitchen and said, "We need to have everything ready in forty-five minutes, so let's get going!"

"Yes, sir!" Zafir responded.

Zafir knew that in just a short time, he would be setting the stage for an international incident. He trembled with excitement as he chopped olives and placed them on the hors d'oeuvres.

The guests from the *Sea Bridge* were assembled in the dining area of the *Valkyrie*. It was cramped quarters for such a large group, with people spilling out to the exterior deck. The leader of the scientific expedition, Max Lindberg, came to the microphone to welcome everyone and give them an explanation of what they were going to see. The guests were hushed, enthralled with the reality of being on an actual recovery mission.

Max addressed the crowd. "Thank you for your commitment to humanity. After all, that is what this whole project is about: preserving humankind."

Nicole was standing in the back of the group and was monitoring their reaction. Just as she expected, Max had them all in the palm of his hand. Nicole was pleased. It had been a good move to put the *Valkyrie* stop on the agenda.

When Max finished speaking, Nicole went to congratulate him. "As always, you have inspired all of us."

Max replied, "Thank you. I appreciate that. If only I could have that impact on governments around the world."

The reception to welcome the guests was winding down, and the tours of the ship were getting underway. The chef and the entire serving staff were in the galley, cleaning up and consolidating the leftover food to be brought back to the crew members on the ship. Everyone was in a jovial mood because the serving of the guests had gone smoothly and they had some time to relax.

Zafir knew that he had only a short time to plant the device before everyone would be heading back to the *Sea Bridge*. He said out loud to no one in particular, "I'm going to the toilet." He reached for the bag he hid earlier but inadvertently bumped into the cooking pots, creating a loud noise. He jumped, but when he looked up, no one was looking his way.

He left the galley and started following the map of the ship that was ingrained in his memory: straight then a right turn. Just a little farther and he would take the stairs down one level to a small toilet adjacent to the ship's mechanical room where he could lock himself in to avoid any interference.

Once again he became anxious as he descended the stairs to reach the deck below, but he only had to go down one deck, much more tolerable than his bunk room on the *Sea Bridge*. He reached the next level and began to worry that maybe the plans were incorrect. Where was the access point? He proceeded farther ahead and then he saw it: the sign designating the toilet room, right next to the mechanical room.

He entered the small space and immediately saw the vent that had been on the ship's schematics. This vent was critically important to his mission because it connected directly to the main ductwork that ran through the entire ship. From this location the nerve gas would enter the main air filtration system and circulate throughout the ship in a matter of minutes.

He locked the door, marked the time on his watch, and went to work. His first task was to open the grate covering the vent that ran from the toilet room to the central air ventilation system. He had to be extremely quiet because crewmen would likely be working in the mechanical room that housed most of the ship's electrical, heating, and cooling systems.

He climbed on the sink cabinet so he could reach the vent cover on the ceiling. When he got closer, he could hear voices and noises coming from the mechanical room next door. He carefully and quietly unhooked the grate. Peering into the vent, he could see the duct work leading into the next room. Farther down the duct he could see the attachment where the larger unit blew the cooled air throughout the ship. All the information he had obtained from the London cell had been correct, and everything was going according to plan.

The crewmen's voices were coming closer to his location and were now only a few yards away on the other side of the wall. Zafir froze for a few moments because they were so close he was sure they would be able to detect his presence. It didn't take long to see that they were on a break and not paying attention to their surroundings. They were laughing and joking with each other.

He tuned in to the level of ambient noise coming from the machinery and decided that it was enough to cover the sounds he was making. Slowly letting out his breath, he decided to risk continuing on. He had to move quickly before one of the men came to use the toilet.

He came down off the cabinet, took out the tools from the athletic bag, and laid the vaporizer unit carefully next to the sink. He reached into his pocket, took out the protective box containing the vial of deadly gas, opened the lid, and gently put the vial in the receptacle well of the vaporizer. Then he connected the cable to the small computer. He only had to input the data for the timing sequence and make adjustments to the velocity of the output based on the atmospheric conditions, a task that was easy for him. The device was set.

In slow motion and with purposeful movements, he climbed back up on the cabinet, reached down for the vaporizer device, and gingerly placed it in the vent. His last task was to trigger the lock mechanism so that it would be difficult to disarm. He took one last look to make sure everything was in order and operating correctly; then he closed the vent cover. He silently got down, put the small hand tools back in the bag, and walked out into the corridor to return to the galley.

Zafir was pleased with himself as he walked back to the galley. He couldn't wait to contact the London cell.

He returned to the galley only twelve minutes later and found that the staff was in the final stages of packing to go back to the *Sea Bridge*. He grabbed a stack of large serving platters, wedged the nylon bag between them, and followed the others. He only had to make it back to the *Sea Bridge* and his mission was complete!

When he turned the corner, he could see that the man named Marcos was checking everyone as they came across the gangway. He was carefully scrutinizing everything they carried, leaving nothing to chance. Zafir panicked. If Marcos looked in the bag, he would see the hand tools and the small computer used to set up the vaporizer device.

Zafir could not risk it. It might cause them to search the *Valkyrie*, which would be a disaster. He did a quick about-face, mumbled that he had forgotten something, and returned to the galley. His eyes frantically searched for a good place to hide the nylon bag. He quickly decided to go back to the same rack that contained the large pots and pans. He chose the stacked steam pots at the bottom of the metal shelves, threw the bag in, and then shoved the pots to the back of the shelf.

He hurried back and walked confidently across the gangway to Marcos, who carefully inspected what he was carrying and then let him proceed. Zafir chuckled when he thought about how the security was aimed at protecting the guests on the *Sea Bridge* but not the workers on the *Valkyrie*.

Chapter Twenty-Eight

Proactive Approach

When the tour on the *Valkyrie* was finished, Nicole went to find Max. He was talking to some environmental policy makers, giving them a funding pitch. When Nicole approached, he excused himself.

Nicole gave him a hug and then said, "Your group was as competent and inspirational as I thought they would be."

"Thank you. I really value your opinion, so I am pleased.

"You continue to motivate me, and thank you for having us."

"The pleasure is mine," Max genuinely said.

After talking to Max, Nicole immediately went back to the *Sea Bridge*. She was determined to go on the offensive rather than waiting for the international "experts" to solve the case. After all, she was closer to the situation and had more knowledge of the facts than all the experts.

She put in a call to Sydney, who answered her cell in a sleepy voice. "Hello."

"Sydney, it's me. I guess I caught you in bed. Not working around the clock tonight?"

"I must have fallen asleep in my comfy office chair. I thought you might be calling."

"So you *are* working. Not a surprise, but it's awfully late."

Sydney was known to spend an inordinate time at the office when she was working on an important project. Nicole could always count on her to be there when she needed her. She was smart and creative and came up with innovative solutions.

Nicole told Sydney, "I have decided to go on the offensive, so we need to figure this out."

"I've been waiting for you to say that. You've not been yourself lately—a little depressed I think."

She could always depend on Sydney to give her honest appraisal of the situation. "So let's review what we know and determine a course of action to make some progress on the case."

Sydney excitedly began, "I've been spending some time examining the photos that were given to you at your hotel in Stockholm."

"So have I, but I'm not getting anywhere with them. What have you come up with?"

"I have been exploring the idea that they were not meant as a threat; instead they might be telling a story. What if someone was trying to help you by warning you about what was going to happen?"

Nicole contemplated the idea and then said, "That's possible. It could make some sense."

Sydney went on to explain her reasoning. "There might be an insider who has knowledge about a plan to stop any breakthrough environmental progress that could change the tide of global economics. This person may be disgruntled, or not agree with the position. If I had to guess, I would say they also fear for their life so must remain anonymous. Of course, this is all conjecture at this point, but the pieces seem to fit."

"If the theory proves true, then this may be an ongoing plot and the violence may continue?"

"That could be the case. You need to be very careful," warned Sydney.

Nicole winced. "But not so careful that we can't figure this whole thing out?"

"Yes, you're right. We should be looking at the bigger picture, so we need to be proactive and take some personal risks."

"Thank you. I need your support since everyone else wants to protect me at any cost. Oh, there is one more thing. Oliver told me Jean Cutter had met with Senator Clarkston on several occasions. I am sure there is a perfectly logical reason, but could you find out what that is about? It would be bad if a director for the Everson Foundation could be traced to any of this."

"I'll see what I can find out."

"Thanks. I'll be in touch."

Nicole terminated the call and headed up to the main deck to look for her favorite Russian tour guide. She was the one person who had legitimate access to all the guests and could be trusted.

"Dosha, there you are. Do you have a minute?"

"Yes, of course."

Nicole went directly to the point. "I need to find out some more information about a couple of the guests on board."

Dosha eagerly interjected, "I've been hoping to be of some assistance besides the usual tour guide stuff. Which guests?"

"I had an interesting conversation with Jack Silverton, who is a VP for Unified Energy. He is very disgruntled and skeptical about the whole sustainability issue. Could you befriend him and learn more about what makes him tick and the inner workings of his company? I can't figure out his motivation for coming here, and he is in fear of losing his job. I think he is an interesting selection to attend the meeting for such a prestigious oil company looking to promote their sustainability agenda."

"No problem. You said a couple of people. Who else?"

Nicole smiled at her enthusiasm. "The other one is Ian Whitehouse, the Oxford professor. He is an interesting man but he wasn't on the original guest list so I don't know much about him. He is substituting for an extremely wealthy philanthropist who we thought might help us finance promising research. I would like to know why Ian is on the cruise instead of the other guest, and what his agenda might be. It's probably a small thing, but it should probably be checked out."

"I'll be discreet but make contact as soon as possible. I'll give you a report when there is new information."

"Thanks, Dosha. I appreciate it."

Chapter Twenty-Nine

Death at Sea

All the guests finally arrived back on board the *Sea Bridge* after the motivating day aboard the scientific ship. The gangway was pulled back and the lines were cast off. Everyone lingered on the deck to wave goodbye to the dedicated crew and scientists of the *Valkyrie*. The ship would leave tomorrow to take the dangerous cargo to be destroyed in a state-of-the-art facility on a remote island off the coast of Sweden. The *Sea Bridge* set sail toward St. Petersburg while most of the guests went to their rooms to freshen up and get ready for dinner.

The two ships parted ways exactly on schedule. The fifty-minute buffer that had been programmed into the device had not been necessary after all. Exactly one hour and fifty minutes later, a colorless gas was released into the ventilation system of the *Valkyrie*. The deadly nerve agent infiltrated quickly, settling into the low-lying areas of the ship first.

Max Lindberg was walking down the corridor to his cabin when he began to cough uncontrollably. He reached for his throat and struggled to breathe as his airway passage shut down. His muscles began to jerk and he started to sweat profusely as he slipped into convulsions and finally unconsciousness. Before he realized what was happening, he was poisoned.

It took only a few minutes for the nerve agent to be dispersed through the ventilation system and invade the entire ship. Within ten minutes of the gas being released, everyone on board was dead. No one had been able to send an emergency signal for help. The ship was deathly quiet.

The painstaking work that Max and his team had accomplished to preserve humanity and the environment was for naught. They had been murdered in a well-planned assault to gain control of the weapons of mass destruction that had lain on the bottom of the Baltic Sea since WWII.

On the horizon, a harmless-looking fishing trawler sailing under a Lithuanian flag appeared. It was an outdated, rusty, Russian side-trawler that was commonly used in the Baltic Sea for bottom fishing. Many of these fishing vessels were illegally trolling for cod that had been under international controls for many years due to overfishing. The trawler's conical nets would normally drag the bottom and take in huge amounts of fish, yet this trawler was moving too quickly through the water to have its fishing nets in tow. It did not waver from its course and was on a direct line for the disabled scientific ship.

On deck there were several men wearing black protective suits. They were preparing lines to hook up to the scientific ship. As they came closer, they put on the protective hoods and portable oxygen tanks. The captain of the fishing trawler maneuvered the trawler to draw parallel to the stricken ship. He didn't cut the engines quite at the right time, so the trawler bumped the side of the larger ship, drawing a curse from the men when they were unexpectedly jolted. They regained their footing and quickly tied the lines to the silent ship.

The rusty trawler had been crudely modified for a specialized task. From a distance, it looked like a normal fishing vessel in the Baltic Sea, but there were no nets on board, and the fish storage tanks had been lined with polystyrene foam to absorb any impact to protect a special cargo. The wooden boxes that held the fish were gone, and in their place were bright yellow plastic containers that looked out of place on the rusty trawler. They were lined up on deck next to the wenches that usually controlled the fishing nets but were now being used for cargo hoists.

One of the men made an attempt to throw a rope ladder over the railing of the bigger ship, but his aim was off. He tried several more times before it caught and could be securely tied off. Meanwhile, two other men went to work hooking the yellow containers on a hoist and lifting them to the deck of the scientific ship.

Once the rope ladder was secured, the remaining men dressed in the protective suits scrambled up, causing more shouts as the ladder bounced around wildly. They carefully backed down and tried again, this time ascending one at a time at a slower pace to steady the ladder to safely reach the deck. When they finally managed to arrive on board, they paused for a few moments to look around and noted in satisfaction that everything was serenely quiet.

The men picked up the empty yellow containers and headed directly for the chemical storage facility. Inside the corridor they had to step over two uniformed crewmen who were sprawled face down on the floor. One had his hands over his head, like he was trying to protect himself from an unseen killer. The men proceeded on and were able to enter the door to the storage facility control room without any setbacks.

Inside the control room, the body of a scientist in a white lab coat was slumped over the control panel that operated the robotic arm used to move the toxic weapons. He had been in the process of moving the canisters of nerve gas into the hull of the ship for storage when the gas overcame him. The men in protective suits pushed the lifeless body to the floor. It landed face up and they saw the frozen expression of agony, a frightening reminder of what would happen if they did not carefully handle the nerve gas.

The meticulous work of the scientists on board the *Valkyrie* had made it possible for the intruders to handle the chemical weapons that would otherwise have been unfeasible to retrieve from the bottom of the sea. The scientists had successfully encased the leaking nerve gas casings in individual canisters for containment to be safely transported for ultimate destruction. The intruders had only to penetrate the security of the containment area to gain access to the weapons, which were now relatively safe to handle.

One of the men pulled out his cell phone from his pocket and scrolled down to the text message that had been sent to him with the security code needed for entry. He punched in the seven-digit code on the keypad outside the door. It slid open with a sucking sound, allowing the intruders to easily enter the weapons chamber.

With their heavily gloved hands, they picked up each individual canister and carefully put it in a bright yellow container for transport. Then they carried the containers up to the deck, where they were hooked on a hoist and delivered one-by-one back onto the fishing trawler's deck. Two more men carefully unfastened the yellow containers from the hoist, carried them to the converted fish tank that would protect the cargo, and then stacked the containers. It was a crude method to transport the deadly nerve gas but the men were more than happy to take the risk.

They repeated the same procedure, getting more efficient with each trip. It took an hour and a half to transfer all forty of the canisters from the *Valkyrie* to the fishing trawler without any interference from outsiders. Everything had gone according to plan. The men shouted approval and congratulated each other as they removed their protective suits. *The first cache of nerve gas that had taken scientists years of planning to retrieve from the bottom of the Baltic Sea was now in the hands of terrorists.*

Chapter Thirty

Sea Bridge

Dosha was motivated to locate the two men as soon as she could. She admired Nicole and wanted to help her obtain the information she needed. Who knows, maybe she could even help with the murder investigation.

Her experience in dealing with so many people helped her realize that most had a weakness that could be exploited. Alcohol and attention from a female was often effective. Or possibly, it was the simple task of appealing to their ego. Whatever it was, she was determined to find out more about the two men in question.

An hour after the departure with the scientific ship, Dosha found Jack Silverton in the bar having a cocktail. She sat next to him and ordered a wine spritzer from the bartender.

"Whew," she said. "These scientists are intense, don't you think?"

"Tell me about it. No one knows that as much as I do," Jack said loudly.

Luckily, he is already tipsy, thought Dosha. "Hopefully, you will be able to accomplish what you came here for."

"I doubt it."

"What do you mean?"

"The CEO has some stupid idea that important things might happen on this cruise. I am supposed to report on everything in detail."

"Really," Dosha interjected to keep him talking as she took a sip of her spritzer.

"Yeah, and there is nothing going on, except these stupid scientists who believe the world is going to end because of a little pollution."

"It seems odd that he would be so interested in a meeting like this," added Dosha.

"He has this crazy obsession with environmentalists. He thinks they will ruin our business and bring America to its knees."

Dosha uncrossed her legs and leaned into him a little. "Wow, I didn't know this group was so powerful."

"That's just it: they're not. I have nothing important to report to my boss, so I'll get fired," said Jack dejectedly. "He is on his way to St. Petersburg to let me go."

"Do you think he would travel all the way to Russia just to fire you?" asked Dosha.

"He said he has an important meeting, but I don't believe him."

"What was the meeting supposed to be about?"

"I don't know. I think he said something about an engineer's castle, whatever that means," said Jack as he took another sip of his whiskey.

Jack didn't have much more to say. He continued to repeat himself, saying he was going to be fired.

Dosha's next target was a little more difficult to track down. She finally found Ian Whitehouse sitting in a chair at the back of the main lounge. He was leaning back in the chair with his arms folded and seemed to be observing the people around him. As she watched, Dosha became aware that Ian's gaze was directed almost exclusively toward Nicole, who was talking to one of the scientists.

Dosha thought, "This is interesting. Is he attracted to Nicole? It would make sense, since she is a smart and a beautiful woman. I'll have to find out."

Then Dosha saw Nicole pick up her things and begin to leave. Ian started to get up as well, presumably to follow her. Dosha quickly interceded. "Ian Whitehouse, you are just the person I was looking for. I need some help for the tour around the environmental practices of Russia."

Ian brushed her off. "No, I am too busy." He started toward the door.

Dosha thought quickly, "That is too bad, because Nicole Hunter had to go to another meeting but she wanted me to check out some things with you."

Ian's head snapped around and suddenly he was interested. "I can make a little time for you."

"We could discuss it over a drink," said Dosha.

"No thanks," said Ian flatly. "What exactly was it that Nicole said to you?" he asked pointedly.

Dosha wondered to herself why Nicole had said this guy was charming. She changed tactics. "Nicole said you were a well-known environmental professor."

"That is true."

Dosha swore she could almost see him puffing up. "She wanted me to find out if you had any interest in working on a project with the Everson Foundation." Dosha knew she was stretching here but she thought that Nicole wouldn't mind.

His eyes gleamed, "Oh yes, yes I would. What does she have in mind?"

Nicole noticed that Dosha had entered the lounge and purposely sat behind Ian Whitehouse. The man had started to annoy her. He turned up everywhere and appeared to be watching every move that she made. She excused herself so that Dosha could move in and work her magic. She had to admire her tenacity. It had been a good idea to give her the assignment because Ian Whitehouse was giving Nicole an increasingly creepy feeling.

Chapter Thirty-One

Dead in the Water

That evening, the *Valkyrie* crew did not respond to the standard communication protocol. All subsequent attempts to contact the ship failed. Emergency procedures were automatically activated and international satellites over the Baltic Sea were positioned above the ship to provide a detailed feed of live visual images. The satellite surveillance showed the ship still anchored to its retrieval location, but zooming in on the satellite feed revealed crew members sprawled on the deck. Something catastrophic had happened on board the *Valkyrie*.

Oliver was on a private jet on the way to Saudi Arabia to personally investigate possible connections to the Abraj Atta Towers. Two hours into the flight, the director of the Global Security Alliance sent an urgent message to Oliver to inform him of the *Valkyrie* crisis. Oliver immediately recognized the ship as the one the *Sea Bridge* had rendezvoused with that same day.

He was informed that a strike team had been dispatched to secure the stricken *Valkyrie* and would be arriving within the hour. The team included several specialized crime scene investigators to determine the nature of the disaster. Oliver immediately ordered his private jet to change course back to St. Petersburg.

He put in a call to Marcos. "Have you heard that something catastrophic has happened to the *Valkyrie*?"

"Yes, I was just informed by Interpol. We left the rendezvous point a few hours ago and everything was fine."

"Do you think they had an accident with the nerve gas?" asked Oliver.

"I suppose that is possible, but the scientists were obsessive about safety," commented Marcos.

"It seems to be a strange coincidence that the accident occurred after the two ships met."

"Exactly the same thing that I was thinking, but what is the connection?"

"I don't know, but we'll have to find out. Does Nicole know about the accident?" Oliver questioned.

"I don't think so. Do you want me to tell her?"

"No, I'll give her a call." Oliver got off the phone and chided himself for leaving the *Sea Bridge*. Every development in the case seemed to lead back to Nicole and that little group attempting to save the world. He started to question himself. So why had he left to pursue leads in Saudi Arabia? Was his judgment being clouded by the personal situation with Nicole?

After a lot of thought, Oliver convinced himself that Sydney would be the best one to tell Nicole about the *Valkyrie* incident. After all, he had only made things more complicated, and besides, Sydney was her confidant.

"Sydney, this is Oliver. I have some really bad news and I thought that you might be the right one to tell Nicole." He proceeded to apprise her of the situation.

"Oh no, what an appalling tragedy! This will be hard on Nicole because Max Lindberg was important to her."

Oliver made one more call to Jake Lanser because he needed Jake to help him think through the different possibilities with the new turn of events.

Recognizing Oliver's cell phone number, Jake answered right away. "Hi, Oliver. This assignment just keeps getting more peculiar."

Oliver lamented, "The death toll is mounting and there are too many open questions."

"Well, I can help you with a few things. We have identified three people with criminal histories who wore the silver parka at the Ice Bar. One of them was a thirty-five-year-old man from the States who has a couple of DUI charges on his record. Another was a Danish woman who had been convicted of shoplifting. But the most interesting one was a professional student who appears to have gone to several universities. The DNA results are in the Interpol database because he was arrested during a violent demonstration in Paris. He suffered a head injury and was taken unconscious to a hospital. The following day, he simply disappeared from the hospital bed."

"That's it? That is the only thing he did? It sounds like he was an impassioned student who was caught up in a cause," observed Oliver.

"Exactly. He sounds like a guy who could be recruited by a militant group."

"So we could be dealing with an extremist who slips into an Ice Bar and kills two environmental scientists?"

"Yeah, I know. It sounds a little odd," admitted Jake.

Sydney sent Nicole a text message that said, "urgent call me." Nicole excused herself from the meeting and took her phone off of silent mode.

"Hi, Sydney. What's up?"

"There has been a horrible tragedy on the *Valkyrie*."

Nicole was devastated. It seemed that everyone she touched was being murdered or grievously injured. The world was a horrible place!

Sydney went on to explain the few details that she knew but Nicole could barely listen. She finished, and there was a long silence. Finally, she asked, "Nicole, are you there?"

Nicole struggled to speak. "Max and the rest of the team were the best people." Her voice was choked with emotion.

"It's simply tragic," sympathized Sydney.

There was another long pause before Nicole finally managed to say, "How can we tell our guests about this? It's just too horrible."

Sydney responded, "We'll take it one step at a time."

Nicole felt that she had to talk to Chen right away. He was the only one who understood what was at risk, and the sacrifice that had already been made. She found out that he was resting in his room, so she took the stairs to the level below. As she turned the corner to enter the main corridor, she had the sense that she was being followed. Footsteps had been behind her on the stairs, and she now heard them a ways back in the corridor.

She backed into the nearest stateroom alcove to avoid being seen. It was quiet. Was she being paranoid again? She waited for quite some time and then heard the footsteps resume. She peeked around the alcove wall and saw Ian Whitehouse looking around tentatively. Nicole stepped out. "Are you following me?"

He startled and then recovered, saying, "Of course not. That is preposterous."

"It seems like I've seen a lot of you lately."

"Oh really, I hadn't noticed. It is a coincidence, isn't it?" he said lightly but his eyes avoided Nicole as she looked at him.

"I am going to visit Chen. Where are you going?" Nicole inquired.

"I was taking a walk, on the way to my cabin. See you later," he said and kept on walking down the corridor.

She continued on to Chen's cabin and lightly tapped on the door. His personal nurse opened it and when she saw who it was she said, "Hi, Nicole. Chen would love to talk with you. I have some things to do in my own room, so I'll come back later."

Nicole was genuinely happy to see him, "Hi Chen! This is the first time I have seen you away from that brilliant group of scientists you're working with."

"Yes, it is so exciting because we are making a lot of progress, but I am on doctor's orders to rest. I must say that I am tired."

"I have to tell you something. It is really bad news, and from my standpoint you are the only one who knows what is at stake. I need your help to figure out if the risk is worth it anymore!" Nicole proceeded to tell him what little she knew about the tragedy on the *Valkyrie.*

Chen reached out his hand to take Nicole's. "Oh my God!" he exclaimed. "What is the world coming to?"

"My thoughts exactly," she miserably said.

They sat together in silence, both with downcast eyes.

After a time, Chen sat up straight and began to urgently speak, "This is even more reason why we can't give up. You must promise me that you won't give up."

"But who else will be hurt or murdered?"

Chen circled his arms wide. "The bigger question is how many more millions will die in the long run if we don't proceed with the work."

Nicole inhaled deeply and then slowly exhaled. "I guess I must have known what you would say. That is why I needed to see you. Thanks, Chen. You are a brave person." She bent forward and gave him a kiss on the cheek.

Chen modestly said, "I appreciate you saying that, but I am really not brave at all. It just needs to be done."

Outside the door, Ian Whitehouse was listening. He had watched unobtrusively from the end of the corridor and returned to Chen's cabin after Nicole went in. It was worth the risk because it was vitally important to know if Nicole was going to pursue her support of the alternative fuel projects, or be smart and give it up. He had a feeling that she would confide in Chen.

It was easy to hear the conversation between the two of them through the thin cabin walls. But he heard someone coming down the hall so he pretended to insert a key in the lock of the cabin door across the way, and then quickly returned to the door to listen after they went by.

The exchange between Nicole and Chen made it clear that she was *not* going to back down. When the conversation appeared to be winding down, Ian decided to not to take any more chances and strode off toward his cabin.

The recovery team, including a medical examiner, biohazard experts, and crime scene investigators, hovered in a military helicopter above the *Valkyrie*. It was obvious from the first sighting that whatever happened on the ship had killed the people without warning. They had no time to escape and died while performing their normal duties.

The team donned their protective suits and then landed on the helipad. They carefully monitored the deck, looking for any indications of what might have caused the deaths, but nothing was readily apparent.

Next they proceeded to the bridge. They found the ship's captain lying awkwardly on the floor, apparently having fallen out of the high-backed, leather captain's chair. Not far from him was the first officer, who had been going over a checklist in preparation for the next day's planned departure.

The medical examiner looked at each body to determine the cause of death. Both the officers on the bridge, and the crewmen on the deck, exhibited the same symptoms: contraction of the pupils, loss of control of bodily functions, and likely death by asphyxiation.

The biohazard experts were well aware that these were symptoms likely caused by nerve gas poisoning. Blood samples were drawn from the fallen bodies to be sent to the lab for the final analysis, but in the expert's opinion, the most likely agent was Tabun, or one of the subsequent G-series synthesized by the German scientists during WWII.

These were chemical weapons that had been produced by the I.G. Farben conglomerate, the same company that manufactured Zyklon B, the gas used in Nazi concentration camps. The company that developed the chemical weapons for the most horrendous crimes against humanity now carried their inhumane legacy forward to the modern era.

Having hypothesized the cause of death, the investigators turned their attention to the method of dispersion. The logical cause would be leakage coming from the cargo bay where the metal containers were kept. They slowly descended, stopping to take readings every few meters, but they still found no significant amounts of the gas. They finally arrived at the secure storage facility and opened the electronic door.

Peering inside, they were shocked to see that the hazardous storage area was completely empty! They looked around in confusion. Could the canisters have been moved to another area? But there was no other space large enough to hold them.

A rescue member exclaimed, "What the hell!?"

They were momentarily bewildered and were trying to comprehend the enormity of what had been done.

Then the reality of the situation set in: the nerve gas had been stolen! The team leader stopped in his tracks and immediately contacted the Security Alliance to report the shocking theft. After delivering the sobering news, they proceeded to work on the mystery of how the people aboard the Valkryie had come in contact with the gas. Due to the speed of delivery, they knew there were only two options: ingesting the poison through the water system, or breathing it in through the air vents. Because it had killed the entire crew almost at once, it was reasonable to search the ventilation system first.

It didn't take long for the team to find the device that Zafir had planted in the vent next to the central air filtration system. The biohazard specialists painstakingly removed the unit and logged in all the evidence. It was now official. The innocent scientists and crew on the *Valkyrie* had been ruthlessly gassed to death.

But the fact that the canisters had been stolen was possibly the most devastating news of all. In the wrong hands, the number of deaths on the *Valkyrie* would seem minor compared to the potential human devastation that was possible.

While sitting in a meeting at the Security Alliance headquarters, Jake Tanser dialed up Oliver on the private jet. "Oliver, we have just been informed of some new developments. You are being routed to a high-security airfield outside of St. Petersburg."

Oliver demanded, "Give me the details."

"Satellite images show that a fishing trawler visited the *Valkyrie* a couple hours after the *Sea Bridge* departed."

"A fishing trawler?"

"It flew a Lithuanian flag and had about six men outfitted with protective suits. They brought plastic containers on board and later transferred them back to the fishing trawler. After transfer was completed, they headed on a route toward St. Petersburg. We are certain these men are now in possession of the chemical weapons that the *Valkyrie* was collecting from the bottom of the sea!"

Oliver moaned, "That's not good, not good at all."

"When you arrive, a helicopter will be waiting for you. We believe that the fishing trawler is headed to the Russian navy base, Kronstadt. Your pilot should be receiving the details of the new flight plan as we speak."

Chapter Thirty-Two

Russia - Kronstadt Naval Base

Oliver peered out the window of the helicopter as they approached the Kotlin Island in the Gulf of Finland. The island was shaped like an elongated triangle, with half of the island occupied by the famous Russian Baltic fleet, and the other half consisted of the town, the School of Marine Engineering, and ship repair facilities. This sea fortress had guarded the approach to St. Petersburg for over three hundred years and was once considered to be one of the most fortified ports in the world.

The island was also the home of Fort Alexander, an imposing fortification on the island, more commonly known as the Plague Fort. When it lost its military value, the isolated fortress became a plague laboratory where a serum was produced from horses contaminated by the disease. Ultimately, the Plague Fort was closed after a tragic outbreak took human lives, including the director of the facility.

Today the island of Kotlin is connected to the mainland by bridges and narrow strips of land and is only twenty-five miles from St. Petersburg, making the island easily accessible by car or truck.

As the helicopter came closer to the landing location, Oliver could see tumbled-down fortresses on small islands that once protected the island from invaders, but now were simply reminders of Russia's turbulent history. On one side of the island, bordering the Gulf of Finland, there were haunting views of rusty ships listing at odd angles, and broken-down submarines from eras gone by. The mysterious island was filled with old naval canals, abandoned storehouses, and docks dating back to the seventeenth century. Most of these old structures were in a state of disrepair and complete dereliction, which added to the eerie atmosphere.

The satellite surveillance over Kronstradt indicated that the Russian fishing trawler entered one of the old canals and then vanished. These coordinates were given to the pilot so the onboard GPS system could guide the helicopter to the exact location where the trawler disappeared from the satellite sweep. It was likely the fishing trawler was docked in one of the abandoned storehouses, possibly to unload and transfer the hazardous cargo.

When they touched down, Oliver and three other agents leaped out of the military helicopter with their automatic weapons drawn. They were only hours behind the fishing trawler, so they were anticipating a confrontation. Making their way along the edge of the old canal, they moved slowly toward a rundown, primitive stone building that connected to the waterway.

As they came closer, Oliver could see that the canal disappeared under a large, rusty metal door that closed off the access to the waterway into the old structure. The passage would have been wide enough for the fishing trawler to pass through and was accessible only by boat. They changed directions and walked along the outside perimeter of the building, looking for an alternative entry.

They came to wooden door on the north wall that was old and rotted. Oliver motioned for two of the agents to put their weight against the door. They shoved the door forcefully, and the decayed wood gave way. Oliver lunged through the doorway into the dark interior and rolled to his right with his gun poised.

In the dark, he could only see a glimmer of light coming from the other end of the warehouse, probably a reflection off of the water. He walked toward the light source, taking care to make sure he had footing on solid ground so he would not plunge into the dark water of the canal. He could hear the soft footsteps of one of the agents behind him and the lapping of the water in front of him.

A few more steps and his eyes began to adjust to the darkness so he could make out some features of the dim interior. He was in a wide passageway with high ceilings and worn tracks on the stones beneath his feet that led directly to the edge of the indoor canal. It was likely that this entrance had been used to haul cargo directly onto the ships that were docked inside the storage warehouse.

He carefully proceeded on the stone surface, which became more slippery as he came closer to the water's edge. In the darkness, he could just make out the narrow ledge that ran along the sides of the canal, covering the entire length of the old, stone structure. He carefully began to traverse the slippery ledge, making sure that he had good footing with each step.

Progressing a little ways down the ledge, he could see that the canal branched off to the right. Another large metal door blocked the entrance to the concealed area. He searched for more handholds on the slippery wall as he slowly moved toward the intersection of the waterways. He finally arrived at the large door that closed off the hidden section of the canal. He held onto a rusty, metal bracket and bent down low over the water, looking under the old metalwork. In this position, he could see the bottom portion of a fishing boat.

He listened closely but did not detect any movement or hear any voices on the other side of the gate. He motioned to the others to retreat and go around the building to look for another passageway into the cordoned-off docking area while he waited on the narrow ledge, listening for any activity.

The agents finally confirmed in his ear piece that they had found another entrance and were going in. Oliver took out his gun and shot open the lock on the gate. He shoved the rusty metal door toward the water to reveal the Russian fishing trawler that they had been pursuing. Then he swung around the column and onto the landing of the inner chamber where the ship was docked.

Still no one. He was now sure that they had been too late. The canisters containing the chemical weapons had been transferred to another vessel or vehicle before they arrived.

"It looks like no one is here," said the first agent who came in from an arched entry on the other side.

"Yes, we missed them. It looks like we will have to go back to the satellite surveillance video to see what transpired after the trawler entered the waterway inside the storage building," commented Oliver as he took out his cell phone to call Jake.

Suddenly, Oliver heard a shout. He shoved the phone in his pocket and raced through the arched entry to the outside. One of the agents had flushed out a man who had been hiding along the perimeter of the storage building. They could see the man running at full speed up the incline.

From a distance, Oliver could see that the middle-aged man was angling toward an old car that was parked on the side of a narrow gravel road leading to the old storage buildings. If he guessed right on the intended destination, he could take a more direct route to the dilapidated car and get there first.

Oliver drew his weapon and stayed low to avoid being seen while moving steadily toward the old beater car. Luckily, the agent was in pursuit from behind so the running man did not see Oliver as he moved to the car. When he reached it, he crouched down behind the hood and watched the man running toward him. He was grimacing and gasping for breath. His progress had slowed substantially and he was stumbling toward the car.

"Stop right there!" Oliver raised himself up just enough for the man to see his gun. The man panicked and quickly raised his hands into the air, yelling, "Don't shoot, don't shoot," in Russian. He had long, sandy gray hair and leathered skin. He was wearing a baggy shirt with a knit cap on his head and looked like a local fisherman. He continued to speak rapidly in Russian, saying something about how he didn't know anything and didn't want trouble.

Oliver frisked the man to make sure he did not have a weapon. Then he asked, "Do you speak English?"

"Little bit."

"Why are you running?"

"I think you kill me. You jump out of helicopter with guns."

"What do you know about the fishing trawler?"

The man put his hands on his hips while trying to catch his breath. "My family owns, but fishing not so good. Authorities fine us for catching cod, so don't catch enough fish to live. Once scoop cod out of sea, but now, can't live as fisherman. We do cargo trips with boat to feed families."

Oliver asked, "Who was the last person to hire the boat?"

The man looked dejected. "My brother use computer to find jobs. We move cargo between Baltic countries. If lucky, couple trips per week."

The man removed his cap and scratched his head. "Someone want boat for whole week. Pay thirty thousand rubles! Need money, so brother agrees to pick up in Klaipeda. He tell me take wife on holiday."

"Were you looking for your brother when we arrived?" asked Oliver.

"Da. Fishing boat there, but no brother. Hear helicopter and run outside. See men jump out with guns. There is trouble … so hide." He pointed to the nearby agent. "This man see me. I run."

"Why was the boat docked in this old warehouse? Isn't this an unusual place to moor a fishing boat?"

"Brother told to end trip in Kronstadt. He question, but top Russian official call for permission. Official say do not ask questions; follow instructions only."

"A high-ranking Russian official? Do you know his name?"

The fisherman shook his head. "Nyet, but brother knows."

"Your fishing trawler was used to kill a group of people on a scientific ship. No one survived." Oliver watched the man's face closely to gauge his reaction.

The man went pale and then he began to plead, "I know nothing. You believe me. Pozhaluista! Help me find brother! Pozhaluista!

"Calm yourself. Tell me about the people who rented the trawler. How was it set up?"

The fisherman pulled out a worn handkerchief and wiped the perspiration streaming off his forehead. "I tell him computer would cause trouble. You look people in eye when do business. But he is smart. Made them pay in full before trip."

"When did you last hear from your brother?" inquired Oliver.

"He call from Klaipeda, Lithuania. He say group is strange foreigners and boat come back today."

He paused to gain his composure and then went on, "My brother is smart one. But now I worry, because trawler is here, but brother is not."

Oliver lowered his gun and asked, "How did they pay for the trip?"

"Send to bank. I use money for holiday," he sadly said.

"We will need your brother's computer to trace the communications."

"If help find brother, you take it."

Oliver pulled out his cell phone and contacted the Security Alliance. He informed them of the current situation and that all operatives on the case should be notified to look for a missing Russian captain. He turned to the exhausted fisherman and asked for a description of his brother and repeated it over the phone. Then he motioned for one of the agents to come forward and said to him, "Please accompany this man to his brother's place to get his computer."

When Oliver arrived back at the storage building, the forensic specialist on the team was gathering evidence on the trawler. He had processed the pilot house and was now working his way to the back of the deck. Every surface was being checked for fingerprints, bodily fluids, or any unusual fragments.

The forensic specialist was unlatching all the doors to the storage compartments when he got a whiff of a familiar smell. He opened a lower door and turned on his penlight to investigate. Stuffed in the dark, cramped space was a dead body with a flexible steel cable wedged into the creases of his neck.

He called out, "Over here! We have a victim!"

Oliver grabbed a pair of gloves from the investigator's bag and carefully stepped around the marked-off area. He peered into the dark, cramped space and saw the lifeless eyes of a man. He had a weather-worn face and was wearing a seaman's cap.

Oliver sighed. "He looks like a local. I bet he is the missing brother, the captain of the trawler. They probably intended to get rid of him all along. "

The specialist said, "He has not been here too long, maybe an hour or so."

"Yeah, just long enough for the intruders to make their escape," Oliver lamented. "One step too late."

Once again Oliver berated himself for not staying on the cruise ship. He was sure that there was some connection between the scheduled stop by the *Sea Bridge* and the subsequent incident on the *Valkyrie.*

The agent who had been canvassing the surrounding area for evidence came into the old storage building to find Oliver. "We have found fresh tracks in the dirt leading to the storage building."

Oliver followed him outside to examine the tread marks. They were parallel wheel tracks that could be clearly seen in areas where the dirt was more loosely packed. They led directly from the old storage building to the service road about two hundred meters up the incline.

"It looks like the tracks were made by one of those compact loaders that attaches to the truck for deliveries. The loader went back and forth several times from that storage door up to the gravel parking area above," explained the agent.

"Which means a truck was waiting for them and they are now transporting the nerve gas on land."

"These people are fearless. Nerve gas containers transported on Russian roads? Now that is scary!" exclaimed the agent.

Chapter Thirty-Three

Fuel for Terrorism

Forty canisters of a deadly nerve gas were on a truck headed to St. Petersburg. The crisis had continued to escalate, and now more innocent lives were at stake. Oliver made a direct call to the Global Security Alliance director to ask for immediate resources to stop the transport of the nerve gas. He also made the case to contact the Russian military to aid in the protection of their own citizens.

As he paced back and forth, Oliver was speaking fast and abruptly. He knew that every second counted. "The truck is on the only road out of Kronstadt. It will travel over a series of dams located on small islands that connect to the mainland."

His voice became louder. "If those canisters arrive at their destination, the consequences will be catastrophic. The gas could be released in one massive killing in a populated area, or be broken down and distributed to terrorist organizations around the world. Either way, the outcome will be devastating."

Oliver was close to barking orders to the director. "I need priority access to global security surveillance, immediately!"

The director understood the urgency. "I will give you the highest priority with the intelligence community. We'll downgrade all other high-level projects."

Oliver ran his hand through his hair as he continued to pace back and forth. "You need to use all your contacts in Russia to have them help us find the truck that left the old dockyard with the chemical weapons."

"Done."

"*And* the Russians must also set up road blocks located on the outskirts of St. Petersburg to deny the terrorists access to an area with a dense population."

"I will contact them as soon as I hang up with you," assured the director.

"I also need scientists to give us an indication of what would happen if the nerve gas was released. If confronted by opposition, the terrorists will destroy the canisters, so I need to know the lethal impact on the population."

The director cleared his throat and asked, "But wouldn't the scientists on the *Sea Bridge* have the best knowledge of the potential effects of the gas?"

"You're right. I'll contact them right away." Oliver immediately hung up and called Nicole.

Nicole was in the middle of a very productive session on carbon fusion when her phone vibrated. She looked to see who was calling. It was Oliver, so without delay she walked out of the room to take the call.

"Hi, Oliver. Where are you?"

"Nicole, I need your help right now!"

She could hear the urgency in his voice. "What is it?"

"Terrorists have stolen the nerve gas off the *Valkyrie*."

Nicole sat on the edge of her chair. "Terrorists? How can that be?"

Oliver succinctly explained the situation and communicated what he needed from the scientists. He finished by saying, "Nicole we need this information to finalize our strike plans. Please hurry!"

Nicole returned to the group and announced in a loud voice, "Excuse me, I need your attention. We have a major crisis for which we need to provide good scientific information right away." Nicole proceeded to convey the message that Oliver had just given her.

There was a horrified gasp from the group. Nicole went on, "Oliver needs to know what will happen if the gas is released from the containers. How far can it travel and how many people could be killed?"

"It is a viscous liquid that is not extremely volatile," the scientist closest to Nicole said. "It is usually disseminated in vapor concentrations, and the higher the concentration, the more deadly it is."

Another scientist was already on his computer, looking up the latest research. "There has been no research on the civilian population for obvious reasons, but there have been a couple of incidences where terrorists released the gas. In Japan, nerve gas was released in five coordinated attacks on the subway. Thirteen people were killed and thousands required emergency care."

The discussion became more intense, and everyone was talking at once. Finally, Nicole said, "Okay, we are out of time. What is the scenario that we can give Oliver?"

One of the scientists stood up. "The bottom line is that the more actively disseminated the gas and the higher the population density, the more deaths there will be. A canister that is breached would kill the people in the immediate area, but would not reach a broader population unless there was a high wind. Other than that, there is no formula to predict the outcome; there are just too many variables."

Nicole put the call in to Oliver. He answered immediately. She wasted no time in filling him in on the scenario provided by the scientists.

"Thanks, Nicole. That is what I needed to know," said Oliver.

"Oliver, you are not planning to be in the immediate area, are you?"

He laughed. "Thanks for the concern. I have to go."

The call went dead before Nicole could say anything else. She had wanted to tell him that he was important to her, and to be safe, but she didn't have the chance.

The Global Security Alliance director contacted the Russian military to first locate, and then track, the progress of the truck. The security at Kronstadt naval base routinely monitored the road in and out of the base with surveillance cameras. With the time frame pinpointed, they quickly identified an old military truck being driven by two young men of Middle Eastern descent. They also observed a white van closely trailing the truck that presumably contained additional members of the group.

Oliver was in a helicopter on his way to intercept the truck carrying the nerve gas when the information about its location was relayed to him. He was notified that the truck was getting dangerously close to the outskirts of St. Petersburg. The only good news was that the late afternoon traffic was beginning to dramatically slow vehicles entering the city. In addition, the Russian military was in the process of setting up the emergency roadblock to further snarl the already congested roads.

Nicole's call had confirmed that the operation underway had the best chance to limit civilian fatalities. Two expert marksmen from the Russian military were meeting Oliver's team southeast of Kronstadt, on the edge of the expansive grounds of the Peterhof Castle. This location was prior to the roadblock and would accommodate the helicopters that could land on the castle's expansive lawn. The plan was simple: use the element of surprise and take out the terrorists before they could reach the densely populated city. It was risky, but there was no other option.

Chapter Thirty-Four

Breakthrough

Nicole was in a meeting that had just taken a short break when she saw Dosha outside the door, trying to get her attention. "Nicole, I'm sorry to interrupt, but do you have the time to discuss the assignment you gave me?"

Nicole figured that Dosha must have come up with something important. "Yes, let's go to the sun deck where no one will hear us."

When they arrived on the top deck, they found a small table away from everyone else.

Dosha asked, "What's up? You look anxious."

Nicole looked at Dosha and realized she was becoming her confidant, someone she could trust. She sighed, "You are very perceptive. Oliver is in pursuit of the people who stole canisters of nerve gas from the *Valkyrie*."

"Stolen? I didn't know."

"It is a very dangerous situation!" Nicole stopped short, suddenly realizing that she did not want to reveal to Dosha that her hometown of St. Petersburg was under possible attack.

"I think Oliver is the best person to handle it!" Dosha said confidently.

"Yes, you are right. Anyway, there is nothing we can do about it from here. So tell me about our two interesting guests."

Dosha was animated when she spoke. "Jack Silverton is an insecure man who is being controlled by his boss. If you ask me, he is being used as an *informant* for what is going on during the symposium. He is required to make reports every day, even on the smallest details discussed by the scientists."

"That is interesting."

"The problem is he often doesn't understand what is going on so he is pretty inadequate at what his boss wants him to do. I wouldn't be surprised if he *is* fired because he *is* very incompetent."

"It sounds like we need to find out more about his boss's agenda. It is interesting that he wants daily reports. What about Ian Whitehouse?"

Dosha went on excitedly, "Now he is an even *more* interesting character. He has an edge to him that is quite annoying."

"Yes, I have discovered that myself."

"First of all, he seems to have an obsession with you. He watches and follows you everywhere you go," Dosha said with emphasis.

"I have noticed, but I wonder why?" Having verification from Dosha made her realize she wasn't imaging it.

"At first, I thought he was attracted to you, but after talking to him, I think he is more concerned about what is going on with the Everson Foundation. I hope you don't mind, but I enticed him to open up by saying that the Everson Foundation was interested in him and his expertise. He *jumped* at that and wanted to know more. I sort of told him that I was asked by you to do an initial screening, just to get him to talk. I hope that is okay?"

"It was a good idea. It confirms to me that he has an ulterior motive for being here."

"He was clearly more intrigued by the financial inner workings of the Everson Foundation than anything to do with improving climate conditions."

Nicole rolled her eyes. "He sounds like a greedy opportunist."

"He was also disparaging when it came to his teaching position. I asked how his curriculum could benefit from support from the foundation. He just laughed! He said the majority of his students were ideological neophytes and didn't know anything. He was *very* cynical and quite caustic."

"Did he tell you anything about the billionaire whose position he took on the cruise?"

"When I asked why he was on the cruise, he said that it was an opportunity he couldn't pass up. His mentor had made it *worth his while*. I asked him what he meant by that. All he said was that professors don't make that much. He wouldn't elaborate any more than that."

Nicole thought for a second. "I'll talk to Marcos about our concerns regarding Ian. I probably should have done it earlier. I also need to find out why the wealthy guest that was originally invited did not come, and why Ian took his place."

Two scientists approached them, waving and smiling. One said, "Nicole! We've been looking all over the ship for you. The group is ready to report back on our findings and we need you there."

The members of this particular team had been drawn together from the beginning of the trip. The group was comprised of a nuclear chemist, a physicist, and even an astronomer. Some of the scientists were from major universities, while others were simply rogue geniuses. Chen looked drawn, but he was tenaciously hanging in there as the team leader. They had been pushing themselves hard to deliver on their commitment to find a breakthrough. Now, they were ready to deliver the outcome.

Chen started out, "I have been privileged to work with the best minds in the world, and I am ecstatic about the results. I will turn this presentation over to them and each one will explain the practical theory behind the solution in their field of expertise."

Nicole listened intently to each of the presenters. Many of them were not polished speakers, but none of them could contain their enthusiasm in the presentations. From what she could gather, the "key to the kingdom" was a new kind of nuclear fusion reactor that was significantly different than the laser chamber.

The proposed solution was based off of the observations of the magnetic fields observed around Jupiter and how the sun and stars are powered. A prototype of this fusion machine was already in the testing phase and had recorded good results. The group was proposing a clear path to converting the research to an affordable result that could be put in operation in the next few years.

As each speaker got up and presented their section of the proposal, Nicole became increasingly more excited. It was evident that the group was onto something big. It was an opportunity to redefine how energy is captured and consumed in the global economy.

After the presentations were done, Nicole stood and clapped. Soon, everyone in the room was on their feet, hooting and hollering. She was convinced that with the brain power assembled in the room, combined with a significant grant from the Everson Foundation, there could be a non-fossil-fuel future where everyone on the planet could have access to cheap and clean electricity!

But she had to wonder, was the success they had achieved going to be overshadowed by the ruthless murders that had occurred? She could not help but think about Oliver heading toward a dangerous encounter with the truck transporting the nerve gas.

Chapter Thirty-Five

The Chase

There was not a second to waste. The Russian sharpshooters arrived at the castle grounds moments before Oliver's helicopter landed. As instructed, the two military men sprinted to the helicopter even before the skids touched down. Oliver yelled in Russian while waving them on, "*Hurry!* We need to take off *now*."

While the rotor blades still turned, the men flung themselves and their equipment into the cabin. Then Oliver gave the pilot the thumbs up to take off.

Oliver sat next to the pilot and handed the men headsets so they were in direct communication. He told them, "I know you have been briefed on the target. We will try to take them out quickly so we don't have civilian casualties. They should be in visual range within the next two minutes. Any questions?"

One of the men declared, "No, but we need to be on the driver's side of the GAZ-66 transport vehicle to shoot."

Oliver looked at the pilot, who nodded that he understood. "That is confirmed."

Orders had been given that under no circumstances could the nerve gas reach its intended destination in St. Petersburg. Since the heist had been so well orchestrated, the analysts at the Global Alliance predicted the gas would first go to a warehouse and then be broken down into smaller quantities. Likely, it would then be distributed to terrorist groups around the world, to execute crimes against humanity.

Oliver's senses were on overdrive because he knew that if he failed in cleanly eliminating the terrorists, many innocent people would die. He had been briefed that if the marksmen were not successful, an armed drone would be called in to eliminate the truck and all of its contents.

Any citizen in the vicinity would be killed, and injuries would occur in the general area, but the death count would be contained.

Oliver had learned long ago that in life-or-death situations, he must completely focus on executing the best case scenario. He had been trained to be calm and in control, but he had learned from experience that there was more to it than that. He had to *will* it to happen. To think anything less was not acceptable.

He had an open line to the Global Security Alliance analysts who were monitoring the progress of the truck and white van. Oliver said into his headset, "We're in position."

A voice at the other end of the line said, "They are now within the specified area. You have a *go* to intercept. Do you have a visual?"

Oliver looked down at the stream of Russian traffic, which included many types of trucks and vans. He eyes searched desperately, seeking the specific combination of the Russian military truck and white van that had been described to him.

There were two possibilities within the prescribed area. He looked through the high-powered binoculars and strained to see the details of each one. Then one of the white vans veered off into another lane, looking for an opening in the traffic, and broke contact with the truck in front of him. It had to be the other van and truck combination, about seventy-five meters back.

"I've got it," he said into the microphone. "It looks like a heavy-duty target, heavily reinforced."

"Yes, we know. That is why the Russian military will be useful. They know what it takes to penetrate their own vehicle. They were properly briefed on the cargo so they could plan a strategic hit."

Oliver looked back to see the two Russian sharpshooters focusing in on the military truck. Oliver told the pilot, "We'll eliminate the trailing van first so they don't attack when we go for the truck. It should take the truck driver a few seconds to figure out what is going on behind him.

Let's go!" Oliver left the copilot seat and moved to the back.

The helicopter immediately dropped from an observation altitude to a combat altitude. Oliver could see the surprise on the faces of the two men in the front seat of the van.

Oliver commanded, "Now!" They opened fire on the driver and the person in the passenger seat. The van's windshield shattered and blood splattered over the white hood of the van.

Instantly the helicopter pulled up, and just as fast dove down, now on the driver's side of the military truck. The Russian sharpshooters pointed what looked like a modified grenade launcher at the door of the truck. Oliver hoped their plan to shoot laterally across to the passenger seat without penetrating the cargo area was going to work, or they would all be dead in a few minutes. This was the time that Oliver hated the most, when the success of the mission depended on someone besides himself.

The blast was decisive and well-targeted. The cab had been virtually blown away, but the cargo area was still intact.

Oliver yelled, "Move to the van!"

The talented pilot deftly complied. They were back at the incapacitated van in an instant. Several of the terrorists were piling out of the back with automatic weapons in hand. They ran toward the bombed-out military truck in front of them, shouting and screaming. They intended to salvage the aborted mission by releasing the nerve gas and killing as many people as possible.

Oliver was able to take out one of the terrorists running to the truck, but another one had already reached it. The man pressed himself flat against the rear door of the truck, so it was impossible to hit him from the helicopter without risking the shots penetrating the door and potentially hitting the canisters.

Oliver ordered the pilot, "Put us on the ground!"

The first terrorist to reach the truck was unlocking the latch and opening the tailgate. He was within seconds of being able to destroy the canisters and release the nerve gas!

"Cover me, but no shots near the truck!" he shouted to the others.

Oliver jumped out of the helicopter before it reached the ground. He ran full speed, hoping that the sharpshooters would take care of the third man running to the back of the truck. He heard a pop and then saw the man fall. He was grateful that the Russians were exceptionally skilled.

Oliver reached the truck, lunging forward to grab the man's ankle before he could level his automatic weapon at the canisters. He twisted his leg, causing the man to cry out in pain. But the last terrorist still alive was operating on adrenaline, with an uncommon amount of strength. He was on a suicide mission and would do anything to detonate the nerve gas.

Oliver wrestled with the man to gain control of the automatic weapon. The man was thrashing about wildly. They fell off the back of the truck and rolled on the ground. The terrorists was kicking, biting, and clawing, but he was no match for Oliver, who gave him two quick blows to the head and neck. The terrorist lay unconscious on the street.

After the man was handcuffed, Oliver turned to the two sharpshooters. "Thanks for your help. You guys are good! Could you cordon off the truck until the police arrive? The Global Alliance is working with the Russian government to safely transport the nerve gas to a neutral location. Your Russian military will clean up. I need to go right away!"

Even though his superiors would want him to stay with the nerve gas, Oliver knew that he must get back to the *Sea Bridge*. He felt an almost overpowering urgency to get there immediately. He knew the Russian sharpshooters would do a great job protecting the cargo. With a little luck, he estimated he could be on the *Sea Bridge* in less than thirty minutes.

The wind suddenly picked up as Oliver turned toward the helicopter. The pilot saw Oliver running toward him, so he started the engine in preparation to take off. Oliver jumped inside and yelled, "Let's go!"

The helicopter was buffeted by wind when it lifted off and gained altitude. It was not going to be a smooth ride.

Chapter Thirty-Six

The Storm

The captain was awakened from an early evening nap by a knock on his cabin door. He was still groggy and a little confused.

He responded slowly, "What is it?" He had put long hours in on the ship's bridge the night before, working well into the early morning. They had passed through a relatively shallow passageway in the night. It was one of those few times on the trip when the captain actually needed to be commanding the ship.

An urgent voice on the other end of the line told him, "Sir, we need you on the bridge. A situation has come up."

A situation: that didn't sound good. The captain was instantly alert. "I'll be there shortly."

He hurriedly pulled on his pants and shirt, grabbed his captain's jacket, and headed to the bridge. On the way, he went through a series of thoughts of what the problem could be. He didn't hear any unusual noises, and the engine sounded like it was humming at an efficient speed.

As he climbed the stairs to the bridge, he noticed that there was a rolling action to the ship. He felt himself reaching for the rail to steady his progress.

When he reached the landing of the last flight of stairs, he paused for just an instant to listen. It didn't take long to realize that the strength of the wind echoing through the hollows of the ship was uncommonly strong. He now knew that the ship was experiencing one of those freakish storms that was becoming more frequent and claiming more lives, most often hitting without notice with great ferocity.

He quickened his ascent and opened the first door that went to an outside deck. He was hit with the sting of the sea spray coming over the deck. The calm, serene sea had quickly changed into an angry, deadly force to be reckoned with.

The captain entered and found the bridge alive with activity. He said to the chief officer on duty, "Give me an update!"

The chief officer raised his voice against the storm noise. "About thirty minutes ago, I noticed a slight chop on the water. Since that time, the storm's force has increased dramatically. There have been no forecasts or reports of bad weather in the area, so I am guessing it could blow over as quickly as it started."

The captain ordered, "Make an announcement for everyone to stay in their quarters."

"Yes, sir. We're lucky because most guests are getting ready for dinner, so they are already in their cabins."

At that moment, the phone rang to the bridge and the chief officer picked it up, "Captain, a helicopter is approaching and is notifying us that it will be landing shortly."

The captain yelled, "It can't land in this weather!"

The first officer relayed the information, and then came back and said, "It's Oliver Odin, and he is not asking for permission; he is notifying us."

The captain sighed because he knew that Oliver was not someone who would be dissuaded. He told the first officer, "Get our best rescue personnel up there!"

The crew could hear the beating of the blades on the helicopter before they made visual contact. The dark clouds and heavy rain obscured the view of the helicopter until it was moments away from the deck. When the helicopter finally came into view, the winds were battering it so that it was pitched at an extreme angle.

The situation was grave; the odds of landing in this weather were almost impossible. The small crew was braced for a catastrophic emergency. Everyone held their breath. Oliver looked down at the ship that was being violently pitched up and down in the waves as the helicopter attempted to approach. A landing would be too risky, and he did not want to kill the pilot or anyone else in the process.

Oliver yelled above the howling wind to the pilot, "You get as close as you can. I'll make a jump for it, and you take off. "

The pilot gave one nod and began to try to calibrate the wild pitch of the ship with the helicopter. Oliver watched intently for an opening, but the pilot called back, "No good. I'll try again." He backed off, and the helicopter rocked erratically in the storm.

"Where the hell did this weather come from?" exclaimed Oliver.

The pilot yelled, "I have heard reports of funnel clouds forming out of nowhere, churning up the sea and wreaking havoc with ships."

"Strange," Oliver spoke, mostly to himself.

"Let's try *now*," shouted the pilot.

He expertly used the wind to his advantage and steered the helicopter to the same angle as the ship's deck below and then dropped to within ten feet of the deck. Oliver held on to the frame of the door, waiting just a few seconds more. He hoped the pilot could get a little closer so he wouldn't miss the deck altogether and be pitched over the side.

At the last second, the helicopter dipped strategically, giving him a better chance to stay on the deck. Oliver hit the deck hard and rolled with the momentum. He could feel himself sliding uncontrollably along the slick, wet deck. He knew he was going overboard, cast out into the turbulent sea, but at the last second he was able to grab onto the outer railing. A large wave washed across the deck, submerging him. He could feel his grip slipping but forced himself to hold on. The water began to drain off, but he could no longer feel his fingers.

In a few more seconds, the water receded. In the distance he could see a figure in a survival suit appear through the driving rain, or maybe he was imagining it. He seemed to be fighting his way toward Oliver, leaning at an extreme angle to brace against the wind. Then Oliver could see that the man had a harness on him to keep him from being washed overboard and was holding a rope in his hand. He threw the rope to Oliver just before another wave broke over the deck.

Oliver grasped at the rope and was able to catch it before the full force of the next wave hit him. He held on with all of his strength as the water drained off the deck once more. He moved quickly to put the rope around his waist before the next wave pitched him overboard.

He could feel the rope pulling him toward safety until an even more powerful wave undercut his legs, forcing him down again. Without the taut lifeline, he knew he would have been washed out to sea. He got back up, staggering like a drunken sailor as the ship pitched up and down, but the rope kept reeling him in. Finally, he was close enough for the man in the survival suit to grasp him around waist. Together, they doggedly made their way through the driving rain. In a few more terrifying moments, they made it to safety, quickly closing the water-tight door behind them.

The captain checked the wind speed and saw the gauge climb from fifteen knots to twenty. The ship was rolling on three-meter waves that were building in rapid succession. The captain gave the silent crew alarm for everyone to man their positions, in case they hadn't seen the worst yet.

The emergency communication system came alive with a crackling sound of an excited Russian speaking. He seemed to be in a panic. The captain asked, "Do we have any crew members who speak Russian?"

"I will find out," the communications specialist said and called the hotel manager's room.

The captain looked at the satellite monitoring screen to see where the radio broadcast was coming from. A distress signal was flashing on the screen, which showed the ship's identification number and location. The ship was sending an international signal, showing its position for rescue.

Dosha was lying on her bed, looking at the ceiling, trying to make pictures out of the wood grain to take her mind off the turbulent sea. Her cabin phone rang and she made a lucky grab for it. An urgent voice said, "We need you to come to the bridge *immediately*. We need a translator!"

"Be right there," Dosha said and flew out the door just as the ship took a strong starboard roll. She lost her balance and bumped hard into the wall. Somehow she managed to stay upright and then noticed a man huddled in a nearby doorway with his head in his hands.

As she got closer, she saw that it was the crew member who she had talked to on deck, the one who had made a point of helping her from time to time.

Dosha said, "Are you hurt?"

He did not respond.

She said louder, *"Are you hurt?"*

He peered at her between his hands with unfocused eyes. There was no time to discuss why a crew member was terrified of the storm, but Dosha could see the fear in his eyes.

"Come with me, *now*." But he only slightly looked up.

She yelled once more, *"Come right now!"* and then started walking down the corridor, supporting herself with outstretched arms when the boat pitched her off-balance.

As she moved forward, she could feel the presence of the scared man behind her, following her every movement. She maintained forward progress, bumping and stumbling all the way. When they arrived at the top deck, they could finally see out a viewing window. It was a chilling sight. A huge wave crashed over the ship's bow, flooding the deck. A second later, the view was totally obscured by a flood of water streaming across the glass.

"Come on. We need to keep moving," urged Dosha. They held on tight to the railing while they climbed the last set of stairs to the bridge.

When they came through the bridge door, the captain looked at Dosha. "Are you translating?"

"Yes, that's why I'm here," she responded.

The captain made a motion to the communications officers. "Listen to this recording. What is he saying?"

Dosha listened attentively as the recording was played back for her. Even though the man was speaking urgently, he was easy to understand. She automatically started listening and paraphrasing at the same time. "His name is Nicolai Rushnov. He is the communications officer for the Russian oil tanker Volganoff 226. He is saying his ship encountered an unexpected storm and has been hit by waves reaching twenty meters in height."

Dosha wiped her forehead with the back of her hand while she translated, "They have heard horrible sounds of metal grating against metal. He says he is not optimistic about the ship weathering the storm. Their current situation is that they are listing to the port side and taking on water. If more waves hit, they will go down. The fourteen crew members have been ordered to abandon ship and are now launching the life boats."

"Make contact with all ships in the area to make sure they have picked up the distress call. We need to get those men some help!" ordered the captain.

The captain knew that he could not respond to the distress call because he had to think about the safety of his own passengers. He had no doubt that the relatively modern *Sea Bridge* would perform better in a storm than a rusty oil tanker. He also noted how fortunate they were to have been in the Gulf of Finland when the storm hit. This part of the Baltic Sea was more protected then the southern waters from which the tanker's emergency signal was being emitted.

Chapter Thirty-Seven

Exhaustion

Nicole was in her room, trying to read, when the ship rolled with a steep wave. She had been trying to ignore the storm when the reading lamp slid off the nightstand and crashed to the floor. The sound of the glass shattering made her jump. The room was darker than at any time since she had been on the trip. Her viewing window was awash with water, and the angry clouds had blocked out the daylight.

In the last few minutes, the storm had taken a major turn for the worse, crossing the threshold from being worrisome to downright scary. The wooden doors on the wardrobe opened and then banged shut with every roll of the ship. She tried to stand up in an attempt to pick up the pieces of glass and quickly realized it was impossible to move about the cabin without being thrown into the furniture. Her injured arm was still sore, and she was having trouble bracing herself to stay upright.

Nicole began to wonder what catastrophe would happen next. She had already experienced an unexpected thunderstorm on the flight out of Seattle and now a freak storm in the Baltic Sea. It was insane! There was a sharp knock on the door.

"Nicole, are you there?"

"Oliver, is that you? What are you doing here?" she exclaimed.

When the ship momentarily rolled into a neutral position, she lunged for the lock on the door and managed to knock it open. Oliver came through the door just as the ship took a dive to the left. He collided with Nicole, and they both landed on the floor in a heap. Nicole winced when she hit the hard floor with her sore arm.

He leaned over and touched her injured arm, saying, "Does it hurt?"

"Not too much." She pointed to the broken lamp. "Be careful; there is glass over there."

"You've had a tough time," he observed sympathetically.

The ship started its roll to the other side, and Nicole found herself against Oliver's soaked shirt.

"You're dripping wet. Aren't you cold?"

"Sorry." He took off his shirt and then put his arms around her. Then he said, "I have you. Hold still."

Oliver and Nicole didn't say anything, but he continued to hold her in place, with his arms wrapped around her shoulders. It did not feel awkward, but instead made her feel safe. She was relieved to see him, and she realized how concerned she had been about losing him. It meant a great deal to her that he had come back to the ship and sought her out. Maybe he wasn't like the other guys she had known after all.

Nicole finally asked, "How bad is the storm?"

Oliver was exhausted and took a moment to respond, "I think it's a freak storm that will blow over quickly."

Nicole nodded but did not move. She had been pleasure boating where the water was choppy or had rolling swells, but had never been comfortable with it. She was thankful that Oliver was here to be a strong voice of calm and reason during a storm of this magnitude.

She said to Oliver, "There's been a lot of press about these out-of-season storms, but until you experience it yourself, it doesn't make an impact."

"The ship seems to be handling the waves quite well and does not appear to be in any distress, so we'll be all right."

Nicole was beginning to feel guilty for monopolizing Oliver's time. "Is there someplace you should be instead of keeping me company?"

With one of his hands, he stroked Nicole's hair. "The captain seems to have everything under control, and everyone else is pinned down in their cabins, so I'll just stay here, if that's okay with you."

"Oliver, were you assigned back to the ship by the Security Alliance?"

He smiled slightly and closed his eyes. "No, it was entirely my choice to come back. They may not even know I'm here."

Nicole put her hands on Oliver's arms, which encircled her shoulders. "Oliver?"

"Hmmm?"

"Sorry I've been a little difficult at times, and thanks for thinking of me when the storm hit."

He put his cheek next to hers and gave her a light kiss. "My pleasure." And then he laid his head back down to rest.

Nicole could feel his taut body relax next to hers. She realized that

Oliver was exhausted beyond what any human could endure. She softly said, "Rest now. You have worked so hard, it's time to rest."

Oliver was asleep before she completed the sentence, and she jokingly thought to herself, *This is the sexiest moment of my life and the guy falls asleep.* But she really didn't mind, because she knew it was the most *romantic* moment of her life. She felt secure in Oliver's arms, so it didn't take her long to join Oliver in a dreamy sleep.

Zafir had blindly followed Dosha to the bridge. But what was he going to do now? He made an attempt to be invisible and fade into the background while the crew members read gauges and shouted updates to each other. He nervously noticed that the security guard named Marcos was also on the bridge, observing the action.

The ship was lurching wildly, so he lodged himself between two consoles. Since he was above deck, his panic level had diminished and he was able to think more clearly. He was fascinated by the ongoing emergency actions and watched intently as Dosha translated the message from the distressed Russian ship. She was so different than any of the women he had ever known. Her confidence and vitality was captivating. He could not help but watch her every move.

The captain asked Dosha to make an announcement to the passengers that sounded like a routine information update. Dosha went on the intercom and, in a friendly voice, told the passengers not to worry because the ship was designed to handle harsher storms than this. The safest thing to do was to stay in their cabins and be calm. She promised to provide an update on the status of the storm every fifteen minutes.

The captain was listening to the sounds of the squall. He became entranced by the intensity and rawness of the sound until he was interrupted. The communications specialist said, "I have a high-security message from Interpol for Marcos."

When Marcos ended the call, the captain asked, "What's up?"

"They told me to be on alert for anyone on board who might be connected to the *Valkyrie* disaster."

Another large wave broke over the ship and carried off the remains of anything that hadn't been anchored down.

Zafir heard what Marcos said. Now he had the confirmation that the mission had been successful. But he was sure everyone must know, making him feel paranoid about being on the bridge. He looked around, imagining that everyone in the room was watching him. They *must* realize that he was the one responsible for the deaths on the *Valkyrie*. He shrank down even further, trying to not be noticed by those around him.

One of the officers got off a call from the engine room. He said, "Captain, there's a problem with the oil pressure in one of the engines. It is likely an electrical problem with the gauge, but I'm going to go down to the engine room and check it out."

This was Zafir's chance to escape from the intense scrutiny he felt. When the officer moved across the bridge, Zafir slipped behind him and followed him through the doorway. Everyone was busy monitoring the progress of the storm, and no one saw him leave. He moved quickly to an outside door, took a quick turn, and disappeared out of sight in the pelting rainstorm.

A few more minutes passed and there was a slight drop in the intensity of the wind. The waves had diminished only slightly, but it was a change in the right direction, thought the captain. He started to relax, knowing that he would not have to order the guests to move to the life boat stations. He predicted the storm would soon blow over and the busiest person on board would be the ship's doctor, giving out sea sickness pills and examining the passengers' bumps and bruises.

Fifteen minutes later, the storm had weakened significantly. As promised, Dosha gave an update to the guests, saying the storm had lessened and would soon be over as quickly as it had started. She went on to remind them of the scheduled lecture on the history of St. Petersburg at six, just prior to dinner. Everyone breathed a sigh of relief because a sense of normalcy had been reestablished.

Chapter Thirty-Eight

Puzzle

When Nicole awoke, she lay there thinking that this time spent with Oliver during the storm was almost surreal. It was as if they had become two different people in the chaos and danger of the storm. They did not do their normal sarcastic and challenging banter. Instead, it was replaced with concern and tenderness.

As she observed him sleeping, she began to realize that there was more depth to this man than he let on. He appeared flawlessly professional on the outside, but she had seen glimpses of his tender side. He seemed to genuinely care for the people he protected. She had first noticed this with Oliver's interaction with Chen and then with herself. Being an agent was just not a job to him, but a way of life, much like her own job with the foundation. She had the feeling that Oliver could be a major player in her life going forward.

Suddenly Oliver stirred and looked around, slightly confused. He asked urgently, "How long have we been asleep?"

Nicole looked at the clock. "I guess a couple of hours, but we both needed it."

Oliver urgently said, "That's too long! Come with me; we need to figure out who is responsible for all of these deaths." Oliver jumped to his feet with renewed energy and gave her a hand up.

They arrived at the library, where one of the passengers was having coffee and reading a newspaper.

Oliver said brusquely, "We need to use this space for an important meeting. Would you mind moving to another location?"

The man gave Oliver a glare and slowly folded up his outdated *Wall Street Journal* in preparation to leave.

Nicole added, "Thank you, sir. We really appreciate it."

Oliver firmly closed the doors behind him.

Nicole said, "If we are going to figure this out, we need to have the right people in the room. Let's have Dosha attend because she has been mingling with the passengers and probably knows more about them than the two of us combined. I also think you might want to have Marcos in the meeting."

She could tell by the blank expression on Oliver's face that he was used to solving problems by himself, mostly relying on the intelligence fed to him through the analysts.

She tried again, "It also wouldn't be a bad idea to get Sydney in the conference call as well."

Oliver stroked the stubble on his chin and finally agreed, "You might be right. So far, running after the usual leads has just lead to more death and destruction. Let's also have Jake from the Global Security Alliance sit in on the conference call. He'll have the latest intelligence."

"Sounds good. I'll set up the conference call while you find Dosha and Marcos."

It only took fifteen minutes to round everyone up, set up the dial-in number for the conference call, and notify Sydney and Jake of the meeting. First Sydney called in, and then a couple minutes later, Jake, who had just returned from the most recent security briefing.

Oliver sat back, looking Nicole's way so she would start the meeting. She began by asking the group some open-ended questions. "Do you think this has all been the work of a terrorist group? It just seems that this is too complex. What is their motivation? Maybe there is a bigger conspiracy?"

It didn't take long for Oliver to jump in. "I'm afraid you could be right. It has to be the front for a larger and more ambitious group that has the ability to connect the dots between US senators and terrorist organizations. What do you think, Jake?"

Jake interjected, "The evidence indicates that someone is paying off people. Senator Clarkston's little soiree in the Ice Bar was funded by a bank in the Cayman Islands, along with several other large payments that were given to his reelection campaign. We also have information that the payment to the fishing boat captain came from a bank in St. Petersburg, but upon closer scrutiny, we found the money originated from a different account, from the Cayman Islands."

Oliver asked, "Can we trace the business or individual who has the account?"

Jake responded, "Unfortunately not. The Cayman Island banks have connections with the private Swiss accounts. They are untraceable."

"That's what I was afraid of."

"So there's a chance there are people out there trying to kill anyone who is associated with the climate forum, or potentially any other scientific breakthroughs in alternative fuel?" Nicole asked incredulously.

Dosha piped in, "It must be someone who hates the idea of progress because it threatens the way things are done now."

They all looked at Dosha. She was right. They were looking for a person or group that was motivated to maintain the status quo concerning energy in the global economy.

"But that could be half the planet!" Nicole said in despair.

"So far, everything has had a relationship to the Climate Forum and the think tank on board the *Sea Bridge*," Oliver noted. "I have ignored it, but every lead has been related to those two events. There has to be a connection to David's death and the plight of the Valykrie."

Marcos relayed, "Interpol believes the device that killed the scientists could have been planted by someone on the *Sea Bridge*. I've been instructed to investigate the possibility."

"We need a complete list of every person who set foot on the *Valkyrie*," directed Oliver.

"I'll work on it as soon as we're done here," responded Marcos.

Nicole turned toward the speaker phone. "Sydney, you've been unusually quiet. What is up on your end?"

"As you requested, I've been digging into our board of directors … but do you want to talk about that now?"

"Yes, we have nothing to hide from this group."

"Well, two of the board members are out of the country right now: Jamal Nasir and Jean Cutter. Jamal is in London, and Jean's assistant would only tell me that she was traveling to Europe. After a little research, I found out that Jean Cutter is also on the flight to London, but had a connecting flight: to guess where—*St. Petersburg*. I find that very odd. It has to be more than a coincidence."

Nicole took a sharp intake of breath. "Yes, you're right. That would be a huge coincidence. What in the world is she doing in St. Petersburg?"

Oliver looked directly at her. "After she checks through customs in St. Petersburg, we will have to discreetly follow her."

"Yes, that is the right thing to do," Nicole agreed in a deflated voice. "If she is involved, we need to know now. Then we will figure out how to deal with it."

The group spent more time discussing various organizations that could be the masterminds behind a bigger plot. Jake and Sydney had the most information on external groups that could have the motivation and ability to strike, but in the end there was no definitive answer. Instead they decided to focus on the facts they knew.

"Everything somehow ties back to the people on this ship," Oliver observed. "The best approach would be to investigate key people on the *Sea Bridge* and their relationships to the outside world."

Dosha and Nicole looked at each other. Dosha had been waiting for Nicole to say something about her little investigation of the VP of United Oil and the Oxford professor. Nicole encouragingly said, "Dosha has done some investigative work herself. Go ahead and tell the group what you found out about the two guests who we found a bit odd."

They listened intently as Dosha told them about her interactions with the two men. Nicole could almost see Oliver gloat when she talked about Ian Whitehouse. He had not liked him the minute he laid eyes on him, and she was sure that Dosha's report would give him plenty of reasons to do a full background check on the deceptive professor.

"Sydney, have you found out anything more about the wealthy man who was originally scheduled to attend instead of Ian Whitehouse?" Nicole asked.

"I'm still looking into it. He seems to be an elusive character. The only reason we invited him was because he is thought to be a multi-billionaire and he expressed interest in sustainability progress about six months ago."

"Yeah, that's what I remember too."

"Jake and I have collaborated, but we haven't been able to trace him. My guess is that he gave us a phony name, which is very odd for someone asking to attend a think tank symposium."

Nicole thought for a moment. "I was the one who originally talked to him on the phone. He told me we had met at a function in DC and he was interested in how the Everson Foundation was helping develop renewable energy. I explained to him a little bit about our new direction. He seemed delighted and said he would like to commit money to the cause. That is when I invited him to the think tank on the *Sea Bridge*. But I must admit, I don't remember meeting him in DC. What does he look like?"

Sydney said, "That's just it. We haven't found identification or any photos of the guy: no license, birth certificate, Social Security number—nothing."

Jake piped in, "We'll keep digging. Nicole, if you remember anything about him, let us know."

"I will."

With that said, they wrapped up the meeting. Oliver and Marcos took off to find the guest list showing who boarded the Valkryie. They decided to split the duties, with Marcos working on the passenger list and Oliver interviewing the crew members.

Marcos' first interviews were with the two suspects who had been brought up in the previous meeting. The VP of United Oil seemed to be immediately defensive when he walked into the room to be questioned. Marcos asked, "Why did you come on the cruise?" A couple minutes later, Marcos finally had to cut him off because he was on a tirade about his boss, his company, and his life. He was an angry man, but his whereabouts during the tour had been accounted for.

Next, Marcos talked to Ian Whitehouse. He asked, "How did you come to be invited to the symposium?

Ian fidgeted in his chair and said, "The invitation came to Oxford, and it is a great opportunity, isn't it?"

Marcos sensed that he was being evasive and probably lying. However, during the tour on the *Valkyrie*, he had been in a group of closely monitored VIPs. So, in the end, both men had alibis that checked out.

At the same time, Oliver started interviewing the crew members who had been on the *Valkyrie* during the reception. He wanted to ascertain if anyone had observed anything unusual. The first person he talked to was the enthusiastic chef. All he could talk about was the excellent food that had been prepared. He had noticed nothing unusual.

Next Oliver talked to three of the crew members who had served food and drinks. They all seemed very frank and honest and accounted for each other's presence. Going back to the list, he discovered he had skipped one name because he was not available. When Oliver inquired where the man named Zafir was, he was told that he was ill. Oliver decided to check him out.

Chapter Thirty-Nine

Despair and Reckoning

Zafir lay down on his bunk down in the depths of the ship. It was quiet and dark. His bunk mates were not around because most of them were working. He felt physically and mentally sick. The storm had not bothered him too much while on the bridge, but when he came down to the bunk room, he couldn't handle it. Inevitably, he knew the hull of the ship would be crushed, and he would die. He would choke on the water as it rushed into his lungs, fighting for one more gasp of oxygen. In the end, he was sure he would breathe in the sea water.

Zafir would have preferred to have a knife plunged into his chest instead of being tossed around in this hell hole below the surface of sea. Drops of sweat dripped into his eyes, causing them to burn. He rubbed his fists into them to try to stop the burning, but in a way, the pain felt good.

He began to think about what he had done to the people on the *Valkyrie*. It made him feel so tired that he could not lift his head off of the mattress. Even the air was thick and oppressive, pressing down on every part of his body. He continually tossed and turned, with no relief from his mental torture.

As he lay on the bed, he became obsessed with trying to remember their faces. In his mind, he could see the scientists and crew members desperately gasping for air, not understanding what was happening. They writhed in agony, until they finally succumbed to the poison. He forced himself to visualize the whole scene in the smallest graphic detail.

Finally he dozed off, but the nightmares took over. The victims were in his face, screaming in a high-pitched shrill that he could not escape. Even though he strained with all his might to make out the words, he could not understand what they were trying to say to him.

Was that his mother over there, in the background? Was she screaming at him too?

He forced himself back into consciousness, fighting to not slip back into the terrifying nightmare. He was sweating and trembling but still could not shake off the torment. It was impossible to get the images out of his tortured mind. He was compelled to go over the scene, over and over, again and again and again.

He was so distraught with the reality of what he had done that it did not occur to him to report to his normal work duties. Somewhere in the back of his mind, he must have known that if he did not show up it would become obvious that he was guilty, but he no longer cared. He would lay in the darkness, tormented, until someone came to take him away.

Oliver arranged to be led down several decks to the small, dark crew quarters by one of the crewman who shared the same bunk space with Zafir. They descended to the lower levels through the "invisible" back staircase used exclusively by the crew. It was the first time that Oliver had seen the ship from the viewpoint of a crew member. The more he saw, the more it made him feel sorry for the workers on the ship. He knew that it must be difficult living in such cramped quarters for an extended length of time, much like the seamen who shared a hot bunk on a nuclear submarine.

Oliver asked the guide, "How do you feel about living so far down in the ship when the guests above live in luxury in their state rooms?"

The question caught the crewman off-guard. He didn't know what to say. Finally he haltingly murmured, "I need the job to feed my family. For this, I will endure anything."

When asked what he knew about Zafir, the man simply said, "He is very private and doesn't talk much. I guess he is a loner."

They came to the closed door of the bunkroom and knocked. There was no answer. Oliver drew his weapon and opened the door. They stepped into total darkness while the crewman fumbled for the light switch and turned on the lights. Lying on the bottom bunk was Zafir, his face turned toward the wall.

Oliver came closer. "I need to talk to you."

There was no response, but Oliver could hear Zafir's shallow breathing so he knew that he was alive. He shook his shoulder to wake him, but Zafir did not move, continuing to face the wall.

After a few more failed attempts at communication, Oliver decided enough was enough. In a swift motion, he put handcuffs on Zafir's limp wrists and then physically turned him over. When his faced was turned toward them, Oliver recognized the man immediately. He had served him several meals in the dining room and had seemed very congenial and helpful.

"What's your name?" demanded Oliver.

Zafir said nothing. His eyes were open, but he appeared to be fixed on some inner turmoil. He could not, or would not, acknowledge anyone or anything.

Oliver took Zafir into custody. Surely, the evidence found at the site of the *Valkyrie* would be used to establish his guilt, whether he ever spoke or not.

Chapter Forty

Passage to St. Petersburg

The *Sea Bridge* was making steady progress toward the port where the guests would disembark and clear customs for entry into St Petersburg. The waterway leading to the port was filled with outdated remnants of rusted ships, dingy warehouses, and obsolete equipment that serviced the shipping trade. The harsh Russian winters had taken a hefty toll on any equipment that was not religiously maintained, resulting in vast areas of industrial litter.

Yet in some trade zones along the waterway, there were also up-to-date facilities, with new containers and tall cranes actively loading and unloading modern ships. This disparate scenery was a visual reminder of the hard times in the Russian economy, but also showed the transition to prosperity in recent years.

Who would have guessed, by the industrial nature of the waterway, that the glorious city of St. Petersburg was only a few miles away? Ultimately, the abrupt change in scenery would make the splendor of St. Petersburg stand out even more when the ship reached its final destination.

Zafir had been on lock down for the past eight hours. He had been visited by the ship's doctor, who had given him IV fluids and a sedative. He slept for several hours, and when he woke up, he had regained some mental clarity. He was handcuffed to the bed and was being closely watched.

For some strange reason, he was beginning to feel comfortable in the dark and oppressive environment below the deck. He no longer felt like he was choking. It was as if he belonged in this evil place. He knew that he had become obsessed with succeeding in his mission, regardless of the circumstances. It was for the greater good, but for the first time in his life, he felt doubt.

Zafir was beginning to develop a deeper understanding of why people chose death when destroying their targets. It would have been much easier to be an ordinary suicide bomber, one who could reap the immediate rewards promised to him. Instead, he was forced to wrestle with the pain of what he had done.

Would it have been better to die along with the people I murdered on board the Valkyrie? he asked himself. But that was not a choice. It had not been part of the plan because of the need to buy time for the nerve gas canisters to be removed from the ship. He had been required to return to the *Sea Bridge* to avoid any suspicion. Yet deep down, he knew the answer was yes: it would have been easier to stay on the ship and breathe the gas himself.

It wouldn't be long until the ship docked in St. Petersburg. It had been planned for a contact to meet him on a side-street not far from the pier, to help him hide and eventually get out of the country. Since the London cell had not heard from him in the last twenty-four hours, would they assume that he was dead? Or would they somehow know he had been caught, and instruct the contact to rescue him from his captors? These possibilities had never been discussed, so Zafir did not know his fate.

The one thing he did know was that he would no longer know the freedom of his former life. He figured the odds were he would be executed for what he had done or, at a minimum, rot in a foreign jail for the rest of his life. Yet a small part of him couldn't help but hope for a rescue from the highly capable London cell. If only he could break free and contact them.

He heard a knock on the door, and then Dosha entered. He had not seen her since they were on the bridge during the dreadful storm. The thought ran through his mind that since she had helped him then, maybe she would help him now. It was so kind of her to come see him in his darkest hour.

Dosha sat in an upright chair parallel to where Zafir was handcuffed to the bed. "I have come to understand why you did this. Maybe it will give you peace," stated Dosha.

"Thank you," Zafir said as he looked shyly at Dosha. He hoped that she would have empathy for what he had done. After all, she had lost her mother as a child too.

Dosha was making an attempt to look at Zafir sympathetically, but was having difficulty because she was boiling with anger.

With an edge to her voice, Dosha asked, "I don't understand what happened. Can you tell me why you poisoned all the people on the *Valkyrie*?"

Zafir detected her anger right away. "You can't understand."

"Understand what?" pursued Dosha.

He now looked at her defiantly. "It is my destiny. I am avenging the greed of the royal family."

"What royal family?" Dosha asked more softly this time.

He said nothing.

She tried again in a more soothing tone. "Do you remember when I told you about my parents in Russia? Tell me about your childhood."

He slowly raised his head and began speaking. "I was born outside of Jidda in Saudi Arabia. My mother was an immigrant from Pakistan who worked as a maid in the royal family's household."

Dosha nodded, trying to encourage him to talk.

Zafir became agitated, "Since she was young and pretty, one of the sons of the royal family took an interest in my mother. She told me he would surprise her with flowers and books to read. But she became pregnant, so she was fired and thrown out of the royal house. I was born four months later."

Dosha tried to sound empathetic. "How did you get money to live?"

"We lived in a slum, sharing a mud-brick hut with two other families. My mother did the cooking and took care of the children while the others begged on the streets. When I was six or seven, I learned to station myself on the streets that led to the business district. I watched for luxury town cars and sold financial newspapers to the bored men being driven to work."

"Your mother must have been a special woman."

"My mother was well educated in her homeland, and she taught me to read and speak confidently. She did not want me to be a poor, illiterate child."

"That must have given you an advantage over the other boys working the streets."

Zafir did not respond. Instead he looked down at his handcuffed hands and continued on with his story. "One day I noticed that my mother's health was not good. She began coughing up mucous. She was tired and depressed. I begged her to go see a doctor, but she dismissed my worries. We did not have enough money for a doctor."

Dosha began to feel an inkling of pity for Zafir. He had known nothing but loss and sorrow, although that did not excuse him from his incomprehensible deeds.

"My mother got better for a while, but then she began to spiral downward. She became too ill to leave her dark room and begged for something to dull the pain. I searched everywhere to find the drugs to make her pain go away."

When Zafir looked up, Dosha could see the pain in his normally stoic face. But he pressed on, "Soon I learned there was a network of runners who brought drugs into the slum area for a dealer who wanted the business in the area without setting foot there. So I became a slum drug dealer to make my mother's life more bearable."

Dosha stood up, folded her arms, and turned away. She was struggling with her emotions because she wanted to detest this man, not feel sorry for him.

"A while later, my mother took a turn for the worse. She lay on a mat and slipped in and out of consciousness. Her fever spiked in waves, and she knew she would not survive much longer. It was during this time I learned that my father was a member of the royal family, but he had never come to see me and would never claim me as his son. When she was delirious, my mother told me how she had tried to bring me to the palace, but she was rejected. All she could do was to watch the limousine pull out of the driveway and hold me up to show them I existed. But the driver quickly accelerated away."

Zafir's voice was getting angrier, and he seemed driven to continue. "Even though my mother was feverish and delusional, she was determined to tell me the truth. She told me not to give up hope because I had royal blood and would someday be a very important person. She never gave up the notion that someday my noble father would come to find me."

Dosha turned back to see that Zafir was clenching his hands so tightly that his knuckles were turning white. "As my mother lay dying, I swore that I would seek revenge on my greedy and arrogant father. I spent every waking moment by her bedside and gave her the pain medicine that she so badly needed. Eventually, her breathing became shallow and she became weaker and weaker. Her eyes grew hollow and blank. Her heartbeat was very faint. I stayed by her bedside until her breathing stopped."

"I'm sorry," whispered Dosha.

Zafir's words were rushing out and he was choking back tears. "My mother was placed on a cart with a coarse sheet over her body and taken away by a public health official. I have no idea where she was taken or what they did with her, but I am certain that she did not have a proper burial. A government official showed up and asked me questions about where my relatives lived. I said they lived in Pakistan. The man put me in a car and I was driven to an orphanage."

Zafir stopped speaking and settled back, trying to regain control of his emotions. He finally calmed down and said, "At the orphanage I could no longer wander the streets and fend for myself. I was a prisoner. If they would have just let me out, I could have done a much better job providing for those children than they did. I was forced into a daily routine of doing nothing."

Dosha cupped her chin in her hand and tipped her head a little. "And that is why you killed the people on the Valkryie? To seek revenge for your mother's death?"

Zafir was irritated. "I seek revenge on the *greed* that drove her to her death."

Dosha decided they needed a break. "I'll get some tea. I'll be right back." She left the cabin where Zafir was held prisoner, walked down the hall, and entered another cabin.

When she came into the room, Dosha was shaking her head from side to side and asked, "This is so frustrating. Have you been able to hear everything?"

"Yes, the wire is working well," commented Marcos.

"How do you think it is going? Am I asking what you want? Do you want me to probe further on anything else?"

Oliver was complimentary. "You're doing well. You are the only person that he has confided in. None of the rest of us could get a word out of him. Thanks to you, we know a lot more than we did before."

Nicole asked, "Can anyone figure out why he picked a scientific ship in the middle of the Baltic Sea to carry out his vendetta? It seems like an unusual target for someone on a Jihad mission."

Oliver nodded in agreement. "It *is* unusual, especially with the amount of secret, high-tech information needed to carry it out. It is likely that Zafir was recruited by terrorists and trained specifically for this mission. He had the right profile: lonely, angry, and looking for a purpose in life. In the end, he is just another terrorist, but the unique angle is that he has to have a network of people providing him with classified information."

Nicole told Dosha, "Then we agree. If you could find out how he was recruited, or anything about his connections, it would be extremely valuable."

"I'll try. I think he likes me. It's all very sad!"

Chapter Forty-One

Interrogation

Dosha knocked on the door and came into the cabin carrying tea and sugar cookies.

"Here. This is for you." She poured him some tea and offered him the cookies.

Zafir was grateful for her generosity. "Thank you."

After he took some sips of the tea and consumed a cookie, Dosha asked, "So how did you get recruited for this mission?"

"Six months after I was sent to the orphanage, two peculiar men arrived. They had foreign accents that made it difficult to understand them. They flashed money in front of us while proclaiming the importance of Jihad. The men talked about how they trained boys like us at a camp far away. They told us that at the camp we would get good food and would be trained to be strong fighters. We would be educated to read and write and be trained in a specialized area so we could execute an important mission. They promised that we would learn computer skills and would have access to the Internet!"

Dosha looked surprised. "That must have been exciting."

"Yes, we would be able to communicate with other camps committed to the same worthy purpose. The strange men went on to proclaim the corruption of Western society and pointed out how the weakness of the royal family had resulted in a corrupt collaboration with the United States. Most of the boys were excited about the money, but I liked how they talked about the corruption of the royal family. These men knew how they squandered the country's oil reserves to buy cars and other luxuries while their own people starved. It all come into focus and made sense. I began to understand why my mother had been wronged and was left to die in the slums."

Dosha poured herself some tea and asked, "So it served your purposes?"

"I wanted to learn and be successful, like my mother wanted me to be. In the speeches given by the men who visited, I learned that I was obligated to hate the royal family and all that they stood for. It felt like a tribute to my mother."

She looked directly at Zafir. "Who helped you obtain the information about the *Valkyrie*?"

There was silence, Dosha had been too direct. She could feel Zafir retract into his shell. He had seen through the reason why she was here. "Okay, Zafir, I'll be honest with you. We want to know why a group of innocent scientists were murdered while working on an important project to save human lives."

"It is for the greater good. They were expendable. So many people suffer. You know nothing," he said sharply.

Dosha shook her head in aggravation. "What good could it possibly do to kill those people?"

Zafir said flatly, "You cannot comprehend." Then he turned his head to the wall in defiance. He had withdrawn and would no longer acknowledge Dosha's presence.

Dosha knew she could not get any more information from Zafir. The conversation had ended, so she said, "You will be escorted off the ship, under guard, and will be transported to a neutral country for trial. You will become a famous man who will be hated around the world."

Zafir mumbled under his breath, "Not *all* of the world."

Dosha raised her voice. "I'm also happy to tell you that your mission failed. The nerve gas was intercepted before reaching St. Petersburg, *and* your terrorist friends were all killed."

He mumbled again, "You are lying … just like everyone else."

Dosha ignored his comment and continued, "Those people on the *Valkyrie* had dedicated their lives to making a better environment for everyone in the world. There is *no* justification for killing them!" Then she wheeled around and walked out of the door.

Zafir hung his head in total despair.

The e-mail history was pulled from the ship's database, and the short messages sent and received by Zafir were reviewed by the analysts at the Security Alliance. It appeared that they consisted of simple status updates given in code. The frequency of the communications appeared to be acknowledgements of specific check points and tasks that had been completed. It was obvious that the entire operation had been planned in great detail, way in advance of the sailing.

The e-mail messages had been sent to Zafir's "home" in Saudi Arabia, but in reality they had been systematically rerouted to alternative addresses, bouncing around the world. The Security Alliance analysts had been working diligently to try to track them to their final origination point. They maintained that the network was devised by creative, intelligent individuals, because so far they had only been able to narrow the trace to Western Europe.

Another piece of information was also passed along to Oliver from the investigators on the *Valkyrie*. An athletic bag with tools in it had been found in the galley. It would only be a matter of time to establish that the bag was in fact Zafir's, and that he had used the tools to place the device in the ventilation system.

It was now apparent that the physical evidence, along with Zafir's confession to Dosha, would be more than adequate to convict Zafir in any international court of law.

Chapter Forty-Two

The Shot

The scenery had suddenly changed from heavy industrial structures to classical seventeenth- and eighteenth-century facades, complete with ornate ironwork gates and groomed gardens. The day was calm and serene, with temperatures in the low seventies: a perfect summer day in the beautiful Soviet city.

The *Sea Bridge* docked at the pier farther down the Neva River than where the larger cruise ships were located. This embankment pier accommodated the small cruise ships, sailing vessels, and private yachts. The location was ideal because the guests could disembark, show their passports and walk to the heart of the city.

The long pier was connected by a walkway to a low metal building that housed an immigration check point. In her briefing, Dosha had warned the group that this immigration station was manned by particularly strict, traditional Soviet officers, mostly women. They were not friendly, rarely smiled, and had old-fashioned, early sixties hairdos. She told everyone to *not* make jokes or do anything else to irritate them. Many tourists had suffered the ire of these proud, traditional Soviet officers.

Oliver had arranged for Zafir to be taken off the ship prior to the other guests disembarking. An armored prisoner transport truck would take him to Kresky Prison, famous for its colorful history. It was once one of the largest solitary confinement facilities in Europe, and was used to hold both common criminals and political prisoners considered state enemies. But in more recent history, the prison was known for its overcrowding, tuberculosis infections, and corruption. In an effort to modernize, most of the prisoners had been moved to a facility built outside the city limits. However, because of the international interest and proximity to

St. Petersburg, Kresky prison had been chosen to hold Zafir in solitary confinement.

Oliver and Marcos led Zafir out of the cabin where he had been kept in seclusion. They climbed the stairs to the main deck where the gangway would lead them down to the pier. When they arrived on the deck, they could see that the guests had lined the entire route, positioning themselves along the railing of the ship. They all wanted to catch one last glimpse of the evil man who had murdered their new friends on the *Valkyrie*.

Everyone was silent. Only the footsteps of the three men could be heard as they walked toward the gangway. Zafir's hands were handcuffed behind his back. He no longer wore his crew uniform, but instead a plain white shirt that was too large for him, and wrinkled, gray pants. He shuffled along, looking down at his feet, trying to avoid the eyes of the onlookers. Oliver and Marcos constantly glanced around them, keenly aware of their surroundings. Because of the gravity of the situation, they both wore crisp dark suits and ties. Their firearms were discreetly tucked in holsters under their coat jackets.

The group of three paraded by the guests who had come out to witness the event. As they stared at him, they felt conflicted and deeply disturbed. Most of them were having difficulty understanding how this pleasant man, who had served them many meals, could be a mass murderer. It was unimaginable that this tragedy had occurred.

As they approached the gangway, the agents continued to be watchful, scanning the entire scene for anything that looked out of the ordinary. Below they saw the Russian Militsiya, looking very official, outfitted in their dress uniforms with brass buttons and black leather belts. Their job was to safely escort Zafir to the transport vehicle and then take him to Kresty Prison until an international tribunal decided his fate.

The rest of the pier was eerily quiet because it had been cordoned off for the transfer of the prisoner. Passengers on the other small ships and pleasure craft had been ordered to stay on board until given further notice. The normal activity around servicing the water craft had ceased. One could feel the tension in the air, waiting for the terrorist to emerge from the *Sea Bridge*.

Without hesitation, Oliver took the lead. He took the first steps down, with Zafir behind him and Marcos in the rear. Zafir hesitated for a few seconds, pausing to look at the people on board the *Sea Bridge* who hated him so much. Then Marcos gave him a touch on the back to indicate he should proceed. Zafir drew in a deep breath, looked straight, ahead and stepped onto the gangway.

Crack! Suddenly his head whipped back and his body folded, falling backward onto the deck. Blood came spurting out of his forehead and gushed down his face and chest. Oliver jumped forcefully back on deck. His reflexes had been activated by the sound of the bullet fracturing Zafir's skull. He flung himself on Zafir's body and knocked down Marcos in the process. The crowd observing the spectacle screamed and hit the deck, realizing that something had gone horribly wrong.

Oliver raised his head and looked at Zafir. He eyes were staring blankly into space. He had been shot in the forehead and died instantly. Blood was soaking the front of Marcos' shirt and Marcos was gasping for breath. Oliver knew that there had only been one shot fired, probably from a high-powered rifle, quite a distance away.

Marcos was making gurgling noises, and Oliver realized that the blood on Marcos' shirt was not only Zafir's. The bullet had passed through Zafir's head and had gone into Marco's chest. Oliver pushed Zafir's body away and turned his attention to Marcos.

"Marcos," Oliver said as he tried to stop the bleeding. Marcos was quickly losing consciousness and slipping away. His eyes focused on Oliver and his lips moved, but words didn't come out.

Oliver cradled his head. He thought about their first meeting when the senior agent made fun of the younger one. If only Marcos would have retired earlier instead of hanging on too long. Oliver held his head in his lap until he was gone. Then he looked up in anger, determined to find out where the shot had came from. He looked beyond the pier to the buildings across the street.

His gaze focused on the Russian Orthodox Church, which was directly opposite the ship, dominating the landscape. From the angle of the entry wounds, it was evident that the bullet came from a higher elevation. The shot likely came from a high-powered rifle positioned in one of the bell towers in the church. It had to have been fired by an expert sniper, because someone of lesser skill would not have been able to execute the shot.

With everyone else, Nicole had watched as Zafir emerged from below deck and walked toward the gangway to disembark. When Zafir passed by with Oliver and Marcos on each side, she was standing near the lifeboats, next to Dosha. She saw Zafir take a glance at Dosha with a pleading look in his eyes. It was a sad moment, one that would stay in Nicole's mind for years to come. She thought, *this was a man who thought he was in the right, when actually he had done the most evil thing in the world.* She should have hated him, but instead she found herself feeling sorry for him.

Like the rest of the passengers, her reaction was to duck for cover when the shot rang out. When she raised her head, she could see blood flowing everywhere. It was all over the deck and covered the three men.

She jumped to her feet and raced toward them. "Oliver!"

He was cradling Marcos' head in his lap and didn't hear her, but as she came closer, she could tell that he was unhurt. Her focus shifted to Zafir, and she could see that he had been shot in the head and had died instantly. She turned away from the awful scene because it was too shocking to absorb. She tried to direct her attention to Oliver and Marcos, but she quickly realized that Marcos was in severe distress. She watched as Oliver gently spoke to Marcos and closed his eyes for the last time. At that moment, she felt distraught and sickened. She swore she could feel the rage racing through Oliver's blood.

He carefully laid down Marcos on the deck and stood up, not caring about his own safety. He rushed down the gangway to the dock below, stopping in front of the stunned captain of the Militsiya. From Nicole's vantage point, she could see him show his credentials and then point to the impressive Russian Orthodox Church located across the street. She could hear snatches of him speaking in Russian, presumably enlisting the Militsiya's help to search the church.

Chapter Forty-Three

Private Yacht

Approximately four hundred meters down the pier, a private ocean-going luxury yacht was moored diagonally from the *Sea Bridge*. It was over thirty meters in length and had a low profile, with narrow dark windows and sleek lines. On the back deck were two men wearing discreet, wireless communication devices. The men looked almost identical to each other. Both of them were clean-cut with short hair, most likely ex-military. They were dressed in black leather jackets, sporting sleek designer sunglasses with reflective shades. A pedestrian walking by on the dock would likely think they were highly paid body guards, probably for some rich tycoon or a famous celebrity.

One of the men was closely watching the developments aboard the *Sea Bridge* through small, powerful binoculars. He saw Zafir's head snap backward and body crumple. He witnessed the dark red blood splatter on the clothes of the men and watched as the first man down the plank tried in vain to get the others to safety, but too late.

He waited a minute longer and saw blood begin to ooze over the deck and form a small drip down the side of the white ship. No one could survive losing that much blood. The man pushed a button and confidently spoke into his headset, "The target has been eliminated."

The other man had his binoculars trained on the Russian Orthodox Church with the large onion-shaped cupolas. He watched as the massive front door opened and one of the workers wearing coveralls carried out an old cardboard box with a paint tarp folded on top. The man walked at an average pace and only paused to look at his reflection in a window, and then turned the corner and disappeared into the neighborhood behind the church.

He reported, "All clear."

Below deck, a stocky man in his mid-forties was relaxing in his private office just outside of the luxurious master stateroom. He was standing at the fully stocked bar, preparing to pour himself a glass of 1977 vintage port. He was wearing proper casual nautical attire, a navy cashmere sweater with white slacks, and matching white shoes. His premature silver hair was fashioned in a style to show off its fullness—one of his best attributes, he thought.

The office, along with the entire yacht, was decorated in a monochromatic off-white and beige color scheme with walnut wood trim. The interior was richly appointed but lacked any individual character. It had likely been done by an interior designer catering to the generic tastes of wealthy clients, but the man believed the décor to be rich and special.

Thinking it would be good luck, he had personally opened the vintage bottle of port a few hours before, making it a ritual using an antique Italian brass cork screw that he had acquired in his travels. Next, he decanted the port with a steady hand, pouring the liquid in one steady stream so the sediment stayed in the bottle. Now, in anticipation of a celebration, he slowly poured the port wine from the crystal decanter to a matching port glass. He held it up to the light to admire the rich, ruby color, noticing with deep satisfaction the clarity of the port.

He kept peering at the port wine sitting in the glass. He thought, *What would it hurt to celebrate a little early?* He simply couldn't resist the tempting port any longer. He took a slow sip and sighed with pleasure as the liquid slid over his tongue and down his throat.

"An outstanding year," he announced to himself. "A great vintage year *and* the year I started my business."

He moved to the Italian leather couch. Between each sip, he reached for the spiced almonds and sugar-coated figs from northern Portugal, put there by his assistant for his consumption. He relished the port and smacked his lips on the figs.

There were two sharp knocks on the door.

"*What*?" he said, resenting the interruption to his pleasurable consumption.

A young man opened the walnut door and came into the stateroom. He had dark, short-cropped hair and was conservatively dressed in dark slacks with a white shirt and blue tie. He had a fresh face and was likely in his late twenties. He was businesslike and professional, having a rather formal demeanor.

He repeated the message that had been given him a few moments before. "I have been informed that the target has been eliminated and all is clear."

The older man looked at his glass of port and smiled in satisfaction. He said, "I knew it." Then he looked back at his young assistant. "Call to finalize the arrangements. The meeting is going on as planned. Also, contact my favorite service. I want a classy red head to celebrate."

"Yes, sir. What time would you like her?" inquired the assistant.

"Right after dinner. She will be good for dessert."

He reluctantly put down his port glass and reached for the mobile device on the elaborately carved, teak Chinese coffee table in front of him. The security of the mobile device was the best that money could buy. The program was updated continuously so no one could hack into it to intercept his messages.

He composed a message to the Guardian Council that said, "Welcome to St. Petersburg from the chairman of the council. I look forward to our ground-breaking conclave. Your driver will meet you at your hotel at the preassigned time."

He pushed the Send button, and then reached into the rosewood cigar box, pulling out an expensive Cuban cigar with his thick fingers. It was very satisfying because everything had gone *exactly* as planned. Now he could relax and enjoy his port and cigar. He sighed and said out loud, "No one else could have pulled this off."

He began licking the cigar along its entire length, sucked on each end, then clipped the end. He thoroughly enjoyed the ceremony of preparing the cigar, even more than smoking it, since there was nothing more decadent than lighting an expensive cigar. He knew well that this was a symbol of the rich and famous men who were in his elite class of society. A symbol that he knew he deserved more than anyone.

He gave one last sigh of pleasure and then lit the cigar with an engraved gold lighter that he had received from his first wife. Over the years he had kept mementos from each of his failed relationships to remind him of how far he had come. Now, he could afford all the women money could buy, so he didn't have to deal with any of the emotional ties and unrealistic expectations set up by needy wives.

His financial position had allowed him to acquire unprecedented power. He knew that he had become one of the most influential men who lived today, because he could orchestrate decisions that would change the future of the world. The power felt good, but his only regret was that he had to stay in the background and use other people to manipulate global political and economic systems. But, he knew that sometime in the near future, he would be destined to receive recognition for his incredible achievements.

He leaned back on the couch and blew the cigar smoke in old fashioned rings above his head.

Chapter Forty-Four

Disembarkation

The shooting had resulted in a lockdown of the ship. The guests were required to stay in their rooms until the Russian police determined that there was no imminent threat to the lives of the passengers. Everyone was quick to cooperate, except Ian Whitehouse, who became incensed and made an issue about not being able to leave the ship immediately. The police said something sternly to him in Russian. He obviously didn't understand what they said, but the result was that he became more compliant.

When the "all clear" was finally given, Ian hurried to be the first guest to disembark. He passed by Nicole on the deck, but purposely averted his eyes, pretending that he didn't see her. He had been cleared to leave the ship because Marcos had not found enough evidence to accuse him of any crime other than being a jerk. He rolled his suitcase down the gangway, almost jogged down the pier, and disappeared into the immigration building.

Next to leave was Chen. Special arrangements had been made to transport him to the airport and fly him back to the States. Through the Everson Foundation, Nicole had set up a medical attendant and a security guard to accompany him on the trip. When Chen prepared to leave, tears came to her eyes.

"Chen, I am so proud that you had the courage to come back and lead the charge on the new fuel technology. It simply would not have happened without you."

"Nicole, you are a big part of this journey. Don't forget that we need you every step of the way."

"Thank you. I know there is no going back now. The press kit for the work done on the ship will be released by the foundation in the next few hours. Soon it will all be public."

Chen said, "It's time. Keeping it secret has not served us well."

The team had made the decision to announce the work immediately. Chen and the scientists were adamant that the project should be open-sourced. This approach would challenge the best minds from around the world to get involved right away. At first, Nicole was worried about the non-traditional approach, but ultimately she had to agree that it was the way to go.

In the last few hours that they were together, the team had set up a framework for the website. They would immediately publish the formula and corresponding data to the global scientific community. Chen felt this would be the only way to ensure that others would not be murdered like David, or poisoned like the scientists on the *Valkyrie*. No private individual, corporation, or government could stop it. All the information would be out in the open—end of story.

Nicole felt an enormous amount of gratitude toward Chen for coming back to the symposium after everything that had happened. She knew that between the two of them, they could drive the result to a successful conclusion.

The remaining guests had tagged their suitcases and were waiting for transportation to their various destinations. Most of them left for the airport since it had been decided to terminate the symposium when the ship arrived in St. Petersburg. But a small, hardy group had decided to stay on to take advantage of the planned tour of the city.

Nicole could see Dosha moving toward the gangway with an enthusiastic group of people following her. She was in her element, happy to show off her native country. Nicole could hear her telling them, "St. Petersburg is the most romantic city in the world ..."

Oliver had been conferring with the Global Security Alliance and the Russian police on the assassination of Zafir. The coordinated search did not turn up anything in the church or the surrounding neighborhood. The only thing that was clear was that the shooting had been done by a professional. For unknown reasons, someone had wanted Zafir dead, and had contracted a specialist to do it. Poor Marcos was simply collateral damage.

As soon as Oliver was done with his meetings, he came looking for Nicole.

"Our agent reported that Ian Whitehouse was picked up at the dock by a private town car. I have the feeling that it might be important to check out where your friend is going."

"He's not my friend. I'm coming with you," Nicole flatly said.

"It would be safer for you to stay on the ship until everything is sorted out."

"No chance."

Oliver frowned. "I guess I know you well enough by now to know there is no hope of changing your mind."

Nicole couldn't help but smile at his remark. She only said, "Smart man."

With mock pleasure in his voice, he said, "I hope you like the back of a motor scooter."

Chapter Forty-Five

Conclave of the Guardian Council

They arrived one by one, scheduled ten minutes apart so a high-tech security sweep could be performed between each arrival. At prearranged times, their private town cars had picked them up from the best hotels in St. Petersburg. Even though each guest was scheduled to arrive separately, the town cars took distinct routes to avoid undue attention. Each passed over a different maze of canals that gave St. Petersburg the nickname "Venice of the North." When they came close to their destination, the route converged and every town car went over the hanging bridge and then passed by the equestrian statue that was cast using the actual death mask of Peter the Great.

The drivers had been given detailed instructions through their individual services. They were told to follow the instructions, *without* deviation, or it would cost them their job. Of course, all the mystery surrounding the secrecy aroused the drivers' interest, causing them to sneak secret looks at their clients. But they were disappointed, because by himself each guest appeared quite ordinary. Only when the group was assembled could anyone guess the significance of the secret meeting.

If they had been observant when they approached the castle, the guests would have noticed that each side looked different from the other, each being decorated in the different motifs of French Classicism, Italian Renaissance, and Gothic architectural styles. The brick-red color of the façade distinguished it from most of the other buildings in St. Petersburg. Surrounded by the Moika and Fontanka Rivers and the specially dug Church and Sunday Canals, the castle stood on its own, completely isolated from the rest of the city.

The guests had not been informed of the colorful history of the castle, which was hurriedly constructed to be the royal residence of Paul I. Considered a mystic in his time, he was thought to have been a mentally unbalanced ruler, who had premonitions about being assassinated.

According to legend, he was visited in his dreams by his grandfather, Peter the Great, who warned him about his impending death. The legend told was that Paul could see the ghastly sight of his own image with his neck wrung when he looked into the Winter Palace mirrors.

Paul had the new royal residence designed in the shape of a fortress to thwart assassination attempts, complete with draw bridges to protect him from his enemies. But even with all the precautions, Paul only survived in the palace for forty days. His murderers found him hiding behind a screen in his own chamber, where he was knifed and strangled.

Rooted in the macabre history of St. Petersburg, Mikhailovski's Castle, now called the Engineer's Castle, was the perfect venue for the secret conclave. The palace was full of intrigue, with secret rooms and passageways built for hiding and quick escapes in case a perceived threat occurred. Throughout history, the very sight of the castle elicited fear and anxiety from the citizens of St. Petersburg, and these were the very emotions that the chairman of the council wanted his attendees to experience.

As instructed, the town cars passed up the main entrance to the castle, arriving at the unobtrusive side door. When they arrived, each guest was met by a tall man in a black overcoat who escorted each one into the dark castle. They walked down the long hallway where the guests unknowingly passed by the royal chamber where Paul I was murdered by the band of renegade soldiers seeking his abdication.

A little farther down the corridor, they stopped in front of a massive bookcase that ran from the floor to the ceiling. The books on the shelves were old and musty, obviously not museum quality. Each guest was asked to step aside while the escort swung open the bookcase to reveal a hidden door. Next, with dramatic effect, the wooden latch was opened, exposing a stone passageway, illuminated only by flickering candlelight.

Once they were inside, the door was closed behind each guest, leaving them alone to find their own way in the dim light. This isolation was purposeful, intended to heighten their sense of awareness and elicit a fear response. The guest had to pause, letting his eyes adjust to the faint light so he could make out the uneven stone steps and the narrow, winding staircase.

Since the guests' arrivals had been planned ten minutes apart, they would not see one another until they reached the meeting room, but they all had the same intimidating experience. The uneven staircase required them to put their hands on the cold stone wall to keep their balance as they slowly made their way down to a small antechamber. By the time each of them arrived in the ground room below, their overall anxiety had been successfully elevated.

The new members asked themselves, "What have I gotten myself into?" But the returning members appreciated the drama.

Unexpectedly, a strong, male voice said, "Welcome to the Guardian Council. I am here to make you comfortable."

In turn, each guest startled. A young man dressed in a black shirt and black pants seemed to appear from nowhere and successfully frightened every one of them.

The young man pointed to the single piece of furniture in the small room: a gilded white neo-classic chair that had been placed directly against the wall. "Please sit down and rest. You must be very tired."

Most of the guests sank immediately down into the chair. But a couple of them had resisted and needed to be coaxed a second time, not wanting to be isolated any longer.

He repeated, "Please sit. I have a special drink for you. It is a welcome drink from the chairman of the council. You will soon join the others."

He handed them a brew of Sbiten, a famous Russian drink normally consumed in the winter but appropriate for the cool underground cavern. The smell of the drink with honey, special spices, chili peppers, and raspberry jam was enticing and made a comforting treat that none of the guests could resist.

Of course the guests did not realize the drink had been spiked with flunitrazepam, a drug that was intended to make them more compliant and induce a moderate amount of antegrade amnesia. It had been formulated for each guest individually, depending on the amount of tested experience they had with the conclave. The chairman of the council had personally determined the dosage for the guests. He had successfully used the drug in the past and knew that one couldn't be too careful when orchestrating a meeting at this level. Too much was at stake!

There were only three returning council members from the inaugural meeting of the Guardian Council, since two of the members who attended the original meeting had not successfully carried out their assignments.

The first was a history professor who had second thoughts and ultimately refused to recruit radical students for the cause. A week later, he had died of an unfortunate heart attack while jogging in Hyde Park. It was a tragedy, because he was only fifty-two years old, an avid jogger, and perceived to be in good health. The man had been popular with his students and fellow professors and was deeply mourned by his family. His obituary stated that he had been struck down in the prime of his life.

The second member of the original council was an American congressman who was simply inept at getting anything done. The chairman wondered how the man had ever been elected to a prominent position. Unfortunately, he also knew too much about the Guardian Council and had difficulty keeping his mouth shut.

The congressman was tragically murdered during a robbery gone wrong in his Virginia home. According to the police report, the violent robbery had been done by a thief who was enticed by the owner's priceless gun collection. Many of his antique weapons from his collection had been stolen, but had not yet shown up on the black market. No one had been apprehended, and there were no leads in the case.

The chairman of the council easily justified the killings to himself because failure *could not*, and *would not*, be tolerated. His authority and power over the council simply could not be compromised.

The congressman was easily replaced by numerous other American politicians, including Senator Clarkston, who had been kind enough to arrange the cocktail party in Stockholm. He had decided it was better to have various politicians in his snare so he could call upon them when needed, instead of having an untested one sitting on the central council.

When it came to the killings, the chairman often thought, *It was such a shame that they could not live up to my expectations and had to be dealt with in this manner.* But really he relished the power that allowed him to snuff out lives, whenever and wherever he wanted.

While the guests were enjoying their drink, a camera hidden behind a dark screen took their photograph. Most of them unknowingly looked directly into the camera lens, ensuring that a clear photograph documented their attendance at the meeting. They did not know it at the time, but the new members' lives had been changed forever. As long as their actions and opinions supported the chairman of the council, they would prosper, but if they disagreed or did not perform, they would die.

After he was sure that each guest had consumed enough of the drug-laced drink, the young man pointed to a heavy planked door. "The others are through the entrance over there." Then he escorted them to the meeting room and politely said, "If there is anything you need, please let me know. I am here to make you comfortable."

By that time, each guest had let down their guard because the drug was beginning to take effect. Most of them walked into the adjacent room feeling relaxed, ready to meet the others.

The next room was larger in size. Its purpose was to hide and protect

Paul I should the palace come under siege. It was designed so he could comfortably stay in the room indefinitely. The walls were adorned with Dutch and Flemish artwork. These paintings were brought from Europe when the Russian Imperials were importing most of their art and decorations. The stone floor was covered with Persian carpets to soften the extreme stark nature of the room. In the middle of the room was a large rectangular table designed in the classic Russian style, easily recognizable because of the fine craftsmanship and the decoration of animals and mythological carvings.

In a loud and warm voice, the chairman said to each guest when they arrived, "Welcome to the Guardian Council. I trust your journey was a pleasant one?"

All guests answered differently.

Guest number one said, "I don't advertise it these days, because it is so unpopular, but I came over on the corporate jet ... very pleasant. So I am the first to arrive?"

"Yes, you are the first. I am pleased with the acquisitions that Unified Energy made based on our last meetings."

The CEO of Unified Energy triumphantly said, "It wasn't easy; we had to run roughshod over the PR Department to keep it quiet, but the board of directors was easier to manipulate than I thought. As you know, we also were able to get a few key US senators on our side. We hired a private investigator to dig up some dirt on them. With everything we found out, it was easy to persuade them,"

"Nice job. What else have you been up to?" asked the chairman.

"I set up one of my VPs to participate in that think tank you told me about. He has been giving me reports on what those kooks are up to."

The chairman tensed. He wasn't too pleased that the CEO was taking matters into his own hands. He was overstepping his boundaries and trying to do the chairman's job. He decided to let it go for the moment but would give him a stern reprimand tonight. Playing to the man's ego, he said, "I am hoping you would be instrumental in guiding the two new members of the council?"

"Sure, I can keep an eye on them."

"Please sit down and make yourself comfortable. The other guests are on their way."

Precisely ten minutes later, the second guest entered the room wearing the traditional robes of his country. Although he usually wore a black suit with no tie in Iran, he liked the dramatic impact of the traditional dress at meetings that involved foreigners. He thought it made him look mysterious and reminded everyone of the riches that he represented.

The chairman was very congenial to the oil minister since Iran was one of the biggest contributors to his personal wealth. "It is great to have you on the council again. Your country is so critical to our success!" emphasized the chairman.

The oil minister agreed in richly accented English, "Yes, it is imperative to all of our countries to continue our essential work. There are so many false rumors regarding fossil fuels. We need to tell the world the truth."

The third guest came into the room looking more confused and uncertain than the others. She was clutching her drink tightly, but not consuming very much.

The chairman immediately said, "Let's have a toast in honor of one of our new council members, Jean Cutter. She is on the board of directors for the Everson Foundation, as well as many other prestigious boards."

The chairman was adept at being gregarious when he wanted to portray himself as charming. "Let's have a toast. We welcome you to our small group and know you will be a valuable member." He drank down his drink, gesturing to the others to do the same. The result was that all the guests took another large swallow of the drug-laced Sbiten drink.

The chairman knew that Jean Cutter was a real gamble. She had ultra-conservative views that fit well with the ideological profile of the council, but other than that, she was unproven. Her invitation was based solely on the fact that she sat on the board of the Everson Foundation, and his inside information reported that she was unhappy with their direction.

The chairman had recently realized that the foundation's wealth and policies were a threat to the council's future success. His employers would take a dim view of his work if he could not stop their current path. The foundation was simply too well funded and had developed too many key partnerships to be ignored. *That* Nicole Hunter was a major pain in the butt. She had made sure the foundation was going to back important research that could make dramatic progress in alternative fuel.

Unfortunately, the assassination of Nicole in the Ice Bar had not been successful. Fortunately, he had already invited Jean Cutter in an attempt to gain control over the Everson Foundation. If she didn't work out, she would be dealt with like the others. He was already formulating the next plan where Nicole tragically dies in an accident in Seattle, but he would not disclose that to Jean Cutter. His sense was that she may not handle it very well. He despised having to handle people with kid gloves and only did it when absolutely necessary.

The fourth guest arrived an unforgivable five minutes late. "Privyet. Kak pozhivaesh?" he said to everyone with a broad smile. "Our Russian traffic is terrible; it is the price we must pay for our success," bragged the Russian deputy premier. Then he slumped down in a chair, took out his handkerchief, and wiped the perspiration from his forehead.

He had been en route to the conclave when he received a disturbing call. The military truck transporting the nerve gas was under siege. It had been his responsibility to obtain the military truck and ensure that the nerve gas arrived safely at the warehouse in St. Petersburg. He insisted that his town car driver deviate from the designated route so he could have a few more minutes to confer with his information sources. But in the end, he knew he could not delay any longer and had to go inside the castle before he knew the final result.

As he entered the secret meeting room, he was beside himself with worry, but he knew that admitting any failure at the meeting could be dangerous to his health, so he didn't say a word.

The chairman of the council raised his glass one more time and said, "Welcome, my friend."

From the chairman's point of view, the deputy premier had proven himself to be a valuable asset in influencing energy export policy. Since Russia's economic growth depended on natural gas and oil exports, he was very motivated to support the council's policies. He was also instrumental in leading the creation of the state-owned export facilities expansion. He had excellent contacts with the Russian military *and*, more important, with the complex Russian mafia. He was a valuable man who could be counted on when needed.

A few minutes later, the fifth and final guest entered. The man entered with confidence and said, "This is an interesting location for a meeting. It is very nice to meet all of you. I am Ian Whitehouse, professor of Environmental Science at Oxford."

The others looked at him in amazement. What was *he* doing here?

The chairman chuckled at Ian's entrance. "Welcome, Ian. I can see everyone is taken aback by your profession. In due time, we will have to explain why you are here. I understand your trip to St. Petersburg was quite remarkable?"

Ian responded lightly, "Yes, we encountered a freak storm and they blamed it on *global warming*." The whole group laughed. "I was also able to witness some of the Guardian Council's achievements …"

"That is wonderful. We'll discuss it in more detail later," said the chairman, quickly cutting off Ian so that he couldn't talk about the *Valkyrie* mission. The chairman needed to test Jean Cutter's commitment and loyalty before disclosing the gruesome details of the operation.

Ian Whitehouse had been the logical choice to backfill the position left vacant by the deceased history professor. The chairman had heard of Ian's reputation through his underworld connections in London. Apparently the "well-respected" professor had a gambling addiction and owed quite a bit of money to a couple of the chairman's business associates. It was also rumored that the professor liked to improve the grades of some the young female college students in his classes, provided he received something in return.

Ian was the ideal candidate for the council: a smart, ambitious professor with exploitable flaws. It was easy to arrange an irresistible encounter for Ian to show his colors. Conveniently, a videographer was set up in a hotel room next door to document the indiscretion between the professor and the underage young lady.

Later, when approached with the reality of his debts and the video, the young professor became very cooperative, even going so far as to ask how he could help. The chairman felt very confident about Ian from the beginning, but he also knew that having leverage over the professor would ensure more cooperation. It would not be prudent for a prominent professor to have a video of his underage consort released.

As it turned out, Ian was even more motivated by the large sum of money given to the council members who perform—a classic pay-for-performance plan. The professor's primary role was to befriend radical students with ties to terrorism and then pass on their names to the Guardian Council. Whenever a diversion was needed, what better method than to use terrorists to throw suspicion in a different direction? The chairman knew it was a genius plan to cover their tracks, almost foolproof.

So far, Ian Whitehouse had performed extremely well compared to his predecessor. In the last three months, the radical students he recommended had carried out their assignments with inventive means and without repercussions. Even though one of the students had failed to assassinate Nicole, his effort had been commendable. The core group of radical students lived in London, but they had far-reaching contacts with other universities and terrorist cells around the globe. If managed correctly, they would continue to be the perfect cover for the Guardian Council's actions, since everyone was quick to blame the terrorists and look no further.

Chapter Forty-Six

Proceedings

"Let us begin!" announced the chairman in a loud voice.

Everyone took their seats at the antique Russian table, and the meeting got under way. The chairman opened with an emotional presentation about the vital need for the Guardian Council.

He began, "We are here to save our planet from those who would destroy it. The irresponsible and irrational behavior of scientists, political leaders, and professionals will bring us to our knees. It is up to this council to curb this behavior and deliver a rational ideology for the world to follow."

There were cheers from the members of the council. Jean Cutter was starting to feel more comfortable. This is why she was here: to save the world from its own stupidity.

The council chairman continued, "In the last six months, the Guardian Council has been able to produce excellent results. We have been able to stop irresponsible groups from changing our global energy interests. We have curbed green legislation in the United States, enabled secure growth in energy exports for third-world countries, and increased off-shore drilling. We have been a vital supporter of increasing global wealth and improving overall economic conditions."

The chairman continued to speak for over an hour, mostly because he liked to hear himself talk. This was his moment of glory when he came out of the shadows and spoke to his followers. He did not go into details on *how* things were accomplished, because each member of the council was assigned separate duties. The more illegal activities were confined to those who had the stomach for it so that the other more sensitive council members wouldn't learn the truth. In this way, the power was ultimately held by only one man, who used any means to influence and cajole the other council members.

In the back of the room the assistant moved around invisibly to refresh the coffee service. He listened to his boss's speech as he worked, which only intensified his hatred for him. The assistant had been doing this job for two and a half long years. He had been recruited out of a conservative private college to be the management assistant for this reclusive business man. He had been shaped and groomed by him. He was paid enormously well, way beyond his wildest dreams. In a couple years he would be able to retire a wealthy man, but at what cost?

Initially, he had been exposed to only the legitimate aspects of the business and was in awe of his boss's contacts and the international scope of the business he ran. High officials in foreign countries and executives from private businesses all called him on a regular basis to seek out his advice.

But after a while, he began to wonder why his mysterious boss, who used clandestine methods in all his business dealings, could charge such exorbitant consulting fees. What exactly was his expertise? He began to listen in to snatches of private conversations and paid attention to the details to figure out the true nature of the business. He finally realized the chairman was in the business of safeguarding the global petroleum-based economy, at any cost.

The firm's client list included sheiks, multi-national corporations, and senior government officials from every part of the globe. But there was also a secret list of consultants who were called on to execute special assignments. The list of names was in a black book that the chairman personally maintained. The assistant happened upon it by chance one day when the chairman forgot to lock it up in his desk.

Most of the firm's wealthy clients did not want to know how things were done, only that the success rate was high and their money was well spent. All communications were filtered, the financial dealings were done at arm's length, and payments were wired to a secret account in the Cayman Islands. It would be very difficult to implicate any of the businesses, individuals, or countries in any of the illegal activities.

Lately, the assistant had begun to realize that the *real* strength of the council was the secret list of underworld figures who were called upon when needed for specialized assignments. This is why his arrogant boss earned the large sums of money: because he knew exactly who to bring in to resolve a situation.

The chairman had both vast amounts of knowledge about the criminal world and a gift for manipulating people. He was simply one of the most powerful people in the world, or possibly *the* most powerful, but it was a well-kept secret.

When the assistant realized the full scope of what his boss did, he began to worry about his own future. How would he be able to escape the far-reaching tentacles of the chairman?

He decided to do his best to anonymously warn others that a second conclave meeting was going to take place. He went so far as to obtain a photo from the last meeting, along with other images that he had found on his boss's computer. He sent them to Nicole Hunter's hotel in Stockholm because he knew his boss hated her and was tracking her whereabouts. He figured that she must be a real threat to him. Someone needed to stop him. He was an egomaniac out to destroy the world.

Chapter Forty-Seven

The Tail

Oliver and Nicole left with a Russian official who accompanied them through the customs office down the pier. They bypassed the normal bureaucratic channels and walked out to the street, where the official pointed to the motor scooter that Oliver had requested. Now Nicole understood the flippant comment that Oliver had made to her earlier.

Before she knew it, Nicole was zipping through St. Petersburg on the back of the scooter, holding on to Oliver. She could tell that he was a little concerned, because he kept touching her arm around his waist to make sure she was secure. Maybe she was slowing him down a little, but she was *not* going to be left behind!

Oliver had on a headset and was talking to the agent, who was tailing the town car that had picked Ian Whitehouse up at the dock. From what Nicole could gather, the car had just dropped off Ian in front of a hotel. But only moments later, the same agent reported that Ian did not go into the lobby. Instead, he looked around and then entered a different town car that had been waiting outside of the hotel. No wonder Ian had been in a hurry: he had an important appointment that he had to make.

Oliver had the agent follow the latest town car for another couple blocks and then had a second car deployed to avoid suspicion.

Nicole held on tightly to Oliver as they made a quick u-turn. She commented, "I hope we don't run into Ian because he would immediately recognize us."

"I think he would recognize you, not me. But don't worry; we won't get close until he reaches his destination. Meanwhile, enjoy the ride," Oliver said.

Nicole had to admit, she was having a thrilling time. Here she was, in the heart of St. Petersburg, riding alongside the Neva River with the baroque and neoclassic buildings of the eighteenth and nineteenth centuries flying by. She was on the back of a motor scooter that was being deftly maneuvered through traffic while holding on to an attractive international agent. It was one of the more exhilarating moments of her life.

They drove by the Hermitage Museum and St. Isaac's Cathedral a couple of times, so Nicole figured they must be back-tracking based on the circuitous route of Ian's town car. It was uncanny how Oliver knew the streets of St. Petersburg so well. They turned down side streets and took shortcuts down alleys. Either he was getting precise instructions on his headset or he had done this before.

Oliver was communicating with the other agents, but Nicole could tell from his body language that things were getting tense. He swore under his breath. They had lost the town car. Oliver stopped the motor scooter in a narrow alley while the conversation continued in earnest.

A minute or so later, Nicole heard the sigh of relief when another agent spotted the black car going across the canal bridge, now going in the opposite direction. They took off again, this time at a faster and more aggressive pace. The town car seemed to be vectoring in on a location, so it was time to get involved.

Oliver and Nicole coasted to a stop and parked the scooter on the side of the road just before the canal bridge. Oliver suddenly took Nicole's hand while they walked nonchalantly across the narrow bridge. They passed a security guard on the bridge, and she realized that Oliver did not have any romantic intentions but was simply using her as a cover. He wanted it to appear as if two tourists were walking toward the large fortress ahead. Nicole suspected that Oliver had brought her along for this specific purpose.

At the other end of the bridge, there was a second guard. This one looked them up and down, and Nicole's guess was that if Oliver had been by himself, he would have been pulled aside and questioned. Instead they ambled on, stopping to look at a large equestrian statue of Peter the Great.

Oliver put his arm around Nicole's shoulders and said to her in a low voice, "This area is under surveillance so we need to look like tourists."

Nicole asked, "Do you know what we are walking into?"

He uncharacteristically smiled at her. "I have no idea, but look: there is Ian Whitehouse getting out of his town car."

She looked over his shoulder and saw Ian exiting the car while a man dressed in a black suit held the door. Ian was escorted to the side entry, where he was met by someone and then disappeared inside the fortress.

The man in the black suit returned to his post outside of the door, where he immediately focused on the two of them.

Oliver steered her directly toward the man, and they walked straight up to him. Oliver asked, "Can we get in this entrance to see the living quarters?"

The man glared at him and vehemently said, "No! This is a private meeting. No one is allowed."

"Which way is the public entrance?" pursued Oliver. Nicole could plainly see that the irritated man had an earpiece on and appeared to be part of a security force.

The man pointed to the right, "That way."

They walked in the direction indicated, and as soon as they were out of earshot, Oliver spoke into his transmitter, "We are going inside. Give me directions from the main entrance to the wing of the fortress where Ian Whitehouse entered."

He turned to Nicole and said, "Follow my lead."

They rounded the corner and entered the main entrance. It was almost closing time, so a lot of people were leaving but no one was going in. While Oliver conversed with the ticket attendant, Nicole perused the English museum guide. She found out the building was originally a fortified castle and the private residence of Tsar Paul I. It was later turned into a college of engineering, where Dostoyevsky and many famous Russian writers, scholars, composers, and military heroes had studied. Today it was a museum that housed several prominent collections and still included the state chambers and private chambers of the tsar.

She saw Oliver give the woman a charming smile, and she could see he had managed to talk her into letting them in. He had told the attendant that they only wanted to see one special painting so it would not take long. He had promised to be out of the museum by closing time.

They walked through a long, narrow room that housed a dark and dreary art collection. Oliver again took Nicole's good arm and steered her to the right, down a gloomy corridor. He said, "I am told that we are going toward the private chambers of the castle."

They stopped abruptly in front of a heavy planked door that said in several languages, "Private—Do Not Enter." The unseen people tracking their position by GPS had given Oliver the information that this was the door to get into the wing where Ian Whitehouse had entered from the outside.

Oliver took out a small tool and easily opened the old lock. He cracked open the large door just a bit to take a look inside and then opened it a little wider, allowing them to slip into the shadowy space. They backed into a recessed area, and Nicole held her breath as Oliver discreetly leaned forward to survey the length of the hallway. There was a large man standing about three-quarters of the way down in front of a huge bookcase. He was dressed just like the guard who had been outside of the castle and was wearing a holster underneath his open black jacket.

Oliver bent down close to Nicole's ear and whispered, "Wait here. Don't move. I'll be right back."

Now what? she thought.

She waited in the dimly lit space. Her senses were on alert and she noticed the musty smell of old wood. On the wall there was a painting of a peasant girl wearing a red scarf with a sad expression on her face. Then she heard a soft thud, followed by a scraping sound.

Momentarily, Oliver returned and said, "It's clear; follow me."

Nicole emerged and could see there was no longer a guard in the hallway. Obviously Oliver had taken care of him, but she didn't want to know the details. She assumed that he was tied up somewhere, out of the way. But if that wasn't the case, she didn't want to know, so she didn't ask what had happened.

They walked straight to the place where the guard had previously been standing. Oliver ran his hands around the outside of the old, massive bookcase. He had been told by his contacts that this was an entrance into the secret chambers below the castle. Nicole went to the opposite side of the bookcase and examined it carefully. There was a hand-carved, decorative border that ran along the entire edge. In regular intervals, there was an additional decorative embellishment with carved muses. She ran her hand over the dark, heavy wood. A little light streamed in from a high window across the hall so she could see quite well. About four feet off the ground, there were symmetrical cracks in the border. She looked closer and could see that the wood was well worn in this area, probably where it had been handled over the ages.

Nicole tugged on the wood trim first in one direction and then the other. The slats of wood had reminded her of the Japanese puzzle boxes her dad used to bring home for her when she was a kid. She felt the wood trim move slightly to the right, so she tugged a little harder and could feel it open smoothly. There was a similar crack directly above the section that had just slid open, so she pulled this piece to left. Again it moved easily.

She could sense that Oliver was now looking over her shoulder. He had realized that she was onto something. It had to be a simple mechanism to open up the entrance. After all, this was designed in the eighteen hundreds so it couldn't be too complicated.

Just like the clever Japanese puzzle boxes, the next board moved vertically, revealing a small cupboard. Inside was an old iron ring. Nicole pulled the ring and heard a click. Something had moved into place. With a minimal amount of pressure, a section of the bookcase hinged open. Behind it was a simple wooden door.

Oliver said quietly, "Nice work. I'm told this will lead us to the area where Ian disappeared. This must be a very secret meeting for someone to go to such great lengths to conceal it."

Oliver motioned for Nicole to get behind him. Then he opened the latch and slightly pressed open the solid door. She could feel a cool, damp draft coming from the underground chamber.

The muscles in Oliver's neck were tight. He had been ready for someone to be on the other side of the door when he swung it open.

Inside it was very dark, and the chilly air made Nicole shiver. Slowly their eyes adjusted to the faint light, and they could see a soft, dancing illumination, probably caused by candles somewhere down the stone stairs. They could hear excited voices coming from the depths below. It sounded like there was some kind of commotion going on.

Chapter Forty-Eight

Interference

Jean Cutter was not feeling well. As the meeting progressed, she became disenchanted with the Guardian Council. Now, she was feeling a little dizzy and was having trouble concentrating on what the chairman was saying. The meeting had moved on to discuss the execution of the Guardian Council's operational plan. She thought she heard him say something about employing students, along with a reference to terrorism. Opposing liberal energy policy was one thing, but implementing an extremist plan was totally unacceptable. Who did think the chairman think he was to railroad an agenda like this? Yet she was feeling so strange that she wondered if she was imagining everything. What was going on?

Jean Cutter began to get alarmed and reached for her Blackberry to get hold of someone, anyone, but to no avail. There was no service down in this dungeon-like room. She looked at the faces of the other members of the council. They appeared to be totally engaged in the speech and almost seemed to be in a state of rapture. She started to panic.

The chairman had been eyeing Jean for some time now. She had been growing more agitated as time went on, and he was now convinced that it had been a big mistake to invite her. She was a troublemaker who kept asking for clarification and had even dared to question his authority. She was definitely an uptight, righteous bitch, someone who should *not* be on the Guardian Council.

The chairman consoled himself that at least he had been smart to have her drink laced with a high dosage of flunitrazepam. She would not remember much of the meeting and would ultimately be dealt with like the others who had failed their assignments.

Jean Cutter became increasingly claustrophobic in the dark room below ground. Something was very wrong and she had come to her wits end. She needed to get out of this place, to go somewhere, anywhere but here.

She muttered out loud, "I'm not well," and stood to leave, but lost her balance and fell over her chair. She went crashing to the floor and cried out in pain.

At that point, the chairman became angry. "How dare you interfere with our meeting! You have said nothing intelligent the whole time, and now this!"

The other attendees nodded. This woman from the United States had nothing to offer, and *none* of them were sympathetic.

Ian Whitehouse added, "It has been my experience that these women from the Everson Foundation have no value, absolutely none."

The chairman yelled for his assistant. "Sean, come here right now!"

The assistant left his post in the antechamber chamber and scrambled to see what his boss was yelling about. When he walked into the council room, he could see that the chairman's face was bright red and his eyes were boiling with anger.

Sean had seen him this angry only a couple of times before. It was always when he had lost control of a situation, making his blood pressure shoot up to dangerous levels. His job was to fix the problem quickly. First, he went to the chairman and slipped him two pills: one to control his blood pressure and another to calm him down. He knew that he must always have the medication available, just in case his boss needed it. This is why the assistant earned his big salary: not because of his intellect, but because of his ability to control difficult situations.

Next, he attended to Jean Cutter, who was still sprawled out on the floor, uttering unintelligible words of contempt. No one had made a move to help her, and Sean could see that she was going to be a "drop out" from the council.

He went over to her, took her pulse, and then said quietly to her, "I will help you."

Then he managed to get her up with great difficulty. He put her arm around his shoulder and literally dragged her out of the room.

Chapter Forty-Nine

Antechamber

With forbidding shadows dancing on rough stone walls, Oliver and Nicole moved cautiously ahead. The short passage led to a stone staircase with narrow, steep steps. They could only make out the first few steps, and then the staircase seemed to drop to nowhere in the dark below.

Placing her hands on the stone walls for security, Nicole found them cold to the touch, without any secure handholds. They took one step at a time, being careful where to put their feet so they did not fall headlong down the treacherous steps.

Oliver relayed, "We have lost the signal to the Alliance."

They went slowly, and Oliver gave Nicole his hand to guide her progress. She had to keep reminding herself to not hold her breath in anticipation of what might be below in the dark. *Be calm, breathe.*

The staircase turned in an arc, so now Oliver and Nicole could see some light coming from below helping to illuminate the last few stairs. The loud voices they had heard from above ground had grown quieter. Now there was only a strange bumping sound and the closing of a door. They stopped on the last stair and peered down the short passage into the room beyond. Looking past Oliver, Nicole could make out the shape of a man bending over a body on the floor. Fortunately, he was so absorbed in what he was doing that he did not notice them.

Oliver motioned for Nicole to stay where she was. Then he stealthily entered the room beyond and circled around the back of the man. Nicole held her breath because a confrontation was imminent. Rapidly, he reached out and grabbed the man's neck and head. He subdued him, gaining control immediately and whispering into the man's ear while he pressed his hand over his mouth, "If you cooperate, I won't hurt you."

The man was quite young, probably in his mid-twenties. He did not fight Oliver's hold on him and seemed quite relaxed. Oliver slowly released the young man, but was ready to grab him again if he didn't follow instructions.

Nicole took a few steps into the gloomy antechamber to look at the person writhing on the floor. As she crept closer, she could see it was a female figure that was erratically waving her arms in apparent confusion and desperation. The woman appeared to be unhurt but seemed to be having some sort of psychotic episode. Nicole came closer until she could make out the person's face.

It was Jean Cutter! Nicole was shocked. The cool professional who she had known at the board meetings had been reduced to a deranged idiot. What was she doing on the floor of a secret room in the dungeon of a Russian castle? It seemed that everything Nicole had refused to believe was coming true. It could not be denied any longer: the Everson Foundation *was* involved in whatever was going on here.

A cushion had been tucked under Jean's head. Nicole wondered if the young man had been trying to make her more comfortable when he was surprised by Oliver.

"Jean, why are you here?" she asked.

Jean focused on her face for a brief instant. Nicole wasn't sure if she recognized her or not. Jean muttered something again, and Nicole thought she heard the word *mistake*.

"What mistake? What do you mean?"

But the effort to make sense was too difficult. Jean said some unintelligible words that trailed off.

The young man spoke softly as if he didn't want to be heard by the people in the room next door. "She has been drugged a little, but she seems to have lost her mind too. Normally the reaction to the drug isn't this extreme."

Oliver quietly demanded, "Who are you?"

"I am Sean Kessler, the assistant to the director of the Guardian Council."

Nicole asked, "What is the Guardian Council?"

Sean avoided the question. "Who are you?"

Oliver said firmly, "I'm with the Security Alliance."

"And I'm with the Everson Foundation," Nicole added.

Sean looked at Nicole with interest. "Are you Nicole Hunter?"

"Yes. How did you know?"

"I recognize you from a photograph. I only know you because my boss hates you."

"Who is your boss and why does he hate me?"

Sean changed the subject. "Did you get the packet of photos I sent you?"

"*You* sent them? Why?"

"To warn you. I figured if he detested you so much, you must have some power over him."

"What's his name?" she asked.

"That depends on what name he wants to go by. I know of five different identities that he regularly uses, *and* he has the passports to prove them."

They could hear several voices getting louder from the room next door. It sounded like they were coming closer to the antechamber door.

Sean said in alarm, "Hurry, they are on a break. You need to hide behind the black screen in back of the chair."

There were only a few seconds before someone would come through the door and find them. Oliver and Nicole rushed forward and slipped through a small space between the screen and the stone wall. In her haste, Nicole almost knocked over a camera on a tripod next to some video equipment that was hidden behind the screen. It appeared that everything at this strange meeting was being documented.

The heavy wooden door opened and a short, stout man with a full head of wavy hair came into the room. The screen worked like the one-way mirror used in focus groups. They could see him, but he couldn't see them.

The man bellowed, "*Sean!* Forget that woman. She is *nobody!* I need you to do something for me."

"Yes, sir. What is it?"

The man was obviously agitated. "I need to check on the progress of the shipment."

"Tell me what I need to do and I'll do my best," the assistant said with a sarcastic tone in his voice.

"What has gotten into you?" he roared, and the man's squinty eyes began darting around the room as if looking for something. Nicole's heart was in her throat. What if he saw them?

Sean countered in a weak voice, "Nothing. I am trying to do what you asked."

Then the short man with the big hair commanded, "Shut up! I'll send Ian Whitehouse to tell you what information is needed!"

The assistant recoiled, "Okay, no problem!"

The man quickly turned and walked briskly out of the room.

Chapter Fifty

Shipment Status

The chairman of the council hurriedly returned to the meeting room and went straight to Ian Whitehouse. "My assistant is waiting to help you find out about the status of the little affair that we have going on."

Ian nodded. "I am confident that everything has gone to plan, but I'll be happy when I know for sure. When the inventory arrives at the warehouse, we need to move quickly to get the shipment to the annual meeting of the New Champions in China. The students have planned to release the gas during the sustainability portion of the conference. It will be a platform to let those leaders know that they can't mess with the global economy."

The chairman cut him off. "*And* execute the simultaneous release of the gas in London and Washington DC. Go talk to my assistant, Sean, right away! He will help you get any information you need so you can give a special report to the council. I will meet you in the antechamber after you're done."

The Russian deputy premier was close by and overheard parts of the conversation. He was immediately taken aback that he hadn't been asked to be involved. After all, he had been the one in charge of the shipment of nerve gas when it arrived on Russian soil. Had the chairman already determined that he would be eliminated because he had failed?

The chairman proceeded to pat several attendees on the back and told them what a great job they were doing. When he reached the Russian deputy premier, he said, "Because you have done a good job, I am using Ian Whitehouse as the bait." Then he nonchalantly worked his way over to the far side of the room, where a black curtain hung as a backdrop to the presentation screen. He checked a connection to the computer and then walked behind the black curtain to make an adjustment.

Ian Whitehouse confidently walked into the small, dark room looking for the assistant he had met on the way in. "Hello, are you there?"

Sean said, "Yes, I'm over here. What can I do for you?"

"I need to make a phone call to confirm the shipment's arrival."

"Which shipment is that? The chairman has several important shipments in play."

"Interesting. I am talking about the nerve gas being transported to the warehouse not far from here."

Sean smiled. "Oh yes. Just give me a minute to check on it. I'll go upstairs to get the signal. You can stay here."

Ian impatiently sat down in the lone chair to wait.

He startled, feeling something cold on his right temple. "Be still, or I will shoot you," Oliver said tersely through gritted teeth.

Ian appeared astonished. "What are you doing?"

"We know about the nerve gas. You just confirmed that you were involved."

Nicole could see a look on Ian's face that she hadn't seen before: sheer dread. He was appealing to Oliver in a desperate tone, "I'm just an innocent professor whose primary interest is in saving the planet."

"Sure," said Oliver flatly.

Nicole emerged from behind the screen, and Ian's demeanor instantly changed. He reverted to a smile and turned on his most charming British accent. "Nicole, it is *so* nice to see you!"

She glared at him.

He tried again, "Nicole, help me out here. Tell this man that I am a well-known professor who teaches Environmental Studies at Oxford." Then he added in an indignant voice, "And I would never do anything to jeopardize my position!"

She looked sternly at him, "Tell that to all the people on board the *Valkyrie* who you murdered."

"No, no, no … I didn't do that! I just gave the chairman some of the names of my students who knew some other students who wanted to help him, that's all."

Oliver interceded, "It's time to break up the meeting."

He handed Nicole the gun. He said matter-of-factly, "If he moves, kill him."

"Happily," she said. But in reality she knew she couldn't shoot him. She tried very hard to look as mean and vindictive as she could, but she probably wasn't fooling anyone.

When Oliver went into the next room, Ian asked Nicole, "Are you aware of what is going on here?"

"No, tell me. *You* seem to be the expert."

"I am part of an international gathering dedicated to help shape the future energy economy. It is so important that even your own board member attended."

"And look what happened to her. She was drugged and is despondent."

"But you are a stronger person than her, and we could use your abilities on the council! The chairman is very generous—"

"Not a chance."

All of a sudden, Ian bolted, heading for the stairs that would lead him to the main floor of the castle.

Nicole did exactly what she knew she would do: nothing. She let him go. She heard him slip on the stairs, groan, get up, and try again. Odds were that the back-up agents would catch him leaving the castle. If not, an Oxford professor would probably be easy to find. Certainly, Oliver would not have expected her to kill the man in cold blood.

She put down the gun and went over to attend to Jean Cutter. Her guess was that she had become involved in something that she did not fully understand. This would not look good for the Everson Foundation, but Nicole was sure that the Jean Cutter she knew would not have voluntarily been involved with terrorists, drugs, and who knows what else. She was more likely a foolish victim that they tried to influence and control.

Chapter Fifty-One

Meeting Breakup

Oliver took out the pistol strapped to his leg and entered the meeting room.

He showed his weapon and said loudly with authority, "Put your hands behind your head and line up against the far wall."

The first man to speak was indignant. "I am the CEO of Unified Energy. You have no right to do this!"

In a thick Russian accent, another man added, "And I am from the Russian Ministry. You are an intruder. This will not be tolerated!"

Oliver commanded, *"Quiet!"* Oliver looked at the group cowering against the wall. He asked, "Where is the chairman of the council?"

They all looked around the room and then questioningly at each other. Where was he?

Finally, the man in the traditional Middle Eastern robe said, "He was here a minute ago."

Oliver said to them, "I am from the Global Security Alliance. You are all under arrest."

They all spoke at once, "Arrest? What did we do? You can't arrest us."

Oliver shot back, "I am arresting you for crimes against humanity."

They stared at him aghast. Their mission was to preserve humanity by eliminating those who would destroy the world. What was this crazy man talking about?

Oliver knew that this international group of government and business leaders would be almost impossible to bring to justice. There would have to be direct evidence that tied them to stealing the nerve gas or arranging the assassination attempt in the Ice Bar. It would be difficult, but he *could* make it difficult for them to continue their sordid work. At the very least, these conservative extremists would be exposed and their actions tracked by various watch groups, including the Global Security Alliance.

The most disturbing problem was that the chairman had suddenly vanished. Oliver reasoned there must be another passageway out of this subterranean room. Oliver said to the group, "It looks like your leader has escaped and left you to face the consequences. Tell me how he got out."

They all looked at each other in confusion. Oliver could see they didn't know. The chairman had tricked them all.

Chapter Fifty-Two

Escape

When the chairman came to see his assistant in the anteroom, he immediately knew that something was amiss. Sean was quite brazen and had the gall to show him attitude. This newfound cockiness immediately aroused his suspicion. He quickly swept the room with his eyes. Everything seemed in order, but when he looked more closely at the only hiding place in the room, his assistant nervously looked in the same direction. The chairman could see a shadow that had moved ever so slightly behind the black screen.

At that moment, everything changed. He had no qualms about minimizing risk and immediately set his escape plan in motion. He had survived for a long time in this business, and he knew how to sever ties when necessary. He had too many remarkable contacts and underworld figures working for him. He had made a rare mistake, becoming too visible, but he knew he could rebuild.

"Damn them all!" the chairman exclaimed as he slogged through the slime and foul-smelling mud in the underground tunnel. He looked frequently behind himself to see if anyone was after him. The route was the one that had been designed for Paul I to escape from his assassins, but he would make it out alive. He was filthy and breathing hard, but resolved to keep going.

The escape plan was always an important factor in determining the sight of the conclave meetings. It was essential to have an evacuation plan in case something went awry. He knew that he alone could guarantee the future success of the global economy. He could leave nothing to chance.

The chairman came to the juncture where the tunnel turned toward the canal, having been designed for the Russian tsar to escape to a waiting boat. To the right, the chairman saw that a storm drain had been added in modern times. It penetrated the original tunnel, providing a drier escape route. He tried to clamber up the steep incline, grabbing onto the bushes for leverage, but they gave way and he slid backward.

The chairman let lose a tirade of profanity, falling into the prickly underbrush. He had torn his expensive Italian jacket and had scratched his face and hands. A rage came over him, and he flung himself at the muddy bank and insanely clawed his way up to the street level. He was dirty and disheveled when he finally made it to the top of the steep bank. Breathing heavily, he stood and tried to brush the caked mud off his clothes as best he could.

He looked around. No one on the street seemed to have noticed his emergence from the storm drain. He smoothed out his suit and ran his fingers through his thick hair and walked to the corner to look for a taxi.

Chapter Fifty-Three

The Result

The threat of the nerve gas falling into the terrorists' hands and being used against innocent people had been averted. In addition, the Guardian Council who had facilitated the plan was left in a state of disarray.

As he exited the Engineer's Castle, Ian Whitehouse was unceremoniously taken into custody. He maintained his innocence throughout the inquiries and the circumstantial evidence was not enough to put him in prison. He was relieved of his duties as a professor at Oxford University when a hearing of his peers determined that his dealings with the students were unethical.

The existence of the council and the individual names of the attendees were made public. Most of the countries initially supported their council members but rapidly realized that it was politically incorrect to do so mostly because the world stage had judged them harshly. They had become liabilities.

Six months later, the Iranian oil minister regrettably drowned while vacationing on the lovely Island of Kish.

The Russian deputy minister ultimately disappeared and was replaced by a younger man who was more understanding of the environmental policies facing Russia.

The CEO of Unified Energy was flogged in the press and ultimately forced to resign by his board of directors. After a makeover by a high-profile public relations firm, he landed several contracts to consult with global energy companies. He was also approached by an international book company to write his memoirs.

Jean Cutter vaguely remembered travelling to the meeting at the Engineer's Castle, but she could not recall actually being in the Guardian Council meeting. She had a difficult time understanding why she was replaced on the Everson board of directors and felt that Nicole had a personal vendetta against her.

The chairman of the council was not found.

Chapter Fifty-Four

Good-bye

Oliver escorted Nicole to the airport. They didn't say much as the town car wound its way through the old streets of St. Petersburg. What could be said after everything that had happened? After all, Nicole owed him her life. His hand was resting on her knee, and she impulsively covered it with her own.

He looked at her sadly and sighed. "I really want to see you, but it would never work."

She laughed and tried to say lightheartedly, "Oh really? I don't know. You would make an impressive philanthropist. After all, you were a great imposter at the reception."

He laughed. "And you would be an incredibly smart and sexy agent!"

A long and deadly silence hung in the air.

Nicole looked out the window, trying to maintain control, blinking back tears. St. Petersburg looked more gray and drab than a few hours ago. They both knew that there was no way around it. They could not pretend. Oliver and Nicole lived in different worlds.

At least that would be the common conclusion, but Nicole had been amazed how much her world had crossed over into the dark world of greed, death, and terrorism.

They arrived at the airport. Nicole did not want to prolong the good-byes. She said firmly, "Oliver, let's say good-bye here."

He leaned over and gave her a prolonged kiss. Then he said, "Please, remember me, because I will remember you."

Nicole fumbled for the door before the driver could come around to open it. She had to get out before her emotions got the best of her. It was likely that she closed the door on Oliver when he tried to get out of the car to help. She grabbed her luggage and wheeled it into the terminal, determined not to look back. That was the way it had to be.

Chapter Fifty-Five

Published

Ninety days after the *Sea Bridge* docked in St. Petersburg, a detailed account of the revolutionary breakthrough in alternative fuel using hydrogen fusion was published on the cover of a prominent scientific journal. The title was "Green Energy: Fact or Fiction?"

The entire odyssey, beginning with the shooting of David and the subsequent symposium on the ship, was documented. Chen was interviewed extensively, explaining the facts around the hypothetical breakthrough. He welcomed other scientists to add to the research that could benefit all mankind.

In addition to Chen, several other prominent scientists were interviewed to critique the feasibility of the green fuel breakthrough. Most offered praise for the effort but then went on to offer varying explanations on why it was not feasible.

Two months prior, the editor of the journal received an anonymous phone call. The person on the other end of the line knew everything about him, his address, his children's and wife's name, how much money he made, and his daily routine. The man said to him in a menacing voice, "You *will* find scientists to refute the legitimacy of the discovery, or you *know* what will happen."

A couple of hours later, the editor received a package. Inside the wrapped package was a box of fine Cuban cigars and a note saying, "Do the right thing. It will be good for your life."

A month later, the journal article was published without fanfare. It concluded that the discovery was a hoax and was the result of an overzealous group of scientists who saw an opportunity to benefit from the death of a fellow scientist. However, if one had researched carefully, they would have found that all the scientists interviewed by the journal worked in labs with close ties to the private sector.

Even though the breakthrough was monumental, there were too many individuals and corporations that did not want it to succeed. It was simply not in their best financial interests. Behind the scenes lobbying and a systematic campaign of negative press took its toll on the merit of the discovery and the ability to get it to market. It would take many years of clever public relations and lobbying to overcome the damage inflicted in the public's mind.

But the small group of dedicated scientists could not be stopped. They vowed to continue on and made a pact to network with independent scientists who could not be bought or influenced. Their biggest asset was the powerful organization they had on their side, one that had the resources to help them break through the disinformation: the Everson Foundation.

Epilogue

The next year, extreme weather events continued to increase.

A record number of super cell tornadoes touched down in the United States, destroying everything in their path. Most of these storms formed quickly and struck without warning, tossing cars around like toys and ripping buildings from the ground.

In Europe, extreme cold temperatures in the winter and consecutive days of torturous heat in the summer plagued the continent. It was not uncommon for temperatures to drop twenty degrees centigrade in less than a half an hour. The demand for power was unprecedented, causing wide-scale power failures and brownouts. The sick and weak did not survive the excessive temperatures.

Extraordinary torrential rains caused flash flooding in low-lying areas throughout Asia. Disease ran rampant, so millions upon millions of lives were lost. Farmland and livestock were wiped out, resulting in another drop in food production. There was a dire food shortage around the world.

Many of those in power, along with global private citizens, still believed the extreme storms were simple anomalies.

CPSIA information can be obtained at www.ICGtesting.com
232630LV00002B/74/P